MIKE BLAKELY

VENDETTA
GOLD

FORGE®

A TOM DOHERTY ASSOCIATES BOOK
NEW YORK

This is a work of fiction. All the characters and events portrayed in this book are either products of the author's imagination or are used fictitiously.

VENDETTA GOLD

A Forge Book
Published by Tom Doherty Associates, Inc.
175 Fifth Avenue
New York, NY 10010

Forge® is a registered trademark of Tom Doherty Associates, Inc.

ISBN: 0-812-58915-7

First Forge edition: September 1998

Printed in the United States of America

0 9 8 7 6 5 4 3 2 1

To Rebecca

Acknowledgments

For helping me understand the land laws of Texas and the ways of the frontier surveyors, I wish to thank the General Land Office of Texas and the Texas Surveyors Association. A special thanks to Ralph Harris, R.P.S., Austin, Texas, for sharing his collection of antique surveying instruments.

ONE

I had just one ambition the day the old Mexican died. One ideal controlled my every action. A single goal for life went before all my daily needs and immediate desires. I had vowed to dedicate the rest of my days on earth to the complete and unceasing avoidance of criminal activity and nothing I could imagine would ever have the power to sway me from that mission.

It may not sound like much of an aspiration or one that would prove particularly difficult to achieve, but to me it was a cause so crucial and absorbing that I felt precariously near to failure at every turn. Dreams of hard labor haunted my nights, and memories of close confinement filled my waking thoughts. I had just finished a stretch of three years and it was my sole aim to make it the only sentence Roy Huckaby would ever serve. Of course, all that began to change the day I met the old Mexican.

When I first saw him, I must have mistaken him for a wooden Indian. He was standing board-stiff in front of a cigar store on Dolorosa Street, across from the Old Southern Hotel. But when I looked his way again, several minutes later, I caught him shuffling along in front of the Buckhorn Saloon and I knew he was human.

He wore the dress of an old-fashioned vaquero except for the faded red bandanna tied on his head in place of a sombrero. Years had cracked his face like parched soil and I couldn't locate a single tooth amid the white stubble of his beard. He wore a frayed vest under a jacket resplendent with patches. The ends of his bowed pant legs disappeared down the tops of boots that had once stood straight as stove pipes but now slouched like the features of his weathered face. The rowels of his spurs had lost almost as many teeth as his mouth. He used a walking stick to maintain his balance and his only means of getting around was to totter a few feet, then rest.

One of San Antonio's municipal water carts was sprinkling the street to keep the dust down. By the time it had circled Main Plaza, the old Mexican had only taken about a dozen steps. A German merchant left his store at the corner of Quinta and Main and walked all the way across the plaza to the Buckhorn Saloon in the time it took the old Mexican to negotiate the width of three or four planks on the boardwalk. A horseman rode by and the old man raised his hand to wave, but too late, and the rider didn't notice. He paused with his hand in the air and watched the horseman ride out of sight.

He continued to inch along until his squint found my horse under the shade of an oak in the gardens of Main Plaza. He stopped and stared for a full minute. Then I caught a glimmer of desperation in his eyes and knew he wanted something of me, so I crossed the street, tipped my hat, and stepped up on the boardwalk. "Good afternoon, sir," I said. "Can I be of some help to you?"

Conversation didn't come easily between us because he spoke no English and I spoke no Spanish. But I soon figured out from his gestures that he wanted to ride my horse somewhere. Given my recent inclination toward acts of philanthropy, I had no objection to letting him borrow a ride.

The old man didn't look spry enough to climb a stirrup so I led my horse to the edge of the boardwalk and helped him get one leg over the saddle. I did most of the work and he simply leaned in the appropriate direction. He indicated that he would have no further use for his walking stick, in fact he scorned the thing once he was in the saddle, so I left it leaning against the wall of the Buckhorn Saloon.

"Which way?" I asked, giving him the choice of turning up or down the street. He began to point so I would know where to lead him, and we turned onto Flores Street and walked slowly south.

It didn't take me long to learn my first two words of Spanish. "*Derecho*" meant right and "*izquierda*" meant left. I was very familiar with those commands by the time we reached the vaquero's destination, which was the beautiful old Mission Conception, three miles south of Main Plaza.

"*Izquierda, izquierda!*" he ordered, and I made the last left turn through the gate of a split-rail fence surrounding the mission.

I helped the vaquero down from the saddle, and he sat on a rock under a tree to rest. With his eyes and a motion of his hand, he asked me to stay with him. So I sat and listened to him mutter in his foreign tongue. He seemed to have a great many things to tell me. He pointed and gestured incomprehensibly as he spoke. I got the idea he was thanking me for the use of my mare so I merely nodded at him as if I understood. "Okay, old-timer," I said. "Whatever you say. Yes, yes, I understand."

Then the old man grinned, patted me on the shoulder, and reached into his jacket. He pulled out a rolled piece of tanned sheepskin tied with a leather thong. He handed it to me. When I took it, he wrapped his rough old hands around mine and shook them weakly. He tried to get up then but didn't succeed until I helped him.

The moment we both got on our feet, I heard the whistling of mourning doves on the wing. Six of them flew between the twin stone belfries of the old Spanish mission and landed in the tree limbs above us. I knew there were six because I had gotten into the habit of counting birds in prison when they flew overhead or landed on the walls, as if they represented some sort of index to freedom from which I was excluded.

The old man noticed the doves, too, and pointed at them as they found their perches among the branches over our heads. He raised his hands to them and spoke as if to a woman he had once loved. A toothless grin covered his face as he turned to me and made his old arms move slowly like wings and then swept his knotty fingers over his head to indicate the great blue expanses of sky over Texas.

Finally he clutched the cloth of his vest and hobbled toward the mission. There was an altar in front of the ancient building with a statue and a cross and some wilted flowers, and the vaquero shuffled over to it and sank to his knees to pray.

I untied the thong around the sheepskin and unrolled it. There was something written or drawn on it in ink. I didn't have time to figure it out because the doves jumped their perches and took to the sky again. They numbered seven when I counted. I glanced toward the statue and found the old man slumped over in front of it, dead.

I remember letting a shameful thought cross my mind: Now you've wasted your time, Roy. What kind of character witness will a dead Mexican make? I rolled the sheepskin up and put it in my pocket.

In the chapel I found a Mexican boy carrying candles into a baptismal chamber. "Hey, boy. There's an old man out here who just died," I said.

"Where?" he asked.

"Out in front by that statue."

"Which one? The image of the Virgin?"

"I don't know whose image it is. How many statues have you got at this church, anyway?"

The boy put his candles down. "Show me," he said.

I took him out to the altar and he explained that it was indeed the likeness of the Virgin Mary from whose feet the old Mexican's spirit had flown. He didn't seem to regard the corpse as any form of novelty.

"He asked if he could ride my horse here," I said. "Who is he?"

He shrugged and said, "Who knows? The old ones sometime come here to die."

The boy let me know I had nothing more to do there, so I mounted my horse and eased back toward Main Plaza. Halfway there I remembered the sheepskin the old man had given me and I took it out of my pocket for another look. It would take me some time to make sense of the thing, but, once translated, the gift of the dying vaquero would both haunt and enthrall me. It would cause me anguish and rapture. It would rob me of control over my own destiny and change my life forever.

TWO

Something more than chance drew me to San Antonio the day the old Mexican died. The Alamo City was part of a plan I had formulated to keep me forever beyond the grasp of felony. The plan had come to me in Huntsville, the day the underkeeper opened the gate of the Texas state penitentiary to let me out. "We'll see you back here soon enough, convict," he said.

"You'll meet the devil before you lay your eyes on Royal Strickland Huckaby again," I replied. Then I walked into the rain and started stomping red mud puddles down the road, as carefree as a boy out of school. When the clouds broke I found a sunny spot at the edge of a pine wood on the east side of a hill, just outside of town. I sat there all morning and strung together the pieces of my plan for a long, free, honest existence.

The last thing I wanted to do was return to my home in Matagorda County, on the Texas Gulf Coast. A few of my sister's letters had gotten through to me, telling me that the feud had died out there after I left for prison. But I couldn't rely on her word even though I knew she would never intentionally mislead me. I was afraid the feud had simply lain dormant for the past three years and might erupt anew as soon as I stepped off the train at the depot. I intended to spend the rest of my days in a place that offered the least potential for violent conflict and Matagorda County was not it. Neither my folks nor my three sisters would understand that, of course, so I decided not to tell them or any other past acquaintance where I would go.

It occurred to me on the hill outside of Huntsville, as the sun dried the cheap freedom suit the state had provided for me, that *people* had caused all my troubles. People as individuals and people as a society. Well-meaning people, ill-intentioned people, people I knew well and some I had never even seen. They had caused all my misfortunes. It made sense to me, then, that I should look for a place where few people lived and go there to start staying out of trouble.

The frontier had the fewest people, but moving to the frontier to shun trouble made no more sense than joining a leper colony to avoid smallpox. I decided I would drift just shy of the frontier, to the edge of the settlements, and find work in a quiet town or on a lonely ranch where I could mind my own business and avoid people. The one product of humanity I most fervently wished to elude was that anomaly of civilization variously known as a vendetta or a blood feud or "a trouble" and my plan would not allow me to come within one hundred miles of such an abomination.

That plan I put into effect at Huntsville. I had made my preparations for the day of my release well in advance and had asked my banker back home to establish an account for me in Huntsville. I drew on it to buy a horse and a saddle. I could have ridden the rails, but trains moved fast and my plan dictated that I take things slow and keep my eyes open for any form of turmoil I might have to sidestep. So I mounted my horse—a five-year-old seal brown mare I named Liberty—and set out for the Alamo City.

San Antonio was not the most likely place in Texas to stay out of trouble, but I reasoned that if I hung around the hotels and stockyards—and avoided the saloons and brothels—I could probably find work and stay clear of vice. I wasn't particular about the type of employment I found, and I was willing to work for little pay as long as I could work alone and mind my own business. It seemed odd that a college-educated man of a wealthy plantation family should consider a career of servility, but circumstances had conducted me to that end and there was nothing I could do about it.

I started out toward San Antonio at such a crawl that even my mare found the pace lacking. I thought I would feel safer if I traveled slow, but the sluggishness only gave me time to contemplate the various species of mischief that could undermine my intricately formed plans. I started to wonder if simply avoiding calamity would suffice. It might prove beneficial, I thought, to actively work against trouble—to begin a practice of doing *good*. That way, if I earned a reputation as one who habitually did his neighbor a kind turn, it could fare in my favor in a court of law. I would have no trouble producing witnesses who could testify to my fine character.

I had no intention of going on trial for anything, but neither had I had that intention in Matagorda County, three years before. I had learned there that a man could find himself at odds with the law simply by going about his business as usual. If I had worked harder at establishing character witnesses in Matagorda County, I might have gotten off with a lighter sentence or been acquitted altogether. My new formula for avoiding incarceration took those kinds of things into account.

So, by the time I reached San Antonio, I had already

carried out a half-dozen feats of good will. I had helped an old man fix a stake-and-rider fence southwest of Bryan. I had caught a boy's saddle horse for him near Caldwell. Just outside of Giddings, I had helped a farmer and his sons get their hay under the barn ahead of a thunderstorm. I had done my part in extinguishing a small kitchen fire in Bastrop. And in San Marcos I had accomplished two acts of benevolence at once by escorting the town cow from the premises of a boarding house whose matron was beating the animal soundly with a broom handle to get rid of it. I had become a virtual samaritan.

The afternoon I tied my horse in the shade on Main Plaza, I was still lumbering through life with one eye trained for eminent disaster and the other for potential deeds of generosity. From my vantage on the plaza, I could watch the door of the Old Southern Hotel and look for cattlemen I might hit up for work.

That was when I met the old Mexican and agreed to let him ride my horse to Mission Conception. Now he was dead and I was wandering back toward my shade tree on the plaza, trying to analyze the peculiar design on the sheepskin he had given me.

I turned it over, around, and sideways several times before I settled on a way to study it. It was essentially a line drawn between two points. One point was labeled "*el tesoro*" and the other "*la piedra del cero.*" If it had said *derecho* or *izquierda* I would have had some understanding of it, but as it was, I didn't have a clue. I swatted at a horsefly that lit on my neck and continued to ogle the gift of the dead vaquero.

There were a few ideas that I could comprehend because they were in numerals and Spanish speakers write numerals the same way English speakers do. A bracket-like manifestation seemed to suggest that the distance between *el tesoro* and *la piedra del cero* was "189 *cadenas*, 7 *varas.*" But of what length a *cadena* was, or a *vara*, I could only imagine. I finally began to grasp the gist of the diagram when I saw "N 49 W" scrawled beside the line that ran between the two points. I recognized "N 49 W" as a compass bearing. The old Mexican had given me a map.

THREE

I remembered the way the old Mexican had gestured and talked at length before giving me the gift. He had probably been telling me what the map would lead to and I hadn't understood a syllable.

I returned to my place under the shade tree from which I had first seen the old man and continued to study the map. *El tesoro. La piedra del cero.* Those were the two key phrases. Two points, a line running between them. North and 49 degrees west.

North was zero degrees. I remembered that much from a cartography lecture I had attended at Southwestern University. I also recalled that there were 90 degrees between north and west. That would cause 49 degrees to bear almost exactly northwest. *El tesoro* stood somewhere to the northwest of *la piedra del cero* and I didn't have the faintest idea what either of them represented.

I almost flagged a passing citizen to ask for a translation, but I remembered my plan and rolled the sheepskin back up. Until I knew what I had, I would not flaunt it in the faces of strangers. Prudence was my hallmark. I leaned back against the plaza oak to contemplate my strategy.

I rolled and unrolled the map twenty times in the next hour until I arrived at a plan to translate it. I would do it one word at a time, using a different translator for each word. I would not mention or show the map to anyone or call the least bit of unnecessary attention to myself. I would go about it casually and carefully. If possible, I would have some knowledge of each translator before I asked for assistance and that was where the Buckhorn Saloon fell into my plan.

I knew the proprietor of the Buckhorn, but was sure he wouldn't remember me. I hadn't seen Albert Friedrich in years and didn't think he had ever known me by name. He was a sober and agreeable man—just the candidate to translate a word for me. Of course, I would have to enter the Buckhorn to talk to him, and I had vowed to stay out of saloons. But one minor violation of my master plan for a crime-free life would matter little in the long run, I decided. Besides, I was burning with curiosity to decipher the old Mexican's map.

"Good afternoon, sir," Friedrich said as I stepped up to his polished cherry-wood bar. He ran a topnotch saloon. "What can I get for you?"

"Beer," I said. Sweet cigar smoke filled the air, glasses clinked together and laughing voices reminded me of the many hours I had spent in saloons before prison. I forced those halcyon memories from my mind, though, because I knew now that beneath the pleasant facade of any saloon rushed an undercurrent of pure wickedness. Some of the same men I had once toasted were now dead.

Friedrich slid a mug to me across the bar. "Say, don't I know you?"

"Nope," I said.

"You look like Champ Huckaby's boy, grown up. Yes, I didn't recognize you in those rags. Have you been ill? You look thin." He turned to a group of businessmen at a nearby table. "Hey, boys, look who's here. I want you to meet . . ."

"How much for this beer?" I said, interrupting him in a severe tone of voice. I had heard of Friedrich's great memory, but never dreamed he would remember me from a single visit to his saloon several years before.

Friedrich instantly caught on to my situation. "Never mind, boys. My mistake," he said to the men at the table. Then he spoke softly to me. "Sorry, Royal. I forgot about the trouble down your way. I thought that was over."

"I'm not Royal. You have me mixed up with somebody else. How much for the beer?"

"On the house with my apologies. I could have sworn you were one of the Huckaby clan." He winked and went to sit with the men at the nearby table.

Friedrich's saloon wasn't called the Buckhorn for the heck of it. He owned a collection of antlers that has never been matched anywhere. Antlers protruded from all the walls and parts of the ceiling, in some places as dense as a bed of nails. A hundred glass-eyed deer heads stared at one another across the billiard and card tables. The most tremendous specimens hung between the marbled columns of the back bar and a few pairs were mounted as they had died, with their antlers locked together in combat. Even the chandeliers were made of deer horns.

Friedrich loved to hunt deer and he loved just as much to talk about deer hunting. He probably remembered me from my only previous visit to his saloon because I had told him a story about a big buck I had killed. As I sipped my beer, I heard him talking about one of his hunts to the gents at the table and he got up to show them the buck he had killed on that hunt. The antlers were tacked to the ceiling with about a hundred other pairs. He used a billiard stick to single it out. "It was this one right here. When that old buck came over the hill, he never knew what hit him . . ." The Buckhorn Saloon virtually bristled inside.

As I turned my beer mug up, five cowboys burst in,

dressed in new boots, hats, or handkerchiefs, and already somewhat drunk even though it was an hour till dark. They had just returned from a drive, I figured, and were bent on trading their wages for fancy clothes and whiskey. They all wore pistols and surged about as one blustering body of havoc, making me nervous. "Look what we brung you from the Sabinal," one of the cowboys said, holding up a huge pair of deer antlers bearing fourteen points. "Old Ben Saddler kilt this buck last winter and throwed the horns up in a tree. We borrowed 'em when we left the ranch. Figured you might trade us a few drinks for 'em."

"I should say I'll trade!" Friedrich said. "That rack will earn a drink for each of you."

"Make it drinks for the house, and we'll swap," another cowboy said.

The men at the table approved and Friedrich began drawing the beer and pouring the whiskey.

"Say," I ventured when he brought my new mug, "do you speak any Spanish?" The cowboys were laughing it up along the bar next to me and covering my conversation with Friedrich adequately.

"Enough to get business done," Friedrich said.

"Well, I don't speak any. But there was a Mexican talking to me today and, of course, I couldn't understand anything he said, but there was one word he used a lot. I was wondering if you could translate it for me."

"It was probably profane," Friedrich said, "so don't get offended at me when I tell it to you. Sometimes they'll smile at you like you mean the greatest compliment and all the while they are cursing every member of your family. What was the word he used so much?"

"The word, as I recall it, was *tesoro*."

Friedrich stood bolt upright and began to laugh. He shot his eyes toward the cowboys lining the bar next to me. "Hey, boys, this young fellow needs a Mexican word translated. Does anybody know what *tesoro* means?"

The punchers thought for an instant and then began

spouting jeers. One of them cuffed me about the neck. "By God, he must have gone and bought him a treasure map!"

The men at the table turned their faces to the antlered ceiling and laughed in unison. "Give him one on us, Albert," one of them said, "he won't have any money left if he's bought a treasure map!"

There was more laughter at my expense and I could not even attempt to deny purchasing the map. Friedrich brought me another beer. "How much did you pay for it? Fifty dollars is the going rate."

"I didn't pay that much."

"No, he got swindled at a bargain!" the cowboy next to me said. "Give him a drink on us. He's a good sport to take such a ribbin'!"

Friedrich continued to set up drinks for everybody. "Don't feel bad," he said to me. "Some of these boys have probably invested in buried Spanish treasure, too. Who took you?"

I shrugged. "An old man."

"The old men sell the most maps," a cowboy said. "I guess they're supposed to be old enough to remember where the damned Spaniards buried the stuff."

They went on about old Mexicans selling bogus treasure maps, but my thoughts drifted as I drank my beers quicker—the mugs were backing up. I remembered what Friedrich had said about Mexicans smiling and cussing one's family members at the same time. Was that what the old Mexican had pulled over on me? Had that feeble old man chosen me as the victim of his final hoax? A last jab at the almighty gringo? After I had let him ride my horse?

I couldn't believe it. He had spoken to me as he had to the doves he dreamed of flying with. I thought I knew enough about deceit that I could have detected it in his eyes at Mission Conception. And I had not paid a red cent for that map. The old man had *given* it to me. That should have accounted for something. Yes, his gift to me was given in sincerity—a map labeled with lost treasure. *El tesoro.*

The beer shone golden through the mug in my hand and glistened through the facets of the glass like polished pieces of eight. Maybe there really was a treasure. But even if there was, I knew nothing about it except that it lay buried 49 degrees northwest of a thing labeled *la piedra del cero.* And just what in the hell was *la piedra del cero?*

"Well, which one was it?" a cowboy asked, nudging me on the shoulder.

"Which one was what?"

"Haven't you been listenin'? Was it parchment or sheepskin?"

"Sheepskin," I muttered.

"That's five you owe me, Dick! Pay up!" The cowboys made good on their bets.

"India ink or blood?" they asked next.

"Blood?" I responded, astounded at the thought.

"It must be India ink, then!" Dick said. "Now *you* owe *me* five," and the money changed hands again. "Where is it? Let's have a look at it."

"No, I better not," I said. "I've drunk my last beer so I better get going."

Friedrich had a full stein in my face before I could reach my hat on a nearby antler tine. I had forgotten how easily beer could flow down one's gullet. "Here's another, friend," the barkeeper said. "Now, let's see that map. Maybe one of these boys will recognize it."

I shrugged and pulled the sheepskin from my pocket and unrolled it on the bar. We bunched our heads together to study it and I could smell three or four different species of liquor riding the rough voices of the cowhands. The gentlemen from the table came over to look, too. They all told some fine jokes on me, but even I was laughing by then. The beer and the visions of treasure had improved my disposition.

"Here's the treasure," one said, pointing at *el tesoro.* "Have you a pickax and shovel, Albert?"

"It lies forty-nine degrees northwest of this, whatever that means," I said, pointing to *la piedra del cero*.

"Let me see," said a businessman from the table. "I speak some of the lingo. I have Mexicans on my payroll."

"I aim to have one on my bedroll, tonight," one particularly randy cowboy said. The rest of them howled like wolves.

"I don't know what it means," the employer of Mexicans said, "but here's the distance between the two points. One hundred eighty-nine *cadenas*, seven *varas*. What in the hell is a *cadena?*"

"What in the hell is a *vara?*"

"A vara is about two or three feet or so," a cowboy said.

"How the hell would you know?"

"My uncle's a surveyor. He's always talkin' about varas and leagues and labors and things like that."

"But what's this part mean?" I asked anxiously, pointing my finger again at *la piedra del cero*.

"I think he's still aimin' to dig!"

A great laugh went up among the deer antlers.

"No, it's not that," I explained. "But I'm going to frame this and put it in my parlor. It will make a better story if I know what all the words mean."

The men around the treasure map became studious. Finally one of the cowboys spoke up. "This here means rock," he said, indicating *piedra*. "I know because me and a Mexican kid I grew up with used to chuck 'em at each other all day and that's what he called 'em—*piedras*."

"The rock of the something-or-other," a businessman said. "Who knows what *cero* means?" He pronounced the word, "care-oh."

"It ain't 'care-oh,' it's 'chair-oh,'" one cowboy insisted. "Or maybe 'share-oh.' Damn these Mexican words!"

The cowboy with the hopes of having a *señorita* on his bedroll spoke up then. "What's your name, gold-digger?"

"Charlie Fischer," I said, quickly assuming the name of a former prison mate.

"Well, Charlie, I know a girl across town that can help us change these last two words to American—this share-oh and this here *cadena*. Stick with ol' Matt Cottle and we'll go see her later."

Stepping into the Buckhorn had been a severe enough transgression against my designs for avoiding trouble but visiting a whorehouse was unthinkable. "No, I have no business there," I said.

"Of course you haven't," Matt said. "You've done all your business with an old mapmaker." The boys howled, especially the one named Dick who seemed to be getting drunk faster than the others. "But we'll loan you a buck a head and you can pay us back when you get your treasure. Ain't that right, boys?"

"Why the hell not!" joyous Dick yelled.

Things looked grim for me. I had five drunken cowboys buying me beer and staking me to a night at the whorehouse. They would not let me refuse their charity. I finally had to give in and decided I could just give my five to a girl and then get the hell out of San Antonio and go treasure hunting and return to the formula I had conceived in Huntsville—the one I was currently straying so far from.

When we left the Buckhorn Saloon after dark, all of us were still passably sober except for Dick. He tried to pick a fight with a stagecoach guard carrying a shotgun, and we had to drag him away kicking.

We mounted our horses and rode toward the whorehouse across town. On the way, there was some discussion about shooting out the gas streetlights, but Matt told his friends to wait until after he had bedded his señorita in case they all had to make a gallop for the ranch.

I was still sober enough to feel uneasy about the prospects ahead. I considered turning my horse to make a break from my corrupting acquaintances, but my mind was still on the treasure map and the two words yet uninterpreted.

And also, though I was uneasy, I was having certain carnal visions about the house of ill repute at which we would soon arrive. I had visited such an establishment on one or two occasions in Matagorda County—a lonely, sequestered two-story mansion where buxom belles played classical music and curtsied to the wealthy ranchers and plantation owners who frequented the place. I was curious to find out how the San Antonio brothel and its personnel would compare.

It disappointed me to find that the cowboys' whorehouse was nothing more than a shotgun shanty. We hitched our horses outside and the boys chipped in their dollars for my benefit before we went in.

The madam was a fat, painted woman who had tried to improve the looks of her establishment on the inside with a bunch of cheap curtains and tapestries. She played an ill-tuned piano with a half-dozen dead keys while a couple of scurrilous jacks danced with the working girls. "Welcome, boys," the madam said when we entered. Dick started dancing by himself and his friends stomped and clapped for him until he whirled himself to the floor.

The girls, about eight or nine of them, were of every nationality, race, and tribe I could imagine in my present condition of inebriation. One yellow-haired girl didn't look a day over sixteen. Overall, the place represented the vilest example of iniquity I had ever stood in outside of the state penitentiary.

"Where's the Mexican girl you know?" I asked Matt.

"She must be busy. Wait a few minutes. She'll show."

Matt and I sat on a dusty sofa and waited. The few minutes turned into half an hour. The rest of the cowboys danced with various whores, "to get a feel for 'em," Dick said. He finally disappeared down a hallway with the young, yellow-haired girl. My head was pounding by that time and I realized I had drunk near two gallons of beer on an empty stomach. I longed to be sober and sleeping alone under the stars.

But the sheepskin map rolled in my pocket made me stay. The old Mexican had *given* it to me. That virtually guaranteed its authenticity. He would have *sold* it to me for a hoax. Wasn't a chance at buried treasure worth the risk of five more minutes in a whorehouse? Then an awful thought occurred to me. The old swindler knew damn good and well that he was about to keel over at Mission Conception. What use would he have for my money where he was going? By *giving* me the map, he had perpetrated the perfect fraud—one I would scarcely suspect in a hundred years.

The lady of the house quit punishing the piano and approached Matt and me. She leaned over and swung her huge breasts in front of our faces. "Are you boys shy?" she asked.

"No, just particular," Matt said. "I'm waiting for Juana. There she is now!"

Juana had emerged from the hallway, a slip of a *señorita.* She came running at Matt when she saw him and, flinging herself at him, wrapped her legs about his waist and bit his ear playfully.

"Ouch, damn it!" he said, and slapped her on the rear end. He began carrying her back toward the hallway and I followed.

"Now, wait a minute," the huge madam said. "You get your own girl. We don't double up here."

I should have made a break for the door, but I had come that far and there were only two more words to translate on the map. Yes, it was probably a worthless piece of sheepskin, but I had done the old Mexican a kindness and therefore there was just the slightest chance that he had given me an authentic map out of gratitude.

"You," I said, pointing at the nearest prostitute, "come on." I felt more depraved than I had in my entire life. I caught up to Matt before he got Juana locked away behind her door. She was prattling nonstop in Spanish.

"Slow down," Matt said. "No savvy." He started to close the door.

"Hey, what about the map?" I asked. The girl I had chosen was a half-dressed half-Indian and she was going through my pockets for money and I was squirming like a wounded centipede, trying to retain some particle of dignity. I won't admit everything I was thinking then, but I had been locked away from women for three years and there was a conflict going on within me between proper moral conduct and acute lust. I was thinking that I had already fallen far enough from grace as it was and would have to give the girl the money anyway ...

"Can't you wait till later?" Matt said.

"No."

"Well, damn it, come on in here and let's let her have a look at it." Matt laboriously used his limited Spanish to let Juana know what we were about. She looked suspicious at first, but finally allowed us all to enter her cubicle and the half-Indian whore kicked the door shut behind us. I unrolled the map and Matt showed it to Juana. He stuttered through some more Spanish and pointed at the words we wanted translated. When Juana stopped laughing, about my having purchased the map, I suppose, she began trying to explain. First she addressed the reference to 189 *cadenas*.

Her words came too quick and Matt had to get her to slow down. She wore a silver chain around her neck and she kept showing it to Matt as she explained.

"I think she's sayin' a *cadena* is like this necklace she's got, but men wear it in jail."

That made perfect sense to me. "Chains," I said. "One hundred and eighty-nine chains. The distance is measured in chains and varas."

"Yeah, but how long of a chain?" Matt asked.

"It's not as if it matters. This is just going to hang in my parlor."

"Oh, yeah. Let me see if I can get her to change this other word to American—this 'share-oh.'"

"Sí, cero," Juana said. *"Como, como, como . . ."* She couldn't find a word Matt could comprehend.

With me the struggle was with morality, not language, for the half-Indian whore had found things in my pockets I had forgotten I kept there.

"Como, como, como . . . Nada!"

"Nada?" Matt said.

"Nada," Juana repeated.

"She says it don't mean nothin'," Matt told me.

"How could it mean nothing? Are you sure?"

Matt asked her again if the word had no meaning.

"No, no, no," she shrieked. *"Es como nada. Cero es como nada."*

"I don't know what the hell she means, Charlie. Let's forget about it. These girls work on time."

Juana punched Matt in the stomach. She did not like being misunderstood. The half-Indian girl was trying to strip me, much to my moral degradation and lascivious gratification. I tried to fasten the buttons as quickly as she undid them, but I was quickly losing ground.

"Mira," Juana said, holding five fingers in front of Matt's face. *"Cinco,"* she said. She turned her thumb in against her palm and said, *"Quatro."* Her fingers went down one by one as she said, *"Tres, dos, uno."* Then she brandished her closed fist in Matt's face and said, *"Cero!"*

"Oh, I git it," Matt said, handing the map to me. "She don't mean that it don't mean nothin'. She means that it means absolutely nothin'. *Cero* is zero."

Of course! Only one letter differed between the two. Zero! *La piedra del cero* was the rock of the zero. That was where my treasure hunt would begin thanks to the generosity of the kind old Mexican. But what and where in the hell was the rock of the zero?

I might have had something of a tussle with temptation at that juncture. With the map translated, the only matter left unresolved was that of the half-Indian prostitute. But a sudden shotgun blast relieved me of my moral responsibilities to resist her advances.

Juana jumped onto her bed, bounced off holding the mattress, and landed in the corner with it on top of her. The half-Indian whore jerked her hands out of my pockets so fast that the rough fabric of my trousers chafed me in a sensitive area. She joined Juana behind the mattress. Matt pulled his pistol out and cocked it.

Another blast went off somewhere in the shack and I could hear the courtesans screaming and doors slamming and one big, loud, angry voice railing above it all. If Juana's room had had a window, I would have leapt through it at that point, but there was no such avenue of escape available. The ruckus outside of the room continued as Matt and I backed speechlessly away from the door, he with his revolver cocked and aimed in that direction, I holding my pants up so they wouldn't fall below my knees—the half-Indian whore had undone most of the buttons. The thundering voice roared again in the hallway and filled me with dread—and disdain for the old Mexican for getting me into this fix.

Suddenly the door burst open and we beheld a huge, grizzled frontiersman in the doorway with a double-barreled shotgun. Matt dropped his pistol and it went off. The frontiersman sent a blast of buckshot through the ceiling in retaliation.

"Who's under that beddin'?" he demanded.

"Just whores," Matt said.

"Let me see 'em!" His voice rivaled the bellow of a crazed bull.

Juana and the half-breed peeked over the top of the mattress and then ducked under again. The frontiersman cursed and moved down the hall. I eased cautiously to the door, holding my trousers up with one hand, hoping to make my break up the hall and out into the street to my mare, Liberty.

Just then drunken Dick fell into the corridor in front of the frontiersman, pulling up his pants and holding onto his pistol. "What the hell is going on out here?" he asked, swaying as he stood. From the same room, now, came the yellow-haired minx, clutching Dick's shirt in front of her naked body. She took one look at the big man with the shotgun, said, "Papa!" and ducked her head of yellow hair back into her room. Other heads ducked into other rooms and only Dick was left standing in front of the double-barrel.

"Why, you whorin' little son of a bitch!" the old settler bellowed. He thumbed back the hammer of his live barrel and leveled it on Dick. I was Dick's only hope for salvation and as such I foolishly disregarded my own safety and used both fists to strike the enraged father on the back of the head, causing him to blow a huge chunk of wall away as he fell.

Dick must have sobered up instantly, because he made a marvelously agile leap over the old pioneer and shot past me at a sprint. Matt ran out behind him and so did several other customers. "Run, Charlie!" Matt yelled to me. That was the last I ever heard from Matt Cottle, however, because my trousers had dropped down around my ankles, hindering my escape. A shotgun barrel tapped me on the skull about then, and I fell into a compulsory form of slumber.

I awoke in the San Antonio City Jail, arrested for causing a drunken row in a whorehouse. I found out the old settler had escaped with his yellow-haired daughter, leaving only me to pay for the damages. Thus, less than one day after my arrival in the city where my permanent avoidance of trouble was to have begun, I found myself jailed, wounded, ashamed, and utterly miserable.

FOUR

The judge let me wire my banker in Matagorda County for the money I needed to pay for my fine and the damages. I included strict instructions that no one in the vicinity should know of my whereabouts. I had to drop my alias and go back to being Royal Strickland Huckaby, which was neither an honor nor a pleasure. Until I could produce the cash, I had to remain in jail. The authorities were rather upset with me and I was furious at the old Mexican. And at myself for having believed in him.

One jailer, however, listened to my story that I was but little responsible for the disastrous outcome of the previous night, and he checked the bank for me at intervals to see if the transfer of funds had been accomplished. This man was a short bundle of muscles whose head consisted of a thick skull and an anvil jaw, the hinges of which he seemed to keep working by greasing their joints regularly with profanities.

"Hey, Huckaby," he said when the beans and bread

came that evening. "The goddamn bank ain't got your money yet. Tomorrow you'll get out for sure, though. Anyway, we'll keep your ass out of trouble tonight." He slid the tin plate through a slot in the grating. "Here, I got you a newspaper to pass the time with."

One of the other prisoners scowled at me from his cell. "I guess if I had me some money in the bank I could buy me a guard, too."

"Shut up, you thievin' bastard," shouted the guard, and spit on the prisoner's food before sliding it through the cell grate.

The newspaper distracted me with satirical commentary and accounts of all the local disasters and social engagements. I remembered the specifics of only two articles, however. One was a cryptic report of the rechartering of the Colorado River Navigation Company that was, according to the newspaper, engaged in clearing the raft at the mouth of the Colorado River to open that stream to steamer traffic. I knew that to be pure bunkum.

The Huckabys owned ranch land along the lower Colorado and I had seen the raft many times over the years and had seen several attempts to clear it fail. The Colorado River Navigation Company was an impotent, graft-ridden governmental entity that, each time it was reactivated, ran out of money before a fraction of the raft could be blasted or carved away.

As a boy I had once walked across the raft and shot a great many water moccasins in the crossing. It was a permanent fixture on the river. Every year, floods tore trees from the banks hundreds of miles along the Colorado and pulled them downstream to add to the driftwood raft. In time, they became waterlogged, sank, and were driven into the riverbed by other sinking debris with the force of a pile driver. The river current seeped through the raft but steamers could not enter from the Gulf of Mexico. Only a couple of land-locked boats serviced the river above the raft.

About once every ten years, some legislator who had

never laid eyes on the tangled mass of timber would undertake to remove it with public funds, and the Colorado River Navigation Company would quit the grave, usually fed by taxes levied on steamers and other merchant boats. It would slow the growth of the raft for a while, until some bureaucrat had sufficiently lined his pockets, then it would fold for lack of funds and hibernate for another decade or so while the great raft remained forever intact.

That brief newspaper article predicting the ultimate navigability of the river made me chuckle a little, sarcastically, despite my aching head and dejected frame of mind. The idea seemed even more peculiar now that railroads served almost every town along the Colorado as high up as Austin. Why did the river need steamer traffic? Besides, I had seen the Colorado shrink to a trickle during drought years. I decided not to fret anymore over it. I had my own concerns to look after and, so far, I had done a sorry job of looking after them.

On the same page with the report of the Navigation Company, however, I found an article that *did* require every particle of my concern. Reading it made my cell darken.

SPECTACULAR MURDER
Four Dead in Burnet County War

The Burnet *Messenger* reports a stunning double murder in the area of southern Burnet County on the 14th inst., the two victims, brothers, being members of the Standard family currently embroiled in a trouble with a neighboring family by the name of Flatt.

The Standard brothers were shot in the back from ambush near their ranch on the south bank of the Colorado River below the Marble Falls, their bodies filled with bullets. These murders bring to four the number of victims killed in the Flatt-Standard feud. Two Flatt brothers died in a battle two months ago.

The *Messenger* credits a land dispute as the source of the conflict, the two families both claiming the same parcel of land along Double Horn Creek where it empties into the Colorado River.

The *Messenger* reports the neighborhood of southern Burnet and northern Blanco counties in a state of extreme agitation. Texas Rangers have been summoned to help locate the boundary between the two clans and end the hostilities.

I could not say where Burnet County was in relation to my jail cell, but I knew I would have to find out before I left the city. I did not intend to get anywhere within fifty miles of any feud between families or any other opposing factions.

I suffered from fitful nightmares of ambush and violence that night. The next morning the guard at the San Antonio City Jail secured my fine from the bank and opened my cell door.

"Your old nag is in the livery around the block," he said. "You'll have to pay the bill there, too."

"Where is Burnet County from here?" I asked.

"Burnet County? Shit, I don't know. What town is in Burnet County?"

"Burnet, naturally."

"Well, how the hell was I to know? Houston ain't in Houston County. Austin ain't in Austin County."

"Just tell me where the town of Burnet is from here."

"Ninety miles due north, past the Marble Falls on the Colorado. Is that where you're heading?"

"Nope. That's the place I intend to avoid."

"Oh, yes, I understand. So, if anyone was to ask where Roy Huckaby was headed after raking hell in San Antonio, I should tell them anywhere but Burnet County."

"Tell them what you like. I simply mean to say that I intend to avoid the place."

"Yes, sir, Mr. Huckaby. I understand. You are going anywhere, but you damn sure as hell are not going to Burnet County. That I will remember."

"I don't care if you remember it or not," I said.

The guard shrugged his burly shoulders and brought

my personal belongings to me, the most conspicuous item among them being the rolled sheepskin stained with India ink.

"What son of a bitch sold you that worthless piece of horse shit?" he asked, snorting out a laugh or two. "Money just sort of has a way of flowing with you, don't it?"

I had no objection to the guard keeping a small stipend for serving as my liaison with the local bank, but for the amount he took from my cash reserves he should have been locked up in his own jail. I had no intention of starting another altercation in San Antonio, however, because I had found them to be accompanied by the most serious of consequences. I let the jailer keep the money and bid farewell to San Antonio, its jail, its whorehouses, its saloons, and its devious, old citizens bearing gifts of bogus treasure maps.

FIVE

Things change northwest of San Antonio. Limestone rears suddenly through the topsoil. Running springs carve it into craggy ranges. Stunted trees spread a general cloak over the hills, but where their roots probe the spring beds they gain ample, even heroic, proportions.

I stopped among these first outriders of the Texas hills and asked myself what I would do now and how I would prevent myself from straying again from my plan to lead a life free of criminal activity. As I had done in Huntsville, I found a hillside to recline against.

Where would I go now? It seemed easier at the time to decide where I would not go. Not Burnet County, where the Flatt-Standard trouble was leading to murder and ambuscade. Not Matagorda County, where my own vendetta was lying dormant, waiting to flair at my return. Not San Antonio. Not the frontier. I unhooked my canteen from my saddle horn and took a swallow. Liberty was staked and grazing nearby.

I wanted to go to the most peaceful town in Texas.

Where was it? After some deliberation, I decided Fredericksburg would be my destination. The Germans who had settled there loved peace and had even managed to get along with the Comanches before that tribe was run into the Indian Territory. I thought I could probably find work on one of the farms or ranches in the area. I was desperate for a job now, willing to work for room and board. San Antonio had proven true the adage about idle hands.

I got up and moved my mare to another part of the hill. She had eaten all the grass in her circle around the picket pin. Then I moved my own place of repose farther into the shadows. The sun had crept dangerously close.

To get to Fredericksburg, I resolved to use the same mode of travel that had delivered me from Huntsville to San Antonio without incident. I would proceed slowly, keeping my eyes peeled for signs of trouble—like decrepid Mexicans with treasure maps and drunken cowboys carrying racks of deer antlers.

For some time I deliberated on whether or not I should give up my practice of doing good deeds. It seemed the kindness I had done the old Mexican had led to all kinds of skulduggery. It became clear after an hour or so of meditation, however, that my curiosity and greed—not my thoughtfulness toward the old man—had led to the incident in the whorehouse. I decided to continue to pursue acts of helpfulness but to desist in any thoughts of buried treasure.

Buried treasure! Consider the lunacy of it. Of all the things I could conceive that would cause me to break into jail, buried treasure seemed the most outlandish. And yet five cowboys on some ranch were probably telling the story of it as I lay in the shade of my scrubby oak tree.

What *was* this supposed treasure the old Mexican's map had misrepresented to me, anyway? I put the canteen under my head and stared into the sky. *El tesoro*. The treasure. Such vagueness! What treasure? In Texas? The land of a thousand legends of buried treasure? From the shifting sand dunes of Galveston where Jean Lafitte buried his pirated booty to Castle Gap, west of the Pecos, where Emperor Maximilian's fortune waited to be unearthed? Treasure indeed! Trunks of it, mule loads, wagon loads, train loads—all for rubes and dreamers!

The clouds above took on the shapes of abandoned mine shafts and caches of gold nuggets; jewels and coins and gems; oaken chests trimmed in brass and bulging with loot.

I sprang up so suddenly that my mare jerked the slack out of her picket rope. I picked up a stone and hurled it into a little canyon and heard it clacking among boulders. I shook my head, spit, pissed on a cedar bush. I had to work all ridiculous thoughts of treasure out of my system and out of my mind—a mind contorted with some nebulous form of greed that was bound to bring me nothing but misery.

The map! The damned treasure map was at the core of my greed. I rushed around under the oak trees and picked up as many sticks as I could find. My mare stood and stared at me, bewildered. I pulled dry grass for kindling and put a match to it. Soon I had a fire going and I reached into my saddlebag for the old Mexican's map.

I made one crucial mistake before tossing the sheepskin into the flames. I unrolled it for a last look. Two points, a line running between them. *El tesoro*—the treasure. One hundred eighty-nine chains, seven varas. Forty-nine degrees northwest. *La piedra del cero*—the rock of the zero.

What and where in the hell was the rock of the zero?

I threw the map onto the fire and watched every grain of it burn to ashes. It gave the smell of a branding iron against a yearling's flank. The flames dwindled and the embers cooled and I scattered the ashes among the stones. I sat and looked back at the sky. The map was gone and the clouds were clouds again and my ambition was to work for room and board, not to dig for buried treasure. The vindictive old Mexican was dead, San Antonio behind me and the treasure map a part of my past. I was, again, a man of one ambition, one concern, one goal for life.

But the Spanish language is odd in its beauty and it rings like music in one's memories. Like an old song, a phrase heard often enough echoes endlessly in the subconscious, weaves itself among one's thoughts, and trips from the tongue in whispers when all else is silent. *La piedra del cero . . . la piedra del cero . . . la piedra del cero . . .*

The first leg of my trip to Fredericksburg proved uneventful. I rode at such a sluggish pace that my mare found it possible to graze on tall stalks of grass as we went. The first day I made it only as far as Leon Springs. There was a fine stone stagecoach inn there where I took a meal. But I shunned drinks at the bar and slept in a field outside of town.

The second day I rode through Boerne, one of the German towns settled northwest of San Antonio. The town had neat stone houses, clean streets, and an overall look of prosperity. I was so pleased with the looks of the place that I stopped in the post office and asked if employment might be found in the area.

The postmaster, an immaculate man in suspenders and a bow tie, looked up and down my dusty assemblage, flared his nostrils, and said, "We have no work here for the likes of drifters and saddle tramps. This is a proper town."

I moved on, acutely aware of my slovenly appearance. I hadn't bathed since New Braunfels, before arriving at San Antonio. Bathing was a habit I had found difficult to keep up during my sentence in the state penitentiary. Convicts were expected to wash their faces and hands daily, but all from a common trough without a change of water.

I found the Guadalupe River running beside the town of Comfort. I decided to avail myself of the clear, cool waters rushing among the huge bald cypress trees. I rode downstream until I found a place where a fallen colossus had stretched its woody carcass clear across the shallow stream, forming a natural dam. I staked my horse, shed my clothes, and jumped in.

It was October but still hot enough to make a man lather nearly as much as his horse. The Guadalupe felt so good that I stayed in it until sundown. At twilight, a flock of wild turkeys wandered to within fifty yards of my bathing place and flew up to roost in a sycamore. I began to wish for a rifle and decided that when I found a place to settle, I would buy one. But I didn't want to carry one on the road. A weapon might attract trouble.

By dark, my clothes were dry—I had washed them, too—so I rode into Comfort and ate at the stagecoach station. Afterward, I found a couple of old boarders whittling by lantern light on the gallery.

"Good evening, gentlemen," I said.

"Vat's dat?" one said. The folks around Boerne and Comfort, I had found, spoke German as often as English. And some of them, when they did speak English, spoke with the thick tongues of the Old World.

"I said, good evening."

"Oh, yah. Goot evening."

"Sit down, stranger," the other whittler said. With him, no accent was noticeable.

"Don't mind if I do. Pretty hot."

"Yah, ist plenty hot."

"And dry, too," the other one said, "except for that rain we had while back." They continued to litter the floor of the gallery with cedar shavings. The smell of the freshly cut wood drifted to me on the evening breeze.

"I don't suppose there would be a place for a fellow to work for room and board around here?"

The knives became still and the two old whittlers looked at each other, then looked at me, then scratched their heads and stroked their beards and looked at each other again.

"*Nein.* Ain't no verk arount here like dat."

"Nope," the other said.

The knives went back to biting cedar, but after a few strokes the whittlers stopped and looked at each other again. They scratched their heads and stroked their beards some more.

"Nope, not around here, son. However . . ."

"Vat *vas* dat feller's name?" said the German whittler.

"Seems to me he had the first name of a woman."

"Yah! Dat's right! Marion. Marion! Hoh, boy, vat a name!"

"Marion Harkey," the second whittler said.

"Who is Marion Harkey?" I asked.

"He's a fellow that passed through here yesterday. He lost his help recently and was putting out the word that he wanted to hire a man."

"What kind of work does he want done?" I asked.

"Vants lots of fences built und den torn down. Lots of verk, ofer und ofer."

"Fences?" I asked, appealing to the other whittler for clarification.

"Yes. Marion Harkey is a traveling drummer selling bob wire. He goes around putting on demonstrations."

"Demonstrations?"

"Yah, but ve didn't git to see no demonstration here. Too many damned sheeps und not enough cows. Bob vire ist for der cows."

"No, we didn't see it, but we read about it in the San Antonio paper. Harkey built a pen of cedar posts strung with seven strands of his bob wire on Military Plaza and he throwed a rodeo. Beer, beef, bronco rides, and roping contests and cuttin' horses and all. Then, he turned a hundred longhorn mavericks from west Texas into the pen and had a Mexican try to spook them through the wire with torches. They got cut up the first time they tried it and wouldn't go at it again."

"Yah, dat vire helt dem vild cows in, alright. Und dat Marion Harkey, he sold plenty of vire."

"But it's a traveling show, son. Harkey needs a man to build his fences and then tear them down and roll the wire back up every place he throws his rodeo."

I tilted back on the rear legs of my chair and thought about the prospects of building fences so that I could tear them down again. "Where did he go from here?"

"Fredericksburg. He left this morning in his wagon."

"Yah. Dat Marion, he's got to go vest und find zum cows to sell lots of dat vire."

I didn't want to become a barbed-wire drifter on the frontier. Not everybody out there liked the thought of bristling strands stretched across what were once public ranges. Some parties made a habit of cutting fences and shooting fence stretchers. Marion Harkey could spend his wages on some other lackey. I wanted to settle.

"And that's the only work available around here?"

"Yah, dat's it."

"Sorry, son."

"Well, thank you, gentlemen. It's been a pleasure talking to you both."

"Yah, und you, too."

"Good luck, son."

I heard coyotes howling that night as I camped beside the Guadalupe. It was pretty country the Germans had settled a generation before. The hills and clear running streams appealed to a flatlander from the muddy end of the rivers. It was a little rocky, but good for sheep and goats on the hills and suitable for farming in the bottoms where the cedars and oaks were cleared. Cattle did well enough out on the flats. Rain could get scarce in the summer, but springs flowed between most of the hills and folks seemed to get by without getting rich. I asked for no more than that for myself.

The next morning I resumed my trek to Fredericksburg. I passed the stone houses and barns of little farms every few miles and envied the occupants. I had once lorded over two hundred laborers on the sprawling Huckaby plantations and never had to pitch a single fork of hay or throw a solitary calf. But now I wanted only to get intimately acquainted with a couple of thousand acres, work there, hunt, mind my own business. I wanted to live in a place where the name Huckaby caused no more of a stir than the name of a common peon.

Not long after crossing the divide from the Guadalupe Valley into the watershed of the Pedernales River, I caught sight of a two-mule wagon, stopped by the side of the road. I immediately reined my mare in to reconnoiter. A lone man was unloading something from the wagon and a wheel leaned against the sideboards. It looked like a good deed in the making, so I moved cautiously forward.

"How do," I said.

Marion Harkey turned with a heavy spool of barbed wire in his hands and regarded me with a suspicious eye. He wore the clothes of a ranch-man—from the bandanna around his neck to the boots on his feet—but the clothes hadn't come between Marion and much ranch work. He had the thick-waisted build of a prosperous drummer. Sweat streaked his shirt and he looked quite put out. "How would *you* do?" he asked. "Can't you see I've got a busted wagon wheel?"

"Yes, sir, I gathered that. Thought you might like a hand fixing it."

Harkey's tune improved almost immediately. "I would be grateful for some help. Yes, I would. Kind of you to offer, Mr. . . . ?"

"Royal S. Huckaby."

"Marion Harkey."

I got down from my mare and we shook hands.

"Royal. That's a fine name for a common man."

"Thank you," I said, rolling a spool of wire from the bed of the wagon. I judged it weighed in the neighborhood of a hundred pounds when I hefted it.

"Just throw that product down," Harkey said. "Manhandle it. It won't bust. The spool will, maybe, but the wire's indestructible. That's a double-steel strand twist with S-locked barbs. More points to the pound than any wire on the market and just one pound per rod—the lightest, strongest, and cheapest wire ever invented. Eight hundred pounds of bawlin' maverick can't bust that product."

I had four spools on the ground by now and Harkey was just rolling his second one out of the bed.

"I know. I've heard about your rodeo in San Antonio. They say you sold some wire there."

"If a man believes in his product, he ain't afraid to demonstrate it. This wire sells itself. I see the day coming when the whole prairie will glisten with these beautiful strands. We'll have better beef, improved breeds—fat, lazy cattle built for a dinner plate . . ."

While Harkey practiced his sales pitch, I lightened the wagon enough to prize the rear axle up so I could remove the broken wheel. Harkey sat on the cedar post we used for a lever while I put the new wheel on.

"I walked all the way to Fredericksburg for that wheel," he said. "I rode part of the way back in a wagon with a farmer, but rolled that wheel by hand the rest of the way. Whew! That's why I'm so give out. Lucky for me you came along."

He talked more about the future for barbed wire while I loaded the spools back into the wagon. "What do I owe you?" he asked when I had finished.

"Nothing. Just being neighborly."

"By Lucifer, that's decent of you, Royal! Where are you heading?"

"Fredericksburg."

"In that case, ride with me. Throw your saddle on those spools and give your old nag a rest."

Harkey drove a little fast for my taste, but I didn't complain. "Business in Fredericksburg?" he asked.

"I'm looking for work there."

"Work! Why didn't you say so? I need a fence builder for my rodeo. I had a couple of hands, but I lost them in San Antonio. They must have got drunk or jailed or something. I'll be damned if I'm going to wait on hired help. You can start—well, hell, you've already started, haven't you? I'll have all the work you can stand between here and Wyoming."

"Actually, I was hoping to settle."

"Settle! I made you for a drifter, Royal. What use have fellows like us got for the sedentary life? The frontier is crying for barbed wire. Let's deliver! I'll start you right now and pay you a full day's wage for today. I've got the money in my pocket."

Harkey handed the reins to me and pulled out a roll of bills that he flashed in my face. He pitched a swell deal, but I had no ear for it.

"The frontier's not for me," I said. "I may look like a drifter, but I'm a civilized fellow." I handed the reins back to him.

The wire salesman had put on a hat with the kind of crease that was popular with ranchmen then. He pushed it back on his head and diverted his eyes from the road long enough to look me over with some surprise. "You've seen rough times, Royal. I can tell that by looking at you. The frontier's the place for you."

"I've seen enough of rough times. I'm just looking for someplace quiet to live."

Harkey persisted with his offers of employment for several miles. I turned him down flat, but he refused to accept defeat and started negotiating.

"So, you want to settle. Well, I'll tell you what I can do for you. Maybe I can find you some work. If I can sell some outfit around here a mess of wire, they'll want me to hire 'em somebody to string it. Cowboys won't have any part of that kind of work—they know a fence will just put them out of a job. Young Bob Wire can do the work of twenty-five old cowhands. And Bob Wire don't eat beef and he don't drink whiskey. Reckon you can build a fence?"

"I've seen it done."

"Can you build a windmill tower?"

"Windmill?"

"Yes, I sell windmills, too."

"Why windmills?"

"Why? You must come from a wet country, Royal, I can gather that about you right away. You must have plenty of water holes where you're from—down on the coast, I'll bet. Down there you can build a pasture just about anywhere and have water in it—a creek or a bayou or something. But in dry country, you need a windmill. You fence cows in a pasture and you better fence some water in there with them or you'll be out of the beef business and into the hide and tallow market. Out west you have to pump water up from the ground. I couldn't sell a single spool of wire out there if I didn't sell a few windmills to boot."

"I guess I could build a windmill tower if I had one to look at for a model."

"I won't sell many windmills around here. Them dang bubbling springs are running all over this hilly country. I probably won't sell much barbed wire, either. The Germans have built rock fences and got more sheep than cows. Awful tight with their money, too. But wait till I get into cow country out west. That's where I'll make my money, among those cattle speculators. I did pretty good south of San Antonio, too, but the high plains is where I stand to make a bundle. That country is made for fences. You ever been out there?"

"No."

"Nothing to get in the way of fences out there, now that the Indians and buffaloes are cleaned out. Ain't even any trees to clear. The only problem is, there ain't nothing to make fence posts out of. Say, now, there's some work for you! Can you chop a fence post?"

"Sure."

We came to the Pedernales River, shallow and running clear among rounded white rocks in its bed. We let the mules drink there and cooled our faces in the stream. Harkey began trying to convince me that my future lay with cedar fence posts.

"You aim to stay at Fredericksburg?"

"I hope to."

"Check the post office every now and then. Don't be surprised if you find me ordering fence posts. I'll pay the going rate if you can chop 'em and freight 'em west. There must be a million posts in all these cedar brakes around here. It's rough work, but if you round up a crew of men whose hands will fit an ax handle, you can turn a profit. Barbed wire is reaching west and they need posts out there on the plains, Royal!"

I took it all for mostly idle talk, so I told Harkey I'd consider throwing in with him as a post supplier. In truth, the thought of becoming a cedar chopper boss made me a little nervous. Too much responsibility. I wouldn't mind swinging an ax, but swinging business deals could lead to misunderstandings. I had seen it happen before. I had seen men get killed over minor disputes in ownership of property.

The mules were full of water and moving uphill from the Pedernales, so Harkey drove them easy. We made Fredericksburg in another hour. The town differed from the sticky, muddy, clapboard-and-brick coastal towns I had grown up around and that made it instantly appealing. They built with limestone and cypress lumber in Fredericksburg, and the Germans knew how to build things for the long haul. The town had sturdy stone houses, churches, public buildings. They weren't fancy, but they answered every aspect of practicality. Low hills surrounded the town and oak trees shaded the homes.

Main street was wide enough for freight wagons to turn around in. Harkey drove his mules past the White Elephant Saloon and the Nimitz Hotel. We proceeded to a wagon yard on the west side of town, Harkey tipping his hat at anyone on the street who looked like a cattleman.

"Let's have some dinner over at the hotel," he said as a towheaded boy unhitched his mules for him.

I didn't know Harkey's habits, but I thought it possible he would desire an after-dinner drink, so I declined to dine with him. "No, thank you. I'm going to ask around about employment."

"Where are you staying tonight?"

"I'm limited on funds. I'll find a field to camp in."

"That's no way to live. It's liable to start raining this time of year. Why don't you share a room with me at the hotel?"

"No, thanks. I'm comfortable outside."

Harkey shook his head. "You're an odd one, Royal. Look, at least do me the honor of sleeping in my wagon here in the yard so you don't get snake-bit. That way I can see you in the morning and tell you whether or not I hear of any work you might be interested in."

That sounded agreeable enough with me, so I accepted the invitation and left my saddle in the wagon and my horse at the yard.

I spent the rest of the day walking around town, looking for work. Every person I met gave me a sidewise glance. I figured the cheap suit from the state penitentiary was making me look like a low-rate confidence man or something so I decided to invest some of my dwindling cash reserves in a new suit of work clothes. I found a dry-goods store and bought a leather belt, a pair of heavy jean pants, a cotton shirt, and the first pair of underwear I had owned in three years. They were long-handles; winter was not too far off.

I took a good meal at the Nimitz Hotel in the afternoon and saw Harkey working the other side of the street, shaking hands, telling jokes, and making acquaintances. When dark came, the little town of Fredericksburg lapsed into silence. I used my old clothes for a pillow and settled comfortably in the bed of Harkey's wagon, surrounded by spools of barbed wire. Maybe the next day I would find a farm that needed a hand. I imagined making a little room for myself in one of the cool rock barns or outbuildings.

I dreamed that night that I was in a room of stone with chains on my wrists and ankles. But there was a hoe in the room and I used it to part the shackles as if by magic.

Then I floated out of the room, dreamlike, and started walking somewhere with the hoe over my shoulder, my legs and arms swinging free, unfettered. It was dawn, cool and foggy. I passed a stone cottage, and a pretty girl, a farmer's daughter, stepped out onto the porch and waved. In a moment there were three girls waving, sisters—like the three sisters I had grown up with, but prettier. I waved back at them, smiled, and strode to a field that appeared through the fog.

The soft dirt felt good under my feet and the magic hoe started cutting weeds between the rows. It went effortlessly up and down. I struck a rock in the dirt, dug it up, threw it to the side of the field. The hoe attacked the weeds again. I struck another rock, lifted it, and tossed it with great facility beyond the furrows, into the fog. The hoe went back to work, and I struck another object in the tilled ground. I stooped and felt for it with my hands. Lifting it, I hurled it high and hard into the mist. But the dirt fell away when it flew and it erupted into a hundred nuggets of gold, a thousand coins of silver, a million jewels of precious stone—all of which sailed away, hopelessly lost in the fog.

Then there was laughter, and when I turned, I saw the old Mexican standing between the furrows. He was doubled over with mirth. His hardened old hands slapped his knees and tears of joy glistened in the creases of his weathered face. His laughter sounded like the quick grating of a rasp against a coffin. He laughed as the fog swirled and thickened, then looked at me and said, *"La piedra del cero. La piedra del cero."* Then he spread his arms like the wings of a flying dove and laughed until he vanished in the fog.

SIX

It was the laughter of Marion Harkey that woke me up. A couple of spools of barbed wire had shifted and rolled in next to me in the night. I slept so soundly that I didn't feel them. On the other hand, maybe I felt them a bit too pointedly.

Harkey said, "Wake up, Royal, before somebody catches you humping that spool!" and "Say, you like them with bristles on, don't you?" and "I guess the rut comes this time of year for you Huckaby bucks," and he interspersed all his comments with spates of laughter.

It was dawn and Harkey was ready to hitch his mules and head west. "There ain't no wire or windmills to be sold in this town. These folks are too tight-fisted. They could pinch the scalp off an Indian-head penny. Here, I brought you some breakfast."

The Germans made a kind of sausage wrapped in dough and then baked. Harkey had brought me a couple of them along with a jar full of fresh milk. I barely had the capacity to finish it all. My stomach had shrunk after three years of near starvation as a convict and I didn't need a tremendous amount of sustenance to keep going.

"I want you to ride with me to a ranch west of here," Harkey said as I ate. "There's a big cow outfit out there, I'm told. If I can sell some wire there, they'll be looking for someone to string it. That ought to keep you busy until I start sending orders for fence posts. You don't know it yet, Royal, but you're going to get rich with barbed wire and cedar posts."

I saddled Liberty and rode with the barbed-wire wagon as the sun rose behind us. Along the way, Harkey warned me about the dangers of fencing.

"Some of the cowboys will come behind you and cut every strand you stretch. These are mostly the lazier, no-account hands that know they'll be the first ones to get fired when the fences are in. Sometimes they'll throw in with rustlers, too. Barbed wire makes rustling more difficult, as you could figure.

"Mostly, it's the big outfits who start fencing because they've got the money for it. Lots of times the little men will throw in together and cut the fences of the big men. Especially when they fence in water holes and such. The fence cutters give theirselves names like the Blue Devils and the Hatchet Gang and the Nipper Brigade. One of those gangs caught a fellow building a fence down on the Nueces and they wrapped him in wire and drug him to death. I suggest you get yourself a pistol, Royal, if you aim to go into the fence-stretching business."

With that bit of intelligence, I resolved to part company with Marion Harkey at the first convenient opportunity. My future did not lie with young Bob Wire. "The wire cutters must be pretty popular if they can get away with all that," I said.

"Popular, hell. Sneakiness can make up for a great lack of popularity. Them fence cutters come out in the dark of night, cut some fence, maybe leave a message or some-thing, then they're back in their beds before sunrise."

"How much damage could they do in that short amount of time?"

"Hell, it takes a while to build a fence, but it don't take no time at all to tear one down. There's all sorts of ways. Some of them carry wire nippers with them and clip every strand between every post for a mile or more. Some of them rope the posts and pull them clean out of the ground, and others chop them down with hatchets. I've known them to pour oil on the posts and let them burn. Once they started a hell of a wildfire that way. Some brave fence busters down in Karnes County took the time to roll up two miles of wire and left it in front of the fellow's house who had stretched it. And down near Laredo . . ."

The longer Harkey talked, the more apprehensive I grew about riding beside a wagon loaded with barbed wire. I expected to meet a gang of anti-fence men at every bend in the road. "Maybe this country isn't ready to be fenced yet, if so many are that set against it," I said.

"Oh, don't think the big-pasture men are just putting up with it," Harkey said. "Down at San Patricio they lynched a fellow because he was carrying wire nippers in his saddlebags. And they patrol them new fences, too. They got a right to protect their property. Fencing is legal, you know. There ain't no laws against fencing your own land. The open-range days are over, Royal. Men are buying up those good pastures and those water holes and they have a right to fence them. You might just as well get used to that . . ."

We traveled on, past orchards of scrubby peach trees and rocky fields of crooked cornstalks. I was feeling grave, but Harkey kept talking. For a drummer, he was likable enough, but he was going to lead me into a fence war just as sure as Matt Cottle had led me into the whorehouse scrape.

I started thinking up excuses to turn back to Fredericksburg. Maybe I could say that I had left something there. But that sounded too lame. Maybe I could pretend to take sick and go back to see a doctor. But I wasn't sure I was enough of an actor to pull that one off. Finally, I came up with a possible solution.

"Harkey, where have you sold the most wire in this part of the state?" I asked.

"Oh, the folks in this rocky country don't care much for the idea of digging post holes. Business is slow around here. I haven't even bothered to put on my rodeo demonstration. I did sell a mess of wire back on the Colorado, though, just downstream of the Marble Falls. An old man there has decided to fence his whole spread."

That was my cue to turn back. The Marble Falls, I knew, was in Burnet County, right where the Flatt-Standard feud was going on. That was the next-to-last place I cared to go. But Harkey didn't know that.

"The Marble Falls! That's not but fifty miles from here. Why haven't you told me about it before? There's some work for me right there, building fences."

Harkey became serious. He twitched his whip nervously and shook his head. "It ain't a good idea to look for work there."

"Why not?"

"Because the old man I sold the wire to is named Eli Flatt and he's right in the middle of some trouble with his neighbors, the Standards."

I shuddered to know that I was in the presence of a man who had driven his barbed-wire wagon among feudists. But I continued to express my false desire to go to work for the Flatts, just for the excuse to travel a different path from Harkey's. "What difference does that make?" I asked. "I'm looking for work, not trouble. Besides, I've seen family fights before."

Harkey twitched his whip more expressively. "I don't know, Royal. Folks are mighty nervous in that country. You see, the Flatt-Standard thing is a *land* feud. Flatt wants to fence a piece of property on Double Horn Creek that both families are claiming. If you're the one doing the fencing, you'll be in the middle of the fight. I'd advise you against it."

"The thing of it is," I argued, "is that I need a job now. I'm low on money. If you sell some wire somewhere up the road here, I'll have to wait for weeks for the freight wagons to ship it all out before I can go to work. You can't let them have any of the wire in your wagon, here, because you'll need that for your rodeo. But since you sold your wire to Flatt some time ago, he's probably received it by now. I think there's a good wagon road from Burnet to the Marble Falls and Burnet is on the railroad." I felt peculiar pretending to argue my way into a feud.

Harkey shook his head and worried. It was gratifying in a way to see him fret like that on my account. "It's dangerous, Royal. Barbed wire is liable to be dangerous anywhere in Texas right now, but especially in between the Standards and the Flatts. I spent a night with the Flatts. You ought to see the eyes of those men—old Eli and the two sons he's got left. The other two are already dead. Seeing family die like that makes a man's conscience turn cold. The Flatt brothers murdered two of the Standard boys while I was stayin' with them."

"While you were there?"

"Well, I didn't see it happen, but I saw the Flatt boys come back to their house when it was over, looking wild-eyed and kind of pale. I didn't figure out what they had done until later that day when I went to the Marble Falls to put in the order for the old man's wire. There was talk about it all over the settlement there and the two dead Standard boys were laid out at the general store, filled with bullet holes. I got the hell out of town before somebody figured out that I had spent the night with the Flatts. I didn't want to be associated with them and I didn't want to answer no questions to no grand jury. The Standards are going to fight back, of course."

"I read that the Texas Rangers were coming to settle the question of who owned the land."

"The rangers are busy on the plains dealing with those

fence wars I've been telling you about. They haven't had time to take care of the Flatt-Standard trouble yet. The way I heard it, the judge ruled that the rangers and an investigator from the General Land Office would come find the old boundary marker between the Flatt and Standard properties to decide who owned what. But right after court was over, they started shootin' at one another on the way home and the Standards killed two Flatts.

"Then, while I was there, like I already told you, the Flatts killed two Standards. That makes four dead. Now they'll keep fightin' one another till they're all dead, unless the rangers get there first. But the question of who owns the land hasn't been figured out yet because the investigator from the Land Office hasn't showed up. He and the rangers are supposed to come and find an old boundary marker."

"What kind of marker are they looking for?"

"I guess it's a stone one," Harkey said, "because they call it the zero stone."

For some reason I didn't grasp instantly, the term "zero stone" sounded familiar to me. Then, just after Harkey said it, a flock of doves flew up from a patch of dove weed beside the road and one of them flew right over me. By the way it beat its wings and by the cadence in its whistling voice, it seemed to be saying, *"La piedra del cero, la piedra del cero!"*

La piedra del cero? The rock of the zero! The zero stone! The point of reference on the old Mexican's treasure map! I flinched so hard that I jerked the reins and almost made my mare stumble. I lost a stirrup and fell halfway out of the saddle. When I pulled myself back into the seat, Harkey was looking at me as if he thought I was suffering convulsions. I belatedly slapped the back of my neck. "Damned horseflies," I said.

Harkey pulled his mules up and started laughing at me. "Horsefly? That son of a bitch almost knocked you off your mare! You sure it wasn't an eagle diving for those doves?"

"I'm not sure I heard you correctly about the Flatt-Standard thing," I said. "Did you say, 'the zero stone'?"

"Yeah, that's what they call that boundary marker."

"What and where in the hell *is* this zero stone?"

"Damned if I know. If they knew where it was, the Flatts and Standards would probably never have started exterminating one another in the first place. The zero stone marks the boundary that they're fighting over."

My mind all but imploded on itself and worked so fast that I lost control of it. "Harkey," I said, "I've made up my mind to go back and work for the Flatts. I've got an idea. First, I'll fence the part of their property that doesn't border the Standard land, then I'll just quit. By that time you'll be sending me orders for cedar posts and I can collect my pay from Flatt and go into business on my own." I did the smoothest lying I had ever done under the influence of the zero stone.

Harkey deliberated for a while. "Well, you're a grown man and I guess you'll do what you want to do. Just be careful. Keep your guard posted and don't trust neither Flatts nor Standards. I'll send for fence posts just as soon as I can and I'll see if I can get the buyer to pay for the first load up front. That way you can get started sooner and maybe get the hell out of Burnet County before the war gets you." He chuckled a little. "I had you figured, didn't I, Royal? I said you'd seen rough times and I can tell they don't scare you. You're liable to see more of them when you get to Burnet County."

His words were wasted on me. I was seeing the zero stone in my thoughts—a tall, polished monument standing above the trees, encircled by cavorting doves. "Good luck, Harkey," I said, moving my horse up next to his wagon seat. "Write me care of the post office at the Marble Falls."

"Count on it." He shook my hand.

I turned Liberty around and coaxed her into the first lope she had run since I had bought her at Huntsville. I heard Marion Harkey shouting behind me: "Trust your future to young Bob Wire!"

But I was seeing my fortune in old buried gold.

By pounding my heels against Liberty's flanks, I managed to goad her into a gallop. Spanish zeros rang in my ears and dashed to bits all my previous resolutions to abandon treasure hunting. I used my hat to fan the rump of my mare and grasped desperately for a mental image of the burned map. The line between *la piedra del cero* and *el tesoro* bore northwest. How many degrees? Forty-nine! The dust rose behind me as if in the wake of a whirlwind. How many chains? How many! One hundred . . . One hundred eighty . . . One hundred eighty-nine! Plus seven varas!

But, oh, my God, of what length was the chain? And of what length, exactly, was a vara? It didn't matter. I would find that treasure if I had to dig a trench ten feet deep and ten miles long from the zero stone, northwest, 49 degrees, to the buried treasure. I would use doubloons for skipping stones and ingots for trotline weights. God bless the soul of the old Mexican!

I rode so hard that I barely saw Fredericksburg when I passed it. I kept the gallop up, heading for the Marble Falls, Double Horn Creek, the zero stone, and the cache of long-forgotten treasure. Damn the Flatts and the Standards and their trifling feud!

The road forked ahead—one branch leading north and the other east—but the Marble Falls were due northeast and I had no intention of swerving. I held a beeline, taking neither fork, but making my own road between them. I plunged my mare into a gully and drove headlong into a tangle of mustang grapevines that yanked me from the saddle like a calf hitting the end of a lariat. It was probably the most fortunate accident that ever befell me, for it knocked a good deal of the treasure-hunting madness clear out of my brain.

Liberty ran halfway up the opposite slope and stopped, heaving. It took me several minutes to get my wind back and crawl to her. I loosened the saddle cinch and let her blow. I would have ridden her to death if not for the grapevine.

It was the zero stone. My knowledge of it thrilled me, but I had to learn control of it. What had happened to my plan? What of working for room and board? What of avoiding anything that smacked of my old vendetta in Matagorda County? I would have wished to God that I had never met the old Mexican, but I feared my wish might come true.

It was time to sit again against a slope and think things through. I dragged myself into the shade to ruminate.

SEVEN

If it was true that the old Mexican had given me the treasure map as his final hoax, then his laughter must have pealed somewhere as thunder when the grapevine unhorsed me. When I thought of that likelihood, I cursed his soul and damned the ashes of his sheepskin map.

If it was true that he had presented the map to me in a spirit of real benevolence, then his smile must have shone somewhere as sunshine when Marion Harkey told me where to find the zero stone. When considering that possibility, I worshiped his spirit and cherished my memories of his chart.

But even when I regarded the treasure map as a blessing, I had also to consider it a scourge. It tempted me with rumors of riches yet tortured me with threats of feud blood. Knowing what I knew about vendettas, how could I even consider approaching the haunts of the Flatts and the Standards? How could I?

Quite easily, really. I simply rationalized: My being in the vicinity of a feud did not necessitate my being drawn into it. True, it had happened to me in Matagorda County because one of the major combatants had been my friend and brother-in-law. But it would not happen with the Flatt-Standard affair because I had made no acquaintances on either side. My previous notion that jeopardy would increase with geographical proximity to a feud was a product of rampant paranoia. The real danger came from intimacy with the feudists.

With that matter settled, I decided I might just as well crawl out of the gully I had fallen in, tighten the cinch on my mare, and proceed to the Marble Falls. There was no longer any use in trying to avoid Burnet County. The lure of the treasure was so strong that even had I turned away, I would have walked back in my sleep. The spell of the zero stone owned me and I would not break it until I found my treasure—or my corpse—buried in the ground.

The trick was to master the spell. I would take no more mounted plunges into blind gullies. I would listen to no more twittering Spanish phrases from flying doves. I would rely on patience, discretion, practicality. And, most importantly, I would not approach the zero stone until I could do so without the slightest risk of injury or incrimination.

It occurred to me that if, as Harkey had said, an investigator from the General Land Office was coming with a company of Texas Rangers to find the zero stone, then I would have nothing to do but wait. Once the marker was found and the feud settled, I could snoop around 49 degrees northwest of the zero stone until I found the treasure—assuming the old Mexican's map was genuine. But it had to be genuine! The zero stone existed! At any rate, until it was located, I would have to find some kind of work around the Marble Falls to keep me busy.

That was my new formula and it made perfect sense. It required nothing but patience. I added to it a few elements from my former plan: be helpful, stay out of saloons, avoid prostitutes.

I backtracked to the fork in the road and took the east branch. It soon crossed the Pedernales and led downstream along the south bank. Questions I had not yet pondered began to arise: What type of boundary marker *was* this thing called the zero stone? Who erected it and when? How did it come to be considered lost? How did the old Mexican know about it? Who had located treasure in its vicinity and plotted the distance between the two by chain lengths? And what length of chain had been used in measuring?

Patience, Roy, patience.

I arrived at the settlement near Johnson Ranch well before dark. The Marble Falls were to the north on the Colorado, twenty-some-odd miles away. I decided to spend the night at the Johnson Ranch settlement, called Johnson City, and finish the final leg of my trip to the falls in the morning.

At Johnson City I realized another ill effect of my crazed attempt to ride cross-country to the zero stone. My charge into the gully had knocked one of my mare's shoes loose. This inconvenience was in addition to the bruises up and down my back that now had me feeling as stove-up as a grandfather.

I found a blacksmith in town. He was a bald-headed, squint-eyed old codger named Samuel Jessom who looked more cantankerous than a roped bear. But I would soon learn that he was a deacon in the Methodist Church and a paragon of decorum.

"Passing through?" he asked me after fixing the shoe.

"Yes," I said, "I'm heading to the Marble Falls."

"You're not going to try to make it there tonight, are you?"

"No, sir," I said. "I'm going to camp by the river and start in the morning."

"In that case, I'll be honored to have you for a dinner guest," he said. "Come on. We better go kill a chicken." Deacon Sam walked abruptly out through the back door of his shop.

"Do you want me to help you lock your place up?"

"No doors," he said. "I leave it wide open. Somebody might need something. Come on."

"Don't you think somebody might run off with something?"

"Nothing in there I can't get along without. Besides, if they were to ask, I'd give them whatever it was they needed, anyway. Why make a person grovel? Let's go."

I had once seen a trained chimpanzee in a traveling menagerie and Deacon Sam Jessom so reminded me of that animal that I expected to see him flip over backward any second. His feet angled outward, his legs bowed rather remarkably, and he tottered from side to side, ape-like, when he walked. His arms seemed to have been lengthened considerably from years of hefting anvils and wagon wheels. His fingers curled severely in toward his palms, permanently molded that way around the handles of hammers and billows and tongs. His shoulders dropped off at the angles of a church steeple, and if he possessed the ability to stand erect, I never saw him exercise it.

I led my mare and followed Deacon Sam down a well-worn trail that skirted a native pecan orchard and came to a tiny cabin near the Pedernales. "How do you like them?" he asked. "Fried? Roasted? We could have some dumplin's or make up some stuffin'."

"Fried," I said.

"Good. That's what I had a taste for this evening myself. Corn crib's over there. Pick out some roasting ears while I kill a fryer."

It took me longer to shuck the corn than it took Deacon Sam to pluck the chicken, yet he seemed to move in the most unhurried way. He shucked the last ear himself. "Might as well fry some okra, too," he suggested. "I'll go pick some if you'll split some stove wood."

I was more than happy to handle the firewood chores, my bruised back notwithstanding, but Jessom had gathered a basket of okra and tomatoes before I could finish.

"Why don't you draw some water from the cistern?" he suggested, and finished splitting the stove wood himself as I picked up the bucket. He had fashioned tin gutters to the eaves of his cabin and outbuildings, all designed to carry rainwater through a system of filters into the cistern. By the time I carried the water into the cabin, Deacon Sam had already lit a fire, cut up the chicken, and started melting the lard.

"Mr. Jessom, I believe you represent the most fluid example of efficiency I have ever known."

"Call me what my friends do: Deacon Sam. And don't be intimidated by my ability to get things done. I'm like John Wesley—always in haste, but never in a hurry. You don't appear to be any stranger to hard work, either—a lean fellow like yourself."

Slices of battered okra dropped, sizzling, into the fat and soon a wonderful aroma filled the tiny cabin. Deacon Sam was stamping biscuits from dough on a chopping block with one hand and setting a coffee pot on the stove with his other.

"Actually, I'm looking for work," I said. "Do you know of anything in this area?"

"What do you do?" he asked, handing me plates to set out on the table. "Milk's in that pitcher," he added.

"Anything," I said. "As long as it doesn't require any particular skill."

Jessom paused to squint at me. "I don't know of anything for sure. But there is a rumor. There's a big granite hill just the other side of the Marble Falls—one huge solid dome of rock. A few years ago the fellows who own it said they'd give enough of it to the government to build a new capitol with. I hear they're getting ready to start quarrying the granite. They're going to build a narrow gauge track to haul the stuff to Burnet and put it on the Austin and Northwestern line there to ship to the capital. That's what I hear, anyway. Maybe they'll be hiring. There looks like enough granite in that hill to last two hundred years. It's hard work, but you might be interested."

I had not envisioned quarry work as my form of livelihood, but for temporary employment it might do. It would only have to last until the rangers came and ended the feud and allowed me to do my treasure hunting. Then a happy thought occurred to me: Something learned in quarrying might prove useful in making excavations for lucre!

"If you don't find work there, you're welcome to come back and work with me for meals and a roof over your head until you get settled," Jessom said.

"Thank you. I might have to accept that offer."

When we sat to eat, the deacon bowed his head and clasped his crooked fingers together. "Let us pray," he said. "Heavenly Father, bless this meal and look after young Roy as he finds his way in this world. Grant him only that which he needs to live in the Christian spirit. In Christ's name, amen."

I said, "Amen," too, habitually. But before I did, under my breath, I muttered a vague appeal for mammon.

Deacon Sam the blacksmith must have whet his appetite on a grindstone that day. He waded through his victuals with both hands, the same way he did his work, and he could lap every morsel of nourishment from a chicken bone or a corn cob. I was more contented in the humble home of Samuel Jessom than I had been in years. His cooking was adequate, his hospitality lacked nothing, and he had put me at ease with his offer of work for room and board. As I cut the lard from the roof of my mouth with a cup of hot coffee, I lapsed into a perfectly serene frame of mind.

I could hear Deacon Sam's beard stubble snagging against his napkin as he mopped his face vigorously. "If you're going up to the Marble Falls," he said, "there's one thing to look out for. There's a fight going on between two families, the Standards and the Flatts. They're crazy with hate for each other and a newcomer wouldn't do himself any service to associate with either clan right now. Don't ask questions about them when you get there. Just keep your mouth shut and your eyes open."

"I've heard about their feud. What do you know of them?"

"I don't know much about the Flatts. Oh, I've seen old Eli around a few times. He was one of the first white men in Burnet County. He was the settler farthest up the Colorado for a few years. But I don't know him and probably wouldn't even recognize his children. Two of them are killed now, anyway."

"What about the Standards?"

"Them I know. Lon Standard is a layman in the Methodist Church, and I see him every year at the camp meeting over at Hamilton's Pool. He's a fine man and it just makes my heart sick to see him in this kind of scrape. Two of his boys are dead, too. I've prayed that he would stop coveting that piece of land they're fighting over and put an end to all the killing."

"But what if the land is rightfully his?"

Jessom snorted. "The earth belongs to God. We may serve as stewards, but what right have we to claim a piece as our own? Land should be for everyone to use."

I grunted as if in approval, but had trouble concurring with old Sam on his ideas of ownership. As a Huckaby, I had grown up acquiring land. My father had lost thousands of acres during the War Between the States but rebuilt during the years I grew into manhood, passing to me the desire to bring the horizons under ownership of the Huckabys. It was a desire I no longer embraced, of course, but one of which I still approved.

After Jessom and I washed the dishes, he spread a pallet of blankets on the floor. Just as I prepared to lay myself down on it, he rolled in ahead of me, uttered a prayer, said good night, and fell asleep as quickly as if an anvil had dropped on his head. I slept in the deacon's bed—narrow but comfortable, the bed frame strung with rawhide and the mattress stuffed with corn shucks. It was the first home I had slept in for more than three years and I was ashamed to find myself covetous of my kind benefactor, the Deacon Sam Jessom.

I felt no compunction, however, over my avarice toward a certain trove rumored to lie under the soil somewhere along Double Horn Creek.

EIGHT

In the morning I took a dip in the Pedernales, washed my working togs, and put on my coarse freedom suit so my new clothes could dry. Jessom had some breakfast and some conversation waiting for me when I got back to his little cabin.

"You speak well," he suddenly said in the middle of our talk. "Are you educated?"

I nodded, my mouth full of bacon and eggs.

"I'm going to let you borrow my Bible, then. If you don't read it, at least read this page marker." He flipped the corner of a card sticking out of the Holy Book. "I have to go fire the forge now, but I hope to see you again. If you have no luck up at the Marble Falls, come back tomorrow and put up with me for a while. The latch string hangs on the outside of my door."

"Thank you," I said, gratified to hear him repeat his invitation of the night before.

"I packed you a lunch. It's in your saddlebag. Good luck." Jessom turned and waddled off toward his wide-open blacksmith shop, leaving me at his table in his cabin, eating his eggs and bacon, drinking his milk and coffee.

As I sopped up the last of the bacon grease with a biscuit, I slipped the book marker out of the Bible Deacon Sam had given me. It was a card printed with a heading that read, JOHN WESLEY'S RULE. Seven lines followed:

> Do all the good you can,
> By all the means you can,
> In all the ways you can,
> In all the places you can,
> At all the times you can,
> To all the people you can,
> As long as ever you can.

Yes, I thought. And you will never suffer a lack of character witnesses. I wondered if John Wesley would have allowed a treasure map to possess him after doing all the good he could by letting an aged Mexican ride his horse. If not, he was a better man than Royal S. Huckaby.

As I crossed the Pedernales and rode northward toward the Colorado, I began to imagine what might have caused the Spaniards to bury their riches in this region. If all I had learned about the conquistadors was true, they came to the hills of Texas not for the clear spring waters or the abundant game or the rolling, rocky vistas or the temperate climate. No, they came for riches.

Assuming that as their reason for going anywhere, they must have found some form of mineral wealth in the hills west of San Antonio and Austin. Evidence of their expeditions had certainly turned up. In Fredericksburg, for example, the earliest German settlers found a weathered wooden cross with Spanish inscriptions surmounting a hill. And I had heard of an Indian chief on the Llano Estacado known as Iron Shirt who wore the armored breastplate of a Spanish cavalryman, long since won on some unheralded battlefield.

Yes, the Spaniards had come here seeking riches, perhaps finding some, perhaps carrying much of it home to the king, and maybe even burying some as difficulties arose, hoping to return for it. The legends of those buried caches had haunted Texans for generations. I was not the first man to let a treasure map possess him. In fact, I had joined the ranks of some rather illustrious adventurers.

Jim Bowie—wielder of the world's most celebrated knife and hero of the fabled Alamo—had crossed the Pedernales River as I had, searching for lost treasure. He and his brother had led a party of treasure hunters in a quest for the legendary San Saba silver mine. They found only hostile Indians and survived a battle against odds similar to those that later killed Jim at the Alamo.

If Bowie and a hundred like him could believe in buried treasure, why shouldn't I? In fact, maybe the treasure waiting for me on the Double Horn had come from the lost San Saba mine—bars of smelted silver. Or maybe my treasure was gold diverted and buried by some corrupt Mexican paymaster who never returned for his ill-gotten wealth. Maybe it consisted of silver candlesticks and precious stones stolen from a cathedral by some fugitive who had hoped vainly to escape to Louisiana.

I had much to unravel. One particular question bothered me more than all the rest. Why hadn't the old Mexican used his own map? Then it struck me: Oh, my gracious, think of the volume of treasure there must be on the Double Horn if the old Mexican had been unable to carry it all away in his pockets! Either that, or there was no treasure to carry away at all and he was laughing at me in hell.

I knew only one thing for sure about the old Mexican. He had heard of a thing called the zero stone and passed the knowledge of it on to me. And until I found it, I would dream his ghost laughter and shrink from the twitter of doves.

A coyote loped, stiff-legged, across the road in front of me and I reached instinctively for a rifle stock under my left stirrup—a throwback to my hunting days on the Huckaby estates. Hunting had once been my all-absorbing avocation. I yearned to own a rifle again. I had enough money left to buy one and a little ammunition for it, and the area between Johnson City and the Marble Falls appeared to offer excellent possibilities for the nimrod. To hunt would be to indulge in the greatest freedom of the savage or the civilized man.

The deacon had familiarized me with the landmarks I would pass on my way to the Marble Falls, and I recognized them from his descriptions. For a long time the washboard wagon road led over successive wrinkles in the topography, slanting mostly upward to the divide between the Pedernales and the Colorado valleys. When I reached that divide, a rather low and inconspicuous one, I stopped in the shade of an old oak to eat lunch.

After a short nap, I saddled my mare and proceeded northward. Before me spread the wide valley of the Colorado River. In these hills the river coursed swift and shallow. Down in Matagorda County it ran slow and muddy through the great raft of driftwood and into the Gulf of Mexico.

To my right I passed a high hill that Jessom had mentioned—a flat-topped rise called Shovel Mountain. To my left, miles away, I saw the landmark known as Packsaddle Mountain where the last clash with Indians in the area had taken place several years before. It indeed struck the shape of a packsaddle against the horizon.

At last I came to a bluff and looked down on the Marble Falls. There was a little settlement across the river and beyond it I saw Granite Mountain—the mound of solid rock nearly two hundred feet high that would build the state capitol. I could tell the work had started there. A single boom was up and pivoting slowly over the virgin quarry.

I got off my horse and put on the clean suit of work clothes I had purchased in Fredericksburg and washed that morning. Thus outfitted, I prepared to procure employment.

Liberty carefully picked her way down the bluff and walked gingerly across the sand just under the falls. The ledge of black stone stood only four feet at the highest, but it stretched three hundred yards or more across the riverbed and split the current into a hundred spouts that gushed through timeworn channels in the rock. Three laughing, bare-chested boys were wearing out the seats of their britches sliding down some of the sluices. Their mothers would switch them through the holes in their pants whenever they got home, but I encouraged them with applause.

" 'At a boy!" I said to one who went headfirst.

"Watch me, mister," another one said. "Watch me, watch me," they all chimed in.

There wasn't much of a town at the Marble Falls—perhaps a dozen buildings. When the quarry got going, the town would probably grow, I thought. There was undoubtedly a saloon or two on the main street so, to avoid them, I rode just west of there on a dirt road down-hill from the main cluster of buildings. It looked as if the road would lead to the quarry and that's where I needed to go to find work anyway.

A couple of steep side streets led up to the buildings on the main street. As I passed the first one, I chanced a cautious glance that way, looking for trouble. All appeared calm.

I didn't look up the second side street because a gaggle of schoolchildren attracted my attention. Their little frame schoolhouse was at the bottom of the side street and the schoolmarm—that poor, haggard woman—had just turned them out. They swarmed like hornets. I knew the mothers of the boys at the falls would have to switch them twice now, for they were skipping their lessons.

I managed to guide my mare through the milling urchins and approached the schoolmarm. "Excuse me, ma'am."

"What is it?" she responded, speaking to me as if I were eleven years old.

"Does this road lead to the granite mountain?"

"Yes, yes," she said impatiently, pointing up the road. But she didn't get a chance to utter another word because at that moment we all—schoolmarm, children, Liberty, and I—heard an unusual but distinct harbinger of impending disaster. Imagine listening to a two-horse surrey racing toward you across a long, wooden-planked bridge and you will have some idea of what the racket sounded like.

The schoolmarm screamed: "Children!" The students ran, seeming to get nowhere. My mare turned toward the noise, trembled with fear, and tried clumsily to back away.

A large barrel came rumbling down the hill, bouncing heavily, swerving, and building speed. It was big enough to smash three underclassmen or two advanced mathematicians and there was nothing between it and the children but a steep pitch and fifty yards of dirt street. Instantly I decided to sacrifice my poor mare by throwing her into the path of the calamity.

Children scrambled, screamed, and fell as I made my mare move in between them and the rolling barrel. Liberty pranced and snorted and jerked her head, but I held her in the street. The schoolmarm was virtually yodeling in distress.

The barrel came on like a boulder loosed by a mountain avalanche. It rolled faster and angled to one side. Just up the hill from me it came hard against the corner of a staircase that bashed in one of the staves. It bounced, whirling, and began spewing a spiral of pure, white, stone-milled flour into the air through the broken stave. My mare reared, kicked, and grunted at the spectacle, but I held her fast in the path of the keg as it hit the ground just in front of her and burst. A tremendous white cloud enveloped me and barrel staves flew like canister, one clobbering me on the ear.

No amount of horsemanship could have held my mare then. She whirled like an outlaw mustang and it was all I could do to hang on. Above the ringing in my ears, I heard the schoolmarm shrieking and the children, blast their ungrateful hides, laughing like a choir of hyenas.

Blinded and choked near to death by the flour, I had no idea where I would light when my mare flung me from her back. I simply covered my head and hoped for a safe landing. Instead, I crashed through a window and came to rest on something that felt like the cargo in Marion Harkey's barbed-wire wagon or the walls of Albert Friedrich's Buckhorn Saloon.

I must have been unconscious for a few seconds. When I came to, I caught myself murmuring, " ' . . . In all the places you can,/At all the times you can,/To all the people you can . . .' " My vision cleared and I could see my legs sticking out of the schoolhouse window. I was on my back, the remains of a previously sound school desk splintered around me. I reached for something that I felt jabbing me in the rear end and found it to be an extremely sharp pencil. I heard scores of little bare feet stomping up the steps and knew the schoolchildren were rushing in to finish me off.

I started to lapse back into unconsciousness, but before I could slip away, I beheld the lines of a marvelously angelic face peering at me through the window between my boots. In my dazed state, she was all waving hair and batting eyes, glistening lips and heaving bosom. I smiled at her crookedly.

"Thank God, he's not killed," she said. Then she turned her angelic face to rail at someone outside and I knew immediately she was made of mortal flesh. "Damn you, Nat! I told you to put that barrel upright in the wagon! I told you the son of a bitch would roll out!"

"Annie Standard!" screamed the schoolmarm. "You watch your filthy mouth around these children!"

Standard? Two minutes in town and I had fallen through a window on account of a Standard.

"Oh, forgive *me*, Miss Teeter," Annie said testily. Then she turned to look through the window again. "Don't just stand there, children. Get him up."

The students had gathered around me and began pulling in ten different directions, but eventually coordinated their efforts and put me on my feet. They bolstered me as I wobbled toward the door. There I saw the full length of Annie Standard, waiting to help me outside. She wore a faded print dress, tied in tight around her waist and rolled up at the sleeves. Everything about her reminded me of fine sand—her tawny hair, her dunelike curves. And her finely freckled skin looked like the smoothest brown beach of the most exotic island. I must have stared at her like a convict at an open door.

She slung my arm over her shoulder and helped me walk outside. Then she sat me down on the front steps of the schoolhouse. She began ineffectually dusting me off with a handkerchief. Through the white cloud she stirred up, I saw that Liberty had completely gotten over the keg scare and was standing patiently as some schoolboys climbed all over her.

Then I spied the two men. One of them, I supposed, was Nat, who had loaded the barrel in the wagon on its side. Both of them, I supposed, were Standards because they were holding rifles, keeping their eyes peeled for trouble, and looking down on me with distaste. Annie appeared to be the youngest of the three.

"Oh, fiddlesticks!" Miss Teeter said, looking in through the broken window. "Sir, you've shattered this glass and crushed an entire desk. What have you to say for yourself?"

I had nothing to say, but Annie did. "Is that all you can think of?" she demanded. "This man was trying to save those children from getting smashed. Why haven't you thanked him yet?"

Miss Teeter gasped.

"That barrel wouldn't have smashed anybody anyway," grumbled one of the brothers. "It busted open right there."

"Shut up, Lum," Annie snapped. "You're lucky it busted or it would have lamed this man's horse and you would have had to pay for it."

"Me?" Lum said. "I didn't put any barrel in the wagon sidewise. Nat did it."

"It was your idea!" Nat said.

"The heck it was," Lum countered.

Annie continued to flog me with her handkerchief while they argued. I took her by the wrist and stood up. "Thank you, miss. I'm alright now. No harm done."

"I was the one that told you not to leave the wagon so close to the hill where somethin' might roll off the tailgate," Nat said.

"You never opened your mouth to say any such thing," Lum said.

Annie followed me as I hobbled toward my horse. "What's your name?" she asked. Lum and Nat ended their argument to look out for their sister. She shooed the children off my mare as I went to put my foot in the stirrup.

"Roy."

"What brings you here?"

"I heard the quarry was hiring," I said, struggling up to the seat.

"If it's work you're looking for, come home with us and we'll put you to work on the ranch," Annie said.

"No, we don't need any hands on the ranch, Annie," Lum said. "You know better than that. Let that saddle tramp alone and get back in the wagon."

Annie's angel face turned fierce. She clinched her fists and took three menacing steps toward her brother, who backed away cautiously. "You go straight to hell, Columbus Standard."

Miss Teeter gasped again.

"Excuse Annie's language, Miss Teeter," Nat said. "She only talks that way when she gets het up. She's been cussin' up a storm here lately. Daddy gave up whippin' her."

"You go on up to the quarry, stranger," Lum said. "They're hiring, alright."

"And you can use your first week's wages to buy a new window and a new desk for my school," Miss Teeter said.

"Lum, pay Miss Teeter for the damages," Annie ordered. She had taken my horse by the bridle, as if she did not intend for me to ride away just yet.

"*Me* pay her?"

"Pay her!"

Lum heaved indignantly and went to negotiate with the schoolmarm.

"We've had some trouble lately," Annie said to me. "We don't have any work to hire out on the ranch right now, but soon we could have. I hope you'll stay around until then. It'll be better work than you'll get at that so-called quarry."

"Thank you," I said. I was still somewhat fuddled—as much by Annie as from my mode of entering the school-house—but I knew enough to recognize a stroke of luck when one dropped into my hands. One of the Standards—undoubtedly the prettiest—had just invited me to work on the family ranch as soon as the trouble with the Flatts had passed. What better way to search for treasure? "That sounds fine," I said. "I'd rather work at a ranch than a quarry, but I have to take what's available for now."

"Come on, Annie," Nat said. "Daddy and Clay are waiting on us. You've slowed us down enough."

I tilted my hat and smiled at Annie. "Good-bye for now, miss," I said.

"Good-bye," she said, turning away. "Well, come on and get the wagon loaded," she said to her brothers. Then she turned and waved quickly to me.

The last I saw of Miss Teeter, she was counting her money.

"What about all that flour?" I heard Nat ask as I rode toward Granite Mountain.

"What about it?" Annie said.

"Well, shouldn't we scrape it up or something? We'll have to pay for it, you know."

"If you want to eat dirt in your hot cakes, Nat, by all means, scrape it up."

"Scrape it up," Lum said. "We'll make mush out of it and feed it to the hogs."

"Why don't *you* scrape it up?" Nat asked, and so the conversation went until I rode out of earshot.

NINE

My seal brown mare looked something like a roan after the sprinkling the flour barrel gave her and I looked like a veteran of the chalk mines. I dusted myself off as much as possible as I rode to the quarry. I was sore on the head and all over the back, but I plugged ahead, dauntless.

Granite Mountain loomed before me—a great bulge of beautiful reddish stone flecked with black and glistening with tiny crystals—overall about the color of a red brindle steer. As I got closer to it, I began to have a strange feeling. At first, I passed it off as an aftershock to the way I had met Annie, or to the fact that I had met her at all. I was thinking more about her than the quarry. She even seemed to make me forget, for the moment, about the zero stone and the buried treasure. But as I continued to approach Granite Mountain, I began to realize that the quarry was the thing making me feel peculiar.

When I rode close enough to see the workers scrambling about the rough face of the monolith, something about them made me uneasy. They had started the quarry work; several huge blocks of granite had been sheared from the flanks of the hill. I dipped down into a creek bed then and lost sight of the laborers. When I saw them again, I was much closer. A pitiful realization came to me and chilled every bit of warmth I was feeling for Annie Standard, the zero stone, and buried treasure.

The workers at the quarry came in two classes. One consisted of white men who sat in the shade and fondled shotguns. The other class wore dirty, striped uniforms. They were lean from a lack of food and an over-abundance of hard labor. Most of them were black men. I reined in my mare, afraid to get any closer. I couldn't work at this quarry. The actual labor was being done by convicts. The only hiring going on was for guards.

As I sat on my horse and stared and pitied the men among the slabs of granite, I noticed that a couple of the guards were watching me. One of them got on a mule and rode out to me. He looked me over carefully, resting his scattergun across the withers of the mule. "What do you want?" he asked.

"Are you the sergeant?"

"Yeah, who the hell are you?"

I could judge a guard at a glance with almost invariable accuracy, and the subject on the mule struck me as the most reprehensible sort of bully.

"I heard y'all were hiring," I said, not attempting to hide the distaste in my voice.

"Maybe. What the hell is that white stuff all over your clothes?"

"That's the bone meal of the last fool I met who couldn't mind his own business."

The sergeant grew red in the face and hooked his thumb over one of the hammers of his double-barrel. Then he settled down and chuckled. "Alright, you're a rough enough customer. Do you know anything about convicts?"

"Yes, I have had three years experience among them."

"Where at?"

"Huntsville."

The bully on the mule seemed impressed. "Come on over and talk to the captain, then."

I sat on my mare for a moment, sick with guilt, for some bizarre reason, that I was not among the quarry gang. If only the sergeant on the mule knew how many times those convicts would like to murder him today. "How much does it pay?"

"Forty dollars and grub twice a day."

I laughed with a mocking tone in my voice. "Mister, I wouldn't take ten times that much to work beside the likes of you."

I turned my mare back toward town and listened for the sound of the hammer latching back on the double-barrel. But the only shot the guard fired was, "Then why in hell did you ride out here, you crazy-assed lunatic?"

I had disobeyed John Wesley's rule. I hadn't done the sergeant at the Granite Mountain quarry one lick of good in any way and I was proud of it. In fact, I probably took more pride in what I had done than any man ever did for any such stupid stunt. "The bone meal of the last fool . . ." What wonderful, wicked inspiration had caused me to think up that reply on short notice?

By the time I got back to the town, however, I was regretting my venomous comments. That kind of talk fit nowhere into my plans to avoid trouble. What I needed was a good dose of Deacon Sam Jessom's virtuous influence. I resolved to start immediately back to Johnson City and stay with Jessom until the Flatt-Standard thing blew over. But I would not show up at his modest cabin empty-handed this time. I had just enough cash left to buy a rifle and some cartridges and I intended to do so and kill a fat deer for Deacon Sam and me to butcher.

I avoided the schoolhouse on my return route and rode up on the main street to the store that I knew to be just up the hill from the site of my late catastrophe. The Standards had scraped up their flour, finished loading their wagon, and gone home. I was still embarrassed about breaking the window out of the schoolhouse and for that reason I was glad Annie and her brothers had left. But for some opposing reason, I wished for another glimpse of her.

I entered an establishment with a hand-painted sign hanging over the boardwalk that read, "Lynn's Store," and below, in smaller letters, "United States Post Office." The proprietor was happily counting the large wad of money Lum Standard had left with him. He glanced up at me once, glanced again, and started laughing. "You must be the poor devil who got run over with the flour barrel!"

I spotted some weapons in a counter and looked them over. "Yes, sir. But I'd rather be addressed by name. Royal Huckaby."

"Glad to meet you. I'm J. L. Lynn. Be with you directly." He put his cash away in a drawer. Lynn stood about six feet and weighed in at over two hundred pounds, I guessed—a healthy-looking fellow who appeared to enjoy life and thrive on the mercantile business. "I guess you're wondering what those Standards needed with an entire barrel of flour."

"Forting up, I supposed."

"Oh, you've heard about their trouble, then."

"Yes, it was in the San Antonio newspapers."

"Lum told me they've been afraid to sleep in their own house for fear the Flatts would lay siege on them. But now they're stocked up with enough food and ammunition to supply a garrison for a month. The rangers ought to be here by then."

"What will they do for water?" I asked.

"They already have water in the house. Annie made them boys put a pitcher pump in the kitchen for Mrs. Standard. The boys didn't want to. They said it would rot the floor timbers out, but Annie usually gets her way. Them Flatts will have to catch them out of the house somewhere if they intend to fight. Of course, I hate to see them kill one another like they have been, but, my Lord, I never dreamed it would be so good for business. I never sold the likes of guns and bullets in my life and now there's a run on foodstuffs."

"I'm interested in buying a rifle myself. I need something in a caliber for hunting deer and turkeys and such."

"Oh, is that right? I figured you had your eye on a shotgun. Lum said you were going to hire on at the quarry."

"No, sir. That's no business for a gentleman. How about this Winchester?"

I haggled with Lynn for a while and we struck a deal that included the rifle, a scabbard, and a hundred rounds. I had only two dollars left after the trade, but I felt satisfied when I hefted the weapon and worked the lever a few times and smelled the grease in the action. It was a beautiful rifle with a checkered pistol grip, a shotgun butt, and an octagonal barrel over a full-length magazine. I picked a popular caliber: .45-60.

"I'm going back to Johnson City," I said. "Any chance of finding some good hunting on the way there?"

"Oh, sure," Lynn said. "If I was you, I'd go across the divide and turn west and hunt along the Sandy. There're turkeys and hogs there by the hundreds and enough deer, too. You might even find a bear, but they're getting scarce. Of course, the best hunting around here has always been on the Double Horn, but I would advise you against going there. That's a war zone with the Flatts and Standards."

"I understand. I don't want to get mixed up in any of that trouble. In fact, I would consider it a favor if you would tell me just where the Double Horn runs, so I can be sure to avoid it."

"Do you know Shovel Mountain?" Lynn asked.

"Yes, I rode past there today."

"Well, Double Horn Creek starts at the foot of Shovel Mountain, runs north about six miles, and then empties into the river a few miles downstream from here. It's all on the east side of the road to Johnson City. That's why I told you to stay on the west side of the road and hunt the Sandy, that way you'll have no chance of making a mistake. Of course, you'd be okay hunting up on the head of the Double Horn, under Shovel Mountain, but being a stranger here you wouldn't know where the Flatt and Standard lands take up along toward the mouth of the creek."

"I guess I'll just go on to the Sandy, then."

"That's what I'd do. There's game enough there for a good hunt."

My eyes had been trained for rifles since entering the store and I didn't think until then to look around at the other kinds of goods Lynn had for sale. He had pretty fair supplies of coffee, salt, sugar, dried beans, bacon and tobacco, plus some dry goods and tools. Behind his counter I saw rows of pigeonholes stuffed with parcels and envelopes of different sizes and colors. Two or three piles of unsorted mail lay nearby.

There were three volatile barrels of flour standing innocently against the wall, looking like powder kegs set to roll and explode in bursts of white smoke. There had to be a mill nearby, I reasoned, to supply that much flour.

I must have regarded the barrels with a little too much caution, making Lynn chuckle. But I soon forgot them when my eyes found the willow basket. It didn't seem to belong in Lynn's Store. His goods stood haphazardly on dusty shelves or hung crookedly from the walls. But the willow basket looked as if the hands of a woman had built it and arranged its marvelous contents in a manner almost artistic.

It was shallow, but all of four feet wide, woven of slender branches stripped of bark. In the center stood a collection of glass bottles filled with a fluid of the most remarkably amber hue, the stoppers sealed in wax. A cornucopia of vegetables surrounded the bottles—red tomatoes, green okra, yellow squash. And the whole of it rested atop a bed of the largest pecans I had ever seen.

"Annie brought that," Lynn said, following my stare. "She and I trade often. Crack two of those pecans together. You've never tasted any like them."

I had squeezed pecans together all of my life and knew how much force to clamp on them to get them to crack. But the shells of Annie's pecans crumpled like paper in my hand. The nuts tasted smoother and sweeter than any county-fair, blue-ribbon winners I had ever sampled.

"Ain't they somethin'?" Lynn said. "Annie's got her a prize-winning pecan tree on their land and she takes limbs off of it and splints them onto other trees and makes them grow. You won't believe it, but that's honest. She calls it the mother tree and its limbs put out these kind of pecans even when they grow on a regular tree."

"You mean she grafts the limbs?"

"That's what she calls it! It sure is! And them are the best pecans I ever et. But just wait till you wash it down with a swallow of this."

Lynn peeled the wax from one of the bottle necks, pulled the stopper, and poured some in a shot glass he kept behind his counter for just such occasions. I sniffed the liquid before tasting it and inhaled an aroma so rich that I thought myself in some parlor holding a crystal snifter. It was the smoothest and most potent brandy I had ever swallowed, flavored of peaches.

"Got her a peach orchard alongside her pecan grove, and a vegetable garden alongside that. A big one, so I've heard, though I've never had the pleasure of seeing it. Nat told me there's a little spring that runs through all of them and Annie uses it to irrigate her plants. She brings me stuff in the spring of the year like dewberries and vegetables and peaches, and in the fall she brings more vegetables and pecans and brandy. She should have some wine ready soon. She makes some good spirits from them old mustang grapes."

"If it's as good as the brandy, you'll have no trouble selling it," I said.

"Hell, no, I'll have no trouble. You better buy a bottle

of that brandy yourself if you want some. It'll all be sold in two days."

"No, thank you," I said. "I normally abstain from drink."

"Oh, I see. Well, that's wise if you have the weakness for it."

"Give my compliments to Miss Standard on the brandy," I said, tipping my hat and leaving with my new rifle.

"I will, sir. Good luck on the Sandy."

I made my way back over the same ground I had passed earlier in the day, before fending off the flour keg and before meeting Annie Standard and her brothers. It was getting late and the good hunting would soon commence. My hand kept reaching down to stroke the gun stock sticking out from under my left stirrup. The wood felt smooth and warm, like the taut skin of a living thing. I longed to level my sights on game, but it was clear that I would not get to the Sandy before nightfall.

As I trotted my mare past Shovel Mountain, I got an idea to ride up on top of the hill and look over Double Horn Creek to get a feel for the lay of the land and try to figure out where the zero stone might lie. I thought I might even camp there and start out for the Sandy before sunrise next morning. That way my scent or that of my campfire wouldn't spook the game out of the vicinity.

Shovel Mountain stood just a few miles to the east. It didn't prove much of a hill to climb, but it put my mare and me high enough above the rest of the territory that we could see for miles in every direction. I saw the colossal Packsaddle lying on the ground out to the northwest. I could see way off toward the Sandy and Johnson City to the south. To the east I found the valley of the Colorado snaking down toward Austin. And to the north I saw an undulation of greenery marking the path of Double Horn Creek. Just as Lynn had said, it started on the north face of Shovel Mountain, right under me, and ran northward six miles to the Colorado. The moment I laid eyes on it, *The Feeling* struck me.

Now, The Feeling was something that gripped me from time to time in life. It was something I never talked about for fear I would be committed to the lunatic asylum. The Feeling smacked of sorcery and mysticism and other things people shunned in serious conversation. The Feeling had even spooked me the first several times I felt it and acted upon it, but later in life I began to welcome it.

I first felt The Feeling as a boy while hunting for deer along the cane brakes of the Colorado River in Matagorda County. I was following a deer trail one day, trying to find a place to take a stand and ambush a big buck, when I came to a fork in the trail. Naturally, I had to decide which fork to follow. They both led into the thick hardwood bottoms along a creek. Each fork looked as well used as the other. I looked down the one to the left and sensed nothing out of the ordinary. But when I observed the trail to the right, The Feeling struck me and I knew, somehow, that I would find success down that path. It was no mere hunch or trifling whim—it was an overwhelming certainty, a knowingness. It was The Feeling.

I snuck down the right fork and crouched behind a fallen tree and within a minute the biggest buck I had ever seen in my life strolled up about thirty yards away from me. I killed it with one shot and went to get a friend of mine, a black boy named Rafe.

Rafe and his family sharecropped some Huckaby land. He had a knack for training dogs and had the finest pack of bear hounds in the county, therefore we became friends and hunting partners. It was a rather lopsided partnership, however—he doing all the work and me having most of the fun.

Rafe gutted the buck I had killed, an old twelve-pointer, and tied him on a mule while I told him what had happened. "How do you think I knew he would be there?" I asked him.

"Don't know," Rafe said. "Let's go ask ol' Uncle Pie."

Uncle Pie was a savant to the black people who lived and worked on the Huckaby estates. He stayed in a broken-down shanty near the river where he sat on his porch all day and cracked pecans or whittled or sharpened knives or gave advice. He had spent sixty years of his life as a slave, but was supposedly as free as I was the day Rafe and I went to him to tell him how I had killed the buck. We had to talk loud, for Uncle Pie was hard of hearing.

When he finally got the story straight, he said, "Boy, you done got The Feelin'."

"The feeling?" I said. "What feeling?"

"The Feelin' that tells you where things is. The Feelin' that shows you where to go to see a turkey if you huntin' a turkey and bear if you huntin' a bear. Some of you white folks calls it a 'sixth sense' and some says you gots to have Indian blood to feel it. But it ain't everybody can have it, boy, so you thank Jesus you gots The Feelin' and you remember ol' Uncle Pie told you about it."

For a long time I considered myself somehow gifted. The Feeling continued to strike me from time to time when I was hunting and never failed me if I waited long enough where it told me I should hunt. I grew to trust it and even found it occurring in places other than the hunting field.

When I looked at a total stranger, for example, and felt a twinge of The Feeling, I knew I could trust that person with life or money. When I looked at a piece of farm land my father, Champ Huckaby, had asked my opinion of and shivered with The Feeling when I saw it, I invariably told him to buy and knew the crops would flourish.

It is a frightful thing to know something and not know why you know it. For this reason, The Feeling disturbed me and I contemplated it often. Finally, to convince myself that I wasn't a mental freak of some kind, I conjectured that everyone must have the power to possess The

Feeling, but that few harnessed it. Most people passed it off as intestinal gas or nervous tension and generally drank some catnip tea and bitters or went to bed when they felt it.

I, on the other hand, would not deny it. As Uncle Pie had advised, I would be grateful for it and rely upon it. The Feeling, I thought, would set me on the correct course in life. I trusted it to point out every advantageous opportunity that crossed my path. The Feeling told me what to do and when to act.

Unfortunately, I had no opposing feeling that could tell me what *not* to do, where *not* to go, and whom *not* to trust. I possessed only the power to recognize the positive things, able to sense nothing of oncoming ill fortune. I had only begun, after three years in prison, to develop the ability to sense disaster. Some kind of feeling had warned me about the guard at the Granite Mountain quarry, for example. But it was not yet a sensation highly advanced enough to steer me away from things like whorehouse fights or runaway flour kegs.

But The Feeling *was* mine and it had become so powerful that I never failed to follow it. Only now will I admit that The Feeling virtually seized me with my very first glimpse of the old Mexican as he tottered along with his walking stick in front of the Buckhorn Saloon. Is it any wonder, then, that I should keep coming back to the possibility that his sheepskin map bore the brand of veracity?

I should explain also that I detected a powerful surge of something in the settlement at the Marble Falls, when I first saw the angelic face of Annie Standard—framed by the broken pane of the schoolhouse window and clouded by the white swirl of drifting flour. But that was not *the* feeling. That was a sensation of a completely original order.

TEN

I had never before disobeyed The Feeling, but I had questioned it on occasion. I had questioned it many times in the past several days as it pertained to the old Mexican and now I questioned it concerning Double Horn Creek.

Yes, there was undoubtedly good hunting along the creek. The Feeling couldn't be wrong about that. There was plenty of cover for wildlife. Brushy draws led into the creek from both sides, like veins to the center of a leaf. Cedars, oaks, and pecans grew thick along the draws. Among the coppices were open meadows where game could browse. Even without The Feeling, I would have wanted to hunt there.

But if I hunted too far down the Double Horn, I might stumble into Flatt or Standard territory and get accidentally murdered. As Lynn had pointed out, I was a stranger to the area and didn't know where one man's land ended and another's took up.

As I stood on the crest of Shovel Mountain and struggled to reason against The Feeling, I heard a rustling of leaves moving toward me up the north face of the hill. It came nearer and grew louder, like the wing beats of waterfowl flocking low overhead. Then I saw branches waving in the oncoming gust and when the blast finally whipped over the summit it knocked my hat off.

The season's first cool front had arrived—an annual cause for celebration in Texas. It was no blue norther and would probably do little more than drop the temperature ten or twelve degrees for the next few days. But when a Texan turns to the north in October and feels the breeze in his face, he knows blessed autumn will come to drive summer down to the tropics. It is a time of year that indulges the children of every generation. Even old men and women step outside to smell the crisp wind as if they had never before seen a summer lapse.

A fresh northern breeze could move a man from a hot climate with mysterious energies. The same energies that make the snow geese long to fly down from Canada. The energies that cause whitetail bucks to polish their antlers against oak saplings. Energies that tell predators of the world to stalk their prey. The wild energies of freedom that a captive creature must deny. I was uncaged for my first norther in three years. Did my will consist of the stuff that would enable me to ignore both The Feeling *and* the northerly draft? I should scarcely think so.

I had only enough sense left to notice that about halfway between Shovel Mountain and the Colorado River, Double Horn Creek ran between two pointed hills. The line between those hills, I decided, would serve as my boundary. I would assume the Flatt-Standard feud began on the far side of it, and beyond it I would not venture. Under the combined sway of the zero stone, The Feeling, and the sudden cool snap, that seemed like a substantial precaution.

Liberty eased down the slope of Shovel Mountain as I sniffed the cool, dry aroma of the north and quivered with its energies. At the first clearing I came to along the rushing Double Horn, I staked the mare to graze. I filled my canteen and looped its strap over my shoulder. I also filled the magazine of my new rifle, levered a round into the chamber, and struck out through the thickets.

I stayed in the shadows to make myself less conspicuous to the wary eyes of my prey. I walked in close to the cedars but avoided the oaks as the ground under them was strewn with dried leaves and crunched loudly underfoot like eggshells. I stopped every fifty yards or so and hunkered down to look and listen. I saw no fresh sign the first mile. No moist deer droppings, no freshly shed turkey feathers, no distinct tracks in the mud or the dust. Ah, but the breeze blew in my favor and the prime hour had yet to arrive and The Feeling called me northward.

I blundered up to a place where one of the brushy draws came in from the east to meet the creek. I heard a whistling snort and turned just in time to see the white, waving tail of a doe disappear up the draw. I heard other sets of hooves escaping with hers. I was out of form as a deer hunter. I should have crept up to that draw and peered into it from behind a bush instead of stumbling into full view. I should have seen the deer before she saw me. It was as if I did not know what I was hunting for.

My failure at that draw did little to discourage me, however. To see a deer within rifle range, to hear her distinctive snort, that was no mean privilege to a recent inmate. I considered taking a stand at the mouth of that draw, thinking that other deer might use the trail before dark. But I looked down the creek bed and I could see one of the two pointed hills still a couple of miles off and The Feeling tugged me toward that place.

I moved more carefully now, pausing longer and walking slower. I found game trails and turkey feathers and tracks in more abundance. Here a squirrel chattered at me from a tree limb and there a cottontail rabbit paused before springing into the bushes. And, try though I did to ignore them, mourning doves burst from the trees in flocks around me as I passed. But I spared the small game. I was hunting for something else. Something bigger. Something farther down the Double Horn.

The best hour for hunting began. Sunlight no longer fell into the little valley of the Double Horn. Soon the deer would be moving to their feeding grounds and the turkey would be returning to their roosts.

I came to another draw, a well-wooded one, and this time approached with more stealth. Everything I knew about hunting told me to make my stand there. Game trails streamed in to the place where the draw slashed the creek bank. A huge live oak had dropped an early batch of acorns that would attract deer and turkeys. Fresh tracks lined the muddy places along the creek. Experience told me to hunt there. But The Feeling differed.

When I looked again at the one visible member of the twin hills flanking the Double Horn, not far from me now, The Feeling drew me there. I protested: Pass up a wooded bottom with still water and game food to hunt a half-bald hill? What did The Feeling expect to find up there? I leaned my rifle against a tree to debate. Should I press against the very boundary I had set for myself and risk crossing into Flatt or Standard territory? Or should I hunt the draw I had found and shun The Feeling for the first time since I had known it?

I tipped my canteen up to drink as I deliberated. I tipped it high into the air above my mouth and let the water pour in. But above the trickling noises from the canteen, I distinctly heard, in the direction of the hill downstream, a metallic click—the muffled but unmistakable ring of a lock tripping in its machinery. Though I knew exactly what instrument had caused that noise, I failed to react with proper haste.

The canteen flew from my hand, and the strap around my neck yanked me to the ground. The noise from the impact of the bullet rang in my ears as I staggered to my feet. I looked at my rifle against the tree, but knew not to reach for it. I had nothing to do but stand at the mercy of someone on the hill. The water from my canteen was spilling out of the bullet hole, down the front of my pants.

"Hands up!" a gruff voice yelled from the hill.

I raised my hands and heard a horse coming to me. Down into the draw galloped a gaunt old man with hollowed eyes and a long, white beard, yellowish at the tip. He jumped from his horse holding a carbine in hands as wide and hard as spades. His clothes had seen much service. The hat on his head was marked with the stains of sweat. He wore frayed suspenders over a patched-up shirt and had the legs of his frazzled pants tucked into the high tops of his boots.

He pointed the carbine at me. "I've got him, Topsy," he hollered over his shoulder, without taking his eyes off of me. Almost instantly I heard another horse coming down from the hill. "How many are you?" he asked.

"I'm alone."

"You better hope you're alone," he growled, "because if I hear somebody comin' besides Topsy, I'll kill you quick."

"I'm alone," I repeated. "Just doing some hunting. You don't mind a man doing a little hunting, do you?"

The old man squinted and moved around to pick up my rifle. "Depends on what you're huntin' for."

About that time, Topsy rode down into the draw, and looking at her, I almost forgot the danger I was in. She straddled a red roan horse about three shades lighter than her hair, which was the color of dried blood, but full and beautiful. She had the same thin face as the old man, with none of the creases worn in it. And where the old man's face wore an expression of grim certainty, hers appeared anxious. She rode lightly on top of the horse, moving with the animal like a part of it. She had fringed moccasins in her stirrups, and when she stopped the horse near me, her skirt billowed up over one knee and damned if she wasn't wearing buckskin britches underneath!

"Who is he, Pa?" she asked.

"Says he's a hunter."

"He looks like a hunter."

"Yes, I'm just a hunter," I agreed. "I'm almost out of money and thought I'd kill some meat on my way to Johnson City."

"Looks like you wet your britches," he said.

"Pa!" Topsy complained. "That's just the water from the canteen!"

"Where's your horse?"

"I staked her up the creek."

The old man gnawed on his lower lip and shot his eyes around in suspicious little glances. "You're a friend of them Standards, ain't you?" he said quietly.

I felt in immediate peril of my life, but Topsy came to my rescue. "I know most all the Standards' kin and I ain't never seen him before."

"Then what's he doin' here?" the old man asked.

I was asking the same question of myself about that time. It was that damned old Mexican's fault.

"He's just huntin', Pa," Topsy said, becoming more insistent. "I could tell by the way he was stalkin' down the creek that last half mile that he was huntin'. Tryin' to, anyhow."

"Who are you, boy?" The old man lowered his carbine a degree or two.

"Royal Strickland Huckaby of Matagorda County."

He stared at me for a moment, the northerly breeze bending the yellow point of his whiskers to the south, as if mockingly indicating the place of safety whence I had strayed. "What would you give for me to let you go? How about this new rifle?"

"Oh, Pa!" Topsy bounded down from her horse. She yanked my rifle away from her father and levered the cartridges out onto the ground. She handed the rifle to me and picked up the rounds and put them in her father's pocket. "There," she said, "now he can't do us no harm even he had a mind to." She turned to me. "Sorry, Mr. Huckaby, but we've had some trouble with land grabbers and Pa's riled over it."

The old man's carbine swung up to cover me again and his eyes flared at Topsy's poor choice of words. "Trouble! Hell, the goddamn bastards are killin' us!"

I could tell he wanted to shoot me badly so I decided I would say something before I died. "I understand your pa's feelings," I said to Topsy. "I spent three years in prison on account of a feud in Matagorda County. Three years just because I did what I had to do there to do right by my family. I figure that's all your pa wants to do."

The old man relaxed a little. "What feud?"

"The fight between the Williamses and the Fitz-hughs. Joe David Williams was my brother-in-law."

The old man lowered his rifle. "I remember hearin' about that. You're the one that killed the ranger, aren't you?"

I shrugged. "They said I did, but they couldn't prove it. They could only convict me as an accomplice. I only did what I had to do."

The old man finally let his guard down. "You'll understand why I treated you suspicious, then. I'm Eli Flatt. This is my baby daughter, Topsy. Maybe you've heard of our trouble with the Standards. They're trying to steal our land and they've murdered two of us."

"I read something in the papers."

Old Eli was watching me with less caution now and it looked as if he might tell me I could leave any second. Then we heard hoofbeats coming in a hurry. "Who's that?" he said, covering me again with his carbine.

I shrugged. "Let's take cover," I suggested, trying to look as if I was on Eli's side. I pointed to the brush up in the draw and Topsy helped out by leading her horse there in a sprint. The old man motioned with his gun barrel for me to follow her and he led his horse behind me.

It didn't take long for the riders to arrive along the opposite bank of the creek. The two men were strangers to me, but obviously cut from the Flatt mold—wild-eyed and hatchet-faced.

"Boone!" Eli hollered.

Topsy stepped out of the underbrush and waved. The two riders crossed the creek. I came out under the guard of Eli's carbine, feeling nervous about the new arrivals. Daylight was slipping away quickly.

"We heard a shot," Boone said. "What happened? Who's this?"

"This feller says he's Royal Huckaby of Matagorda County. Either of you seen him around?"

The brothers shook their heads.

"Pa, why don't you be more polite?" Topsy said. "Mr. Huckaby, these are my brothers Boone and Tobe."

I nodded. "Roy," I suggested.

Neither Boone nor Tobe returned any courtesies. "Looks like he peed in his pants," Tobe said.

"Tobe!" Topsy scolded.

"What are you doin' here?" Boone growled. He was obviously the oldest brother of the clan—a full-grown man, graying in the sideburns and probably twenty years older than Topsy.

"He just wanted to shoot a deer," Topsy said.

"That's not what I mean," Boone said. "What brings you to this part of the country?"

"I came looking for work. I heard they were hiring at the Granite Mountain quarry."

"They was," Tobe said. "How come you didn't hire on if that's what you were after?"

"They were only hiring guards for the prisoners. I don't have much use for prison guards."

"He says he was in prison himself for killin' a ranger in that fight between the Fitzhughs and the Williamses down in Matagorda County," Eli said.

"I ain't never heard of no fight down there," Tobe said.

"I have," Boone said. "Whose side were you on?"

"The side in the right. Joe David Williams was my brother-in-law." I was praying that Boone Flatt had no affinity for Fitzhughs.

Boone grinned. "The side in the right," he repeated.

"Maybe you'd care to help us fight Standards, then."

"Oh, Boone!"

"Shut up, Topsy. What about it, Royal? You might as well throw in with us, you bein' experienced at feudin'. Unless maybe you think the Standard side is the one in the right."

"I have nothing against the Standards or the Flatts," I said. "I just got out of prison on account of a fight like yours and I don't care to go back right away. I'd just as soon go look for some less dangerous work somewhere else."

"We can't let him go," Tobe said. "He may be going to join Lum and them. I'll bet you a two-bit cigar they hired him like a professional gun to work with them."

"That's just stupid," Topsy said. "Does he look like a killer to you? He's a little rough, but he don't look mean. He don't even wear a pistol!"

"Tobe's right," Eli said. "We can't let him go now just so maybe he can shoot us in the back of the head later. He's either got to be with us or he's again' us and if he's again' us, we'll have to shoot him."

"I just wanted to kill a deer to eat until I could find some work," I complained.

"Will you throw in with us or not?" Boone asked.

I tried to retrace my steps since my release from prison, attempting to figure out how in God's name I had ended up exactly where I swore I would never venture, but I could not think of a thing for the life of me. I could think of nothing to say and nothing to do.

Topsy saved me. "Look, if you want to keep an eye on him, just put him to work till we find out who he is. Pa, you said yourself we needed to start chopping fence posts since the bob wire got here. He says he's looking for work. There's no need to kill him if it turns out he's telling the truth. And if he hunts Standards as good as he hunts deer, you don't want him on our side, anyhow."

There were no immediate objections, but Tobe sighed heavily and frowned. He was about my age and size and

looked tough as rawhide, but I didn't see any real mean-
ness to him. I sensed that a simple fear of strangers was
behind all his hard talk.

"Can you swing an ax?" the old man asked.

"Yes, sir."

"Twenty dollars a month and board," he offered.

I accepted by not refusing.

It turned out that I was not such a big liar after all in
regard to what I had told Marion Harkey. It looked as
though I really was going to join the ranks of cedar choppers and go to work for the Flatt family. And I was happy
about it, too, inasmuch as it compared to being shot.

"Tobe," Eli ordered, "ride up the creek and get his
horse for him."

Tobe frowned but followed the instructions immediately.

It was dark by the time we started riding to the Flatts'
place. Eli questioned his sons about the movements of the
Standards as we went along.

"It ain't good, Pa," Tobe said. "Lum and Nat went up
to the Marble Falls and got their wagon loaded with supplies. They got enough stuff to hole up in their house
now."

"What?" the old man shouted.

"He's right, Pa," Boone said. "They had their wagon
loaded dang near full."

Eli cussed and pulled savagely at a branch he happened
to pass by. "They sleep in their beds tonight and we still
camp out like curs! Why in hell didn't you stop 'em,
Boone?"

"Couldn't," he said.

"Yeah, they had Annie with 'em," Tobe said. "The
cowards made her ride right between 'em so we wouldn't
shoot."

"Not that they would have shot," Topsy said to me.
"Us Flatts ain't no bushwhackers."

We stopped at the dark edge of a clearing.

"Go ahead and look around," Boone said to Tobe.

"What for? Lum and Nat couldn't have finished unloading those supplies yet."

"We haven't accounted for Clay and Lon," the old man said. "Just do what your brother tells you."

"Half brother," Tobe said before riding away. He was gone for about five minutes while the rest of us sat on our horses, perfectly silent. "No sign of anybody," he said when he came back. We started to ride again and soon arrived at the Flatt home, a weathered board-and-batten structure surrounded by the usual spate of outbuildings.

"You see what cautions we have to take?" Eli said. "We never know when they'll hit us again. They have us outnumbered now with Lon and his three boys. It's only me and Boone and Tobe left on our side—the three of us altogether. I don't count Topsy. She shoots better than her brothers, but it ain't a woman's work to have to kill men."

"It shouldn't be nobody's work." Topsy turned away and went into a little log kitchen next to the house. In the moonlight I saw the form of a burly little dog moving beside her.

The rest of us put our horses in the barn, merely loosening the cinches of our saddles. I knew we would not sleep in the house that night. Men who expected trouble from their neighbors could not be so predictable as to sleep in their own beds unless, like the Standards, they were prepared for a long siege.

Tobe and Boone disappeared somewhere in the night with their rifles while Eli and I went to sit in the dark under a tree. A light came on in the kitchen and I could hear Topsy rattling skillets. I saw the dog again, a mottled, bobtailed cow dog, standing just outside the doorway of the kitchen, licking his chops. About halfway between the dog and me, I saw a pile of objects I would never have recognized in the dark if I hadn't slept among them in the bed of Marion Harkey's wagon.

"You see those headstones right there?" Eli asked, pointing to a group of grave markers illuminated by the lantern light from the kitchen. "The one on the south belongs to Boone's ma, my first wife. The one next to it is my second wife. She died after Topsy was born. It was just their natural time to go, both of them.

"But those two new graves are for Reed and Bass, my next-to-oldest and my next-to-youngest. Standards killed 'em. Jumped 'em after the trial. They knew they would lose the land they were claiming and it riled their greedy souls. But it ain't their land to claim. Never was. It's mine, and they know it."

I thought I should acknowledge Eli's talk with some kind of response. "How did they ever come to claim it in the first place?" I was hoping to make use of my predicament by learning something about the zero stone, but I was prepared to take Eli's account with the proper measure of incredulity.

"I suspect old Lon had it on his mind to steal that land when he first set foot on his claim. Just took him several years to work up the nerve for it. Him and his family were ruined in the war back in Virginia. Lost all their land. So they scraped together everything they owned and sold it and used the money to buy their spread here, just upstream of mine. I had already been here twenty-seven years by that time. I was the first white man to live this far up the Colorado.

"Anyway, Lon and them didn't have a thing when they come here, so I taken 'em in, fed 'em, helped 'em build a house and all. It was Lon and Charlotte and all their offspring. The youngest one was just a sprout."

That would be Annie, I thought to myself, but I dared not mention any Standard names.

"They worked hard—I'll give 'em that. I was glad to have help in the neighborhood because the Indians had been pesterin' us like heel flies. Lon and me both was in on that last fight with 'em over to Packsaddle Mountain. He really had me blindfolded, thinkin' he was the finest kind of neighbor a man could get."

"When did he lay claim to the land?"

"The courthouse up at Burnet burned in '74," Eli said. "After that Lon started claiming Double Horn Creek was his, which was a damned lie. The creek's mine. Always has been. I settled here first and I have always owned that creek."

"What does the courthouse burning down have to do with it?"

"Can't you figure it out? Everybody thought for some time that the courthouse was burned by rustlers trying to destroy all the brand records. But I believe Lon done it. He done it to burn up our land patents, so it would be just my word again' his."

It had been my job in the Huckaby enterprises to evaluate land and oversee the development of it once purchased. My father had handled the details with the deeds and patents and courthouse records, so I was almost completely ignorant of them. When it occurred to me that records of cattle brands and rightful titles to land and such things could be completely lost by destroying a courthouse, I ceased to wonder why so many Texas counties had converted theirs to ashes.

"Why did it take so long to bring the case to court," I asked, "if the courthouse burned back in '74?"

"Because I'm a fool with generosity. I asked Lon one day why he would claim the Double Horn when he knew it was mine and he looked me dead in the eye and lied like a thief and said I should know damn good and well that it belonged to him. We might have fought right then if I hadn't been such a fair man. You see, boy, it didn't make any difference to me who owned the land because we both used the creek and our herds ran free on each other's land. There weren't no fences—and won't be till you get them posts chopped.

"So I compromised with Lon, bein' generous. I told him we would just keep sharing the creek and call it our boundary. I was giving up maybe a hundred acres along the other side of the creek by doin' that, but I figured that was a small price to pay to stay on good terms with my neighbors."

"And then?" I asked.

"Then Lon decides earlier this year that he wants the whole creek to hisself and starts talking about fencing it off. That's where he drew too hard on my generosity and I fought back. But I done it proper. Took him to court. That's the difference between us Flatts and them Standards. They done their fightin' like a mob. Jumped us after court. His boys murdered two of my sons."

"I was sorry to read about that in the papers," I said. "Land isn't worth the lives of good young men. That was a sore way for them to act just for losing the case."

"They haven't lost yet, but they will."

"You mean the trial isn't over?" I asked.

"No. The judge ruled that a company of rangers and a Land Office investigator would have to come and find the zero stone to locate the original boundary."

At last, the term I had waited to hear! "Zero stone? What in the hell is the zero stone?"

"It's a sack of shit, if you ask me. There's a sort of legend around here that a party of men who surveyed this place back in '38 left some kind of monument or somethin' chiseled in a rock. I've lived on this land forty-seven years and I ain't never run across it."

I let Eli's notion upset me for a moment—the notion that no zero stone existed. But then I remembered the old Mexican's map. Eli could waste his words on the stars. I knew better. But I played along. "You mean the survey party never was here?"

"No, that ain't what I mean, damn it. They were here, alright. I saw 'em. I talked to 'em the day before the Indians got 'em."

"Indians?"

"Yes. It was way back yonder in '38 when I was a pup about like you. I come up the day before it happened to see how them surveyors were coming along. They were platting my head rights for me. This was wild country then. Thirty miles from nowhere. They showed me about where the boundaries to my property would run and I can tell you the Gospel truth that my claim included Double Horn Creek as they showed it to me. But them surveyors never told me nothin' about no blasted zero stone."

"Why did those men come all the way out in the wilderness to survey a piece of land?" I asked.

"The Republic of Texas was trying to get settlers to take up the Indian lands, so they was givin' it away for almost nothin'. A man could get as much as forty-five hundred acres and not have to pay anything but the survey fees.

"The surveyors come all the way out here because they planned to make a great big survey of this whole valley, to open it up to settlers. When I heard about them getting up a survey party in Austin, I went to them and told them that I wanted the first plot myself. I wanted to be the first settler. So I asked them to pick out the finest piece of land along the river and start their big survey there and I would patent that first piece of land for myself. I offered them a bonus over and above the survey fees to do that for me.

"I rode up here several days after they got started to see what my land looked like. It included Double Horn Creek and a good portion of land along the Colorado and several little springs here and there. I asked them to send the field notes back to the General Land Office as soon as they got them written up so I could go ahead and get my patent. Then, the next day, I rode back down to Austin."

"And the Indians got them that day?"

"That's right. This piece of land was all they got surveyed before the Indians got 'em. The reds must have figured out what was up. They knew settlers would come after the first survey crew. Them surveyors must have let their guard down, because Indians killed and scalped 'em all except for one."

"One got away?"

"Yep."

"Who was he?"

"Hell if I know. But lucky for me he got away and took the field notes back down to Austin and turned them in, so I could use them to patent my land."

The old Mexican! The old Mexican had been a member of that survey party—maybe a cook or a guard or a horse wrangler. Being a young Mexican back then, he had managed to escape the Indian attack and had taken the field notes to Austin. He had probably found the treasure with the rest of the men in the survey party a day or so before the massacre and they had used their surveying equipment to plot the exact location of the treasure so they could come back for it later.

Yes, that explained the 49 degrees northwest, measured by the surveyors' compass! And the 189 chains! Didn't surveyors use chains to measure land? They all would have become rich if not for the Indians. And the old Mexican—the young Mexican, that is—was too badly scared to come back after the treasure himself, so he simply made a map of it. That dear, old vaquero had bequeathed to me a buried fortune!

My mind amazed me with the speed at which it could conjure up such possibilities. I wanted desperately to ask old man Flat if he remembered any Mexicans being part of the survey crew or if the surveyors had seemed strangely excitable about something they wouldn't mention the day he talked to them. But what would Eli think of those kind of harebrained inquiries?

I heard the hinges creak as the door to the log kitchen opened wider. Topsy walked out carrying a big pot and a cake of cornbread. She paused to look for us, her dog watching for some morsel to fall from her hands.

"Over here, Topsy," Eli said.

She approached and put the food down in front of us. The dog moved around downwind of the stew pot and started sniffing the air, inching nervously toward the steaming vessel.

"Git out of there, Speck," the old man growled.

Speck cowered and followed Topsy as she went back to the house for some plates and spoons. By the time she got back, Boone and Tobe had snuck in under the shadows with me and Eli. We all ate our stew and cornbread in silence, the Flatt men with their rifles across their laps, watching the dark, Speck sitting expectantly on his haunches.

I saw Topsy save a corner of her cornbread. She scraped a little stew onto it and gave it to the dog. I ate my fill and still had a little left on my plate, too. When I gave it back to Topsy, I gestured toward the dog and she understood I intended the leftovers for her pet.

We tightened our saddle cinches again, except for Topsy. She stayed home while Eli, Boone, Tobe, and I rode a mile or so into the oak thickets and made a dry camp with no fire. Topsy had loaned me a blanket from the house. The cool front made me grateful to have it. The Flatt men stretched out beside me, their guns in their hands.

My back was too sore from breaking school desks and the ground too rough with rocks to make sleep come easy for me. But the air was clear and the stars brilliant. I was still staring at them when the snoring started. If the Standards had come out to slaughter us that night, they could have located us from three miles away by the noise—provided they could have distinguished it from a chorus of sonorous bullfrogs. The grating lullaby eventually put me to sleep and, in my dreams, became the creaking and groaning of timbers as I wandered aimlessly through the shafts of an abandoned silver mine.

ELEVEN

A gun butt nudged me about an hour before sunup. I rolled out from under my borrowed blanket and saddled my mare. No one spoke as we rode back to the house. When we got there, Topsy already had eggs, bacon, biscuits, and coffee ready for us. We ate out behind the barn. Topsy was the only one who went in or out of the house.

By dawn Eli, Boone, and Tobe had mounted fresh horses. "We're gonna try to get some work done today," Eli said to Topsy, "after we account for them Standards. We'll look for some calves to brand back at Cypress Creek. You might want to take a rope and check them bogs along the river and pull out any cows you find."

"Alright," Topsy said.

Then Eli turned to me. "You'll find you an ax and a file in the barn. Topsy will show you." He took a canteen down from his saddle and tossed it to me. "Here, I believe I owe you a canteen."

"Where do you want me to start chopping?" I asked.

"Use your sense, boy. Find a big cedar brake where we can get a wagon in to load the posts. Cut them about as big as you are around the knee. Hundreds of 'em."

"Might as well chop some skinnier ones, too," Tobe said. "We can use 'em for pickets around the pens and staves on the bob-wire fence to keep the wires from saggin'."

"Alright," Eli said, "cut some smaller ones, too."

"And find you a few great big ones for corners and gate posts," Boone suggested. "Big as you are around the middle and ten feet tall."

"Ten feet," Eli repeated. "And don't take no ideas of pullin' stakes. We'll catch you wherever you run. You're with us now whether you like it or not until we find out just who the hell you are."

I nodded and the Flatt gang trotted to the south. When they called Speck, he kicked up a cloud of dust a whirlwind would have envied as he made his pursuit. Topsy watched them leave, then showed me where to find my tools.

In the dim light of the barn, her hair looked jet-black. But when she passed in front of the morning light streaming in through the open barn door, it shone with the color of rubies. Her moccasins moved silently across the dirt-and-straw floor. "Here's your ax." She handed the tool to me. "I'll get you a file. There's a vise by the door if you want to put an edge on it now."

I clamped the ax head in the vise and started smoothing the burrs from the blade with the file Topsy brought me. She went out with a bridle and brought a big gelding around to the barn door.

"He looks strong enough to pull those brutes out of the mud," I said.

"Yes, he's a strong one, alright." She went to the room the bridle had come from and came out carrying a saddle. She was only a switch of a person, but she didn't let the load slow her down. "Did everything stay quiet last night?"

"Yes," I said, "except for the snoring. I appreciate that blanket you loaned me. I slept well under it, but your pa and your brothers sure must be nervous to camp in the rocks like that."

"They're expecting trouble from the Standards."

"Do you think they'll give you any?"

Topsy was stroking the big gelding's back with a brush. She ducked under his belly to get to his other side. "I don't think they'll come after us. But if any Flatts and Standards happen to cross paths, they're sure to start shooting."

I turned the head of the ax around in the vise to work the other face. I was grateful that it was a double-bladed head so I could spend twice the time on it and work Topsy for more information. "Last night your pa told me how the trouble got started between y'all and the Standards. Too bad about your brothers, Reed and Bass."

Topsy grunted. "It's too bad about Virgil and Cal Standard, too. It's too bad about all of them. But I'm sure Pa didn't tell you how he's the cause of it all. I bet he forgot to mention that."

I stopped in midstroke with the file, shocked to hear Topsy speak out against her father. "What do you mean?"

"It's none of your concern," she said, "but I guess I better tell you so you'll know how much trouble you've stumbled into. It was Pa that caused us to go to war with the Standards."

"I thought the Standards grabbed some of y'all's land."

"They didn't exactly grab it. The boundary never has been marked that any of us know about, so we just sort of shared the creek as a boundary and that worked out fine for years."

"Until the courthouse burned down," I suggested.

"No, that had nothing to do with it. That's just Pa's story. He's told it so often that he's got Boone and Tobe believing it and I think he may even believe it hisself."

"Well, what was it that caused the land dispute, then?"

"You may not believe me but I'm going to tell you." She swung the saddle around in a half circle to get it on the gelding's back. "Pa was the first settler to come to this part of the country. He's always bragged about that and thought he should get more credit for fightin' Indians and all. When they formed the county, he wanted them to name it after him—Flatt County, Texas. Only problem is, this ain't no flat county. So they called it Burnet County, after that old politician, David Burnet. That burned Pa up double because he's an old Sam Houston man and Houston hated David Burnet."

"I don't understand what that has to do with . . ."

"Just hold your horses," Topsy said, "I'm gittin' to it. Since he couldn't get the county named Flatt, Pa's had it on his mind to get a town named for him around here. Well, a few years ago, we had a wet year and the river stayed up running deep all summer. There was a steamboat in the Colorado then—I've heard it sunk down at La Grange since then—but that little steamer came all the way up to the Marble Falls because the river was so high."

"Yes, but what has a steamboat to do with . . ."

"Dang it, Mr. Huckaby, just keep your shirt on. I'm going to make sense in the long run." Topsy was hanging by the cinch strap, using her weight to snug it through the saddle rings. "That steamboat gave Pa the idea that he should start a town on the river and name it Flatt, Texas, and let the steamers service the town. And he figured he'd put this town where that steamer tied up on its way to the Marble Falls. And guess where that was."

"The mouth of the Double Horn?" I asked, finally beginning to grasp the route Topsy had taken.

"Yes, and so Pa figured that's where he'd put his docks."

"But that was all several years ago, you said."

"Yes, and we didn't hear no more whistles from no more steamers this high up the river and Pa more or less forgot about that idea. Then, a few months ago, the papers had a story about the Colorado River Navigation Company. Pa read it and got all excited because this company was going to clear the raft out of the mouth of the Colorado and open up the river to steamboats that could come in and out of the Gulf of Mexico. Pa figured we'd get rich if we had our own steamboat town, so he up and told Lon Standard one day that he was going to fence off the Double Horn and start his town."

"Now, wait a minute," I said, working the last face of the ax. "Your pa told me that Lon Standard was going to fence *him* out."

"That's not true," Topsy said. "It was Pa that said he would fence first. Well, the Standards have always believed that that land was theirs, so they took Pa to court to try and prove it and that made him madder than a hornet. He wanted that town bad. He wanted it so much that he couldn't think straight. And he still wants it. He keeps sayin' that we could be rich as kings if only that damned Lon Standard would stay away from what didn't belong to him."

I began to see what drove Eli Flatt. He was an old man who felt life had shortchanged him on his dreams. He wanted to leave his name on something and he was ready to grasp any idea that could turn his fortunes before he had to die poor. And that was a polite way of saying he was a greedy old bastard.

But of all the nonsensical schemes to pay for with the lives of one's own sons! Steamboats on the Colorado! What did Eli Flatt know of building towns? What did he know of the indestructible raft at the Colorado's mouth? What did he know of steamers? To think that he would go to war with his neighbors in hopes that a line of steampowered vessels would ply the river this high up! This river—the Colorado—that jumped its banks every other year and all but dried up the years in between! The idiot who would follow his greed into that kind of ridiculous speculation had no more sense than the fool who would . . .

The fool who would risk his life and his freedom against the sorry chance of digging up some unknown treasure once mentioned on an old Mexican's map.

"Well, just who *is* it that rightfully owns the creek?" I asked. "The Flatts or the Standards?"

"I don't know. I always thought it was us, but now I'm not sure. The Standards always thought they owned it and said the land patents that burned in the courthouse would have proved them right. But now I just don't know who's right. For so many years it just didn't matter. We *shared* the creek."

"What about the zero stone?"

Topsy had coiled a hemp lariat and was fastening the end of it to her saddle horn. "Nobody knows where it is. Sometimes Pa says there ain't no such thing. Other times he says that if there ever was a boundary marker like that, the Standards would have already dug it up anyhow, so they could steal our land."

If I had to hone the ax head much longer, I would reduce it all to shavings. I paused to take a drink from the canteen Eli had given me. "How come you said your pa caused the killing to start between your brothers and the Standards? He told me last night that the Standard boys jumped your brothers after the trial."

"It was Pa that told all my brothers to take their guns to the courthouse the day of the trial," she said. "He had told them that if the judge couldn't settle the case that day, that us Flatts ought to settle it ourselves. That's what Reed and Bass tried to do and that's why the Standards shot them down."

"You mean to say that the Standards only shot in self-defense?"

"Yes, and the grand jury saw it the same way. Then Pa sent Boone and Tobe out to get even."

"What do you mean get even?" I said.

"You know what I mean. You must have heard how Virgil and Cal Standard got shot."

"You mean Boone and Tobe ambushed them?"

"I told you last night us Flatts ain't no bushwhackers. Boone and Tobe said they came across Virgil and Cal on the road to the Marble Falls. Virgil and Cal started shooting first and so my brothers had to shoot back."

"I read in the paper that the Standard boys were shot in the back," I said.

"It was a running fight. They turned their backs at the wrong time. The point is Pa shouldn't never have sent Boone and Tobe out looking for them in the first place. Now two more are dead and everybody thinks Tobe and Boone are murderers.

"There was a bob-wire salesman staying with us then and Pa wanted to kill him, too, so he wouldn't say anything about where Boone and Tobe had been that day. I talked Pa out of it, though, just like I talked him out of shooting you yesterday."

"I have neglected to thank you for that," I said.

"You can thank me by not letting Pa know what I've told you today."

"I won't say anything." I took the ax out of the vise and slipped the file into my hip pocket to take with me to the cedar brakes. "In fact, there's a secret or two I would like you to know, since you told me yours."

Topsy tossed her red hair over one shoulder as she turned to look at me. "What do you mean?"

"I didn't say anything to your pa because I was afraid he would misunderstand me. But I think I better tell you in case he finds out and takes it the wrong way."

"Finds what out?" she asked.

"I've met some of the Standard family."

"What?" she said. "Which ones?"

I told her about my altercation with the flour barrel. I told it as humorously as I knew how to, but Topsy only cracked a smile for a second or two.

"What about Clay?" she said. "Was he there, too?"

"No, just Lum and Nat and Annie. They did mention Clay, though. Said he and their pa would be waiting."

Topsy sighed and looked beyond me. It made sense

now how she could go against her father when her own brothers were getting killed. She was in love with Clay Standard. If not for Clay, she would have hated Standards as much as old Eli, and she might have shot me herself the day before for getting too close to Flatt land.

"What are the Standards like?" I asked. We were standing in the doorway of the barn, ready to go to our jobs.

"They were good neighbors. But there was always something between Pa and Mr. Lon, even before the land argument."

"What was it?"

"Mr. Lon came from Virginia. He fought four years in the war. I think he was a major or something. When the Yankees won, he lost almost all his land and property. His house burned. He had to turn his Negroes out. He didn't have work for them all after the war. So he came here to start again."

"And your pa?"

"Like I said, Pa is an old Sam Houston man. He voted against Texas going with the Confederacy, just like old Sam did. In fact, most of the people in this county voted against quitting the Union. We ain't never had no slaves around here and we didn't want no war. Pa said we never should have gone to war."

"So your pa and Lon Standard differed about the war?"

"I never heard them argue out loud. But whenever they were together and Pa said something good about the Reconstruction Government I could see Mr. Lon getting sort of hot. And whenever Mr. Lon would talk about Jeff Davis or something, Pa would just get up and leave. Boone and Reed fought with the Confederacy, and Pa was proud of them for it, but he never thought Texas should have been in it in the first place."

"What about the rest of the Standards?" I asked.

"There was five brothers and two sisters before the feud started. Cal and Virgil are dead now. Susan got married to a fellow she knew in Virginia and went back there. Lum is the oldest and used to lead the militia before the Indians were run out. Some folks wanted him to run for sheriff here while back, but he didn't do it.

"Nat's about your age, I guess. It was Nat and Cal who shot my brothers after the trial. Nat's got him the fastest two racehorses around here.

"Then there's Clay," she said.

"What's he like?"

"He's a nice feller. Took me to a dance once last year."

"You like him?"

"Sure, I like him," she said, fiddling with the gelding's bridle. "He treated me nice. He liked to joke around a lot. Always told me I was the prettiest one of the Flatt family. I ain't got no sisters, you know."

I smiled and looped the canteen strap around my neck. "What about Annie?"

"Annie? She's a friend of mine now—or would be if it wasn't for the feud—but in school we used to fight every day."

"Fight?" I asked.

"You bet. Rasslin' and fistfights, too. We got so tough the boys wouldn't even pick on us."

A bizarre image came to mind. It *would* be a good fight, I was thinking. Topsy versus Annie in a hair-pulling, toe-to-toe bout of fisticuffs. I felt strangely disloyal when I thought I would have to put my money on Topsy in the long run.

"We've growed up since then," Topsy continued. "She's a better cook and keeps a better house than I can. Course, she's got her ma to help her. And she's got the biggest garden and orchards you ever seen. She used to send over lots of it for us."

"I guess she must be the prettiest one of the Standard family," I said, before I could stop myself.

Topsy caught me blushing. "Why, Mr. Huckaby! I do believe you took a shine to her yesterday at the Marble Falls! You better watch yourself. She's a hellcat. I have never heard the likes of cuss words in my life as when Annie gets riled!"

"I know," I said. "Well, I guess I better start chopping."

"Yes, you better before you turn any redder," she said. "I'll bring you some biscuits or something to eat this evening. As long as I don't have too many cows to look after." She hitched her skirt up over the knee of her buckskins, took a short hop to get her foot in the stirrup, and then sprang into the saddle. "There's a good cedar brake on that road to the Double Horn," she said, pointing. "You can't get in any trouble as long as you don't cross the creek."

I watched Topsy ride away, then I walked past the spools of barbed wire, past a post-and-rail corral where Liberty was standing with some of the Flatt horses, and on toward the creek. A cool, pleasant stroll of two miles or so brought me to the edge of a cedar brake just off the road. It was a good place to start chopping.

I got my muscles limbered up on two or three trees, then began lopping limbs off at such a clip that the whole out-of-doors smelled like the inside of a brand-new cedar chest. The smaller limbs I piled up in one stack, to be used as the pickets and staves Tobe had suggested. The larger limbs would become posts, big around as I was at the knee, as Eli had specified.

Most of the cedars branched right above the ground into multiple trunks of the fence-post size. It was a rare one that had a single trunk and then the trunk would be just a little bigger around than my leg—still too slender and short for corner or gate posts. I would have to find some old trees for the big posts Boone had ordered me to produce.

As I swung the ax, I began to take Lon Standard's side in the land dispute. His side was Annie's side. His side was the side that went against Eli Flatt and if Eli's own daughter could blame him for the dispute, I figured I could, too.

But, most prominent in my mind was the hope that Lon Standard was right because, if he was, it meant the lost zero stone stood somewhere east of the creek, where my ax was currently making fence posts of cedar trees. It was foolish to hope for such things, but I held to a fancy that I might actually stumble across the rock of the zero somewhere in the cedar brakes while chopping posts.

Why not? I had stumbled across the old Mexican and Marion Harkey and Annie Standard and Topsy Flatt. Why couldn't I stumble upon a lost boundary marker the same way the old Mexican had happened across a lost treasure in the years of his youth? I felt a gold coin or a faceted gem drop into my pocket with every limb I hacked from the brakes.

TWELVE

Topsy must have come across more bogged cows than she expected, for she didn't arrive with any edibles that afternoon. I subsisted on water from Eli's canteen and a couple of biscuits I had saved from breakfast.

It was almost dusk when I saw Tobe riding toward me, leading my mare, picking his way around the cedar stumps. He stared at the piles of posts and pickets around him as if he had never before seen a day's work thus accounted for. "My word, Royal," he said. "Did you have an ax for each hand?"

I had almost finished stacking the day's posts in their appropriate piles and Liberty was a welcome sight. "Thanks for bringing my mare," I said.

"If I didn't know better, I'd think Topsy spent the day chopping with you," he said. "She can rough it with the best of 'em but she's got nothin' on you." He helped me carry the last couple of dozen posts to the stack I was building of them. "She's cooking us some game and some roasting ears," he said as we mounted. He took a last look over his shoulder at the wreckage I had made of the cedar brakes and shook his head in wonder and admiration.

We ate in the dark again, this time in a thicket out beyond the corral. The Flatt men ate three squirrels and two roasting ears apiece. Topsy and I split a rabbit.

"He don't burn much hay," Tobe said, "but he sure makes splinters fly."

Boone scoffed. "The man's bein' paid to work, ain't he?"

"How much you reckon he chopped in one day?" Tobe asked.

"How much *did* he chop?" Eli asked.

"I'll bet you a plug he cut four hundred pickets and two hundred posts and he's got 'em all ricked up like cordwood."

Boone risked a low laugh. "Tobe, you'd bet on spoilt milk."

"That would be almost a post every minute," Topsy said, having figured the question mathematically in her head.

"He couldn't have chopped that much," Boone said.

"Yes, he could have, couldn't he, Pa?" Tobe asked.

"I guess mite near anybody could cut sixty posts in one hour, but I don't know whether or not he could keep it up ten hours straight."

"We'll go count 'em in the mornin'," Tobe suggested.

"The hell we will," Boone said. "Got better things to do."

"Boone's right," Eli said.

After tossing my rabbit bones to Speck, I rode with the men to another campsite somewhere in the dark. I didn't know the trails the way they did, so I just had to follow along. We left our horses in a hollow and threw our bedrolls down nearby. Tobe still hadn't stopped bragging on my prowess with the ax.

"Let me see your hands," he said, once we had seated

ourselves among the rocks and tree trunks.

I held them out, palms upward. Tobe felt them.

"Good gracious, Pa, they feel hard as hooves. I thought *I* had thick skin."

Boone and Eli had to inspect my hands then. It was almost pitch-dark, the moon having not yet risen, but Eli was about to light his pipe, so he let his match illuminate my calluses after his tobacco had taken the flame. In the flickering light, I saw that his long white beard had snagged a few kernels of corn. Then it was dark again and the Flatts smoked silently.

"I don't know why in hell a man would want to work that hard afoot," Boone finally said.

"I didn't have much choice in the matter," I replied. "I built those calluses in the penitentiary."

"What did you do to get put in there, anyway?"

"Hush, Tobe," Eli said. "That's a dangerous question to ask of a man."

"That's alright, Mr. Flatt," I replied. "It might do you all some good to hear what I did because it was not much different from what y'all are doing right now. I was just trying to do what I thought was right by my friends and my family."

There was another stretch of silence. "How long you say you stayed in prison?" Tobe asked.

"Three years."

"How'd you like it?"

Boone started laughing. "Hell, it wasn't a damn holiday he went on. They put chains on him and made him earn his keep. What did you think?"

"That right?" Tobe asked me.

"More or less. Except it wasn't my keep I was earning. It was the contractor's."

"The contractor's? What's that mean?"

"The prison's been under the lease system since '71. They hire convicts out like mules at so much a head to various contractors who work them as hard as they want. When I was in there, sometimes they even subleased us to somebody else. They paid for us by the day, so, of course, to get their money's worth out of us, they worked us as long as we could stand up. Boone's right about the chains, though. We wore them often enough."

"What kind of work did you do?" Tobe asked.

"All kinds. I worked in hide yards and brick yards, built railroads, made charcoal, chopped cotton, dug ditches, pitched hay."

"They must not have fed you too good," Eli said. "Or have you always been that skinny?"

"No, sir, not always," I replied. "I cut a wider wake before I went to prison. The amount of food we got depended on the generosity of whoever it was that was leasing us at the time. Some of them fed us better than others, but none of them fed us enough."

Boone snorted as if he thought I was telling windies.

"What's the hardest you ever worked?" Tobe asked.

"The hardest I ever worked was the time I was given the choice to pump or die."

"What in hell's name is that supposed to mean?" Boone asked.

"I'll explain it to you. You see, I never did much work before I went to prison. Not the kind of work you men are used to, anyway. My daddy owned a lot of land and it was my responsibility to oversee it and make sure other folks were doing the work. My hands and my muscles were soft then."

"Nobody asked you to back up that far," Boone said.

"I'll get to the point quick enough," I said. "When they sent me off to prison I'll admit I was scared. I imagined it would be something like a big dog pit and I knew I wouldn't be the toughest dog to get thrown in. Like I say, I was soft then. But the real danger of the state penitentiary was something that never even crossed my mind until I found out about it firsthand."

"What was that?" Tobe asked.

"The danger that I would be worked or starved or beaten to death by the guards."

"I thought you were gonna tell something about pumpin' for your life," Boone reminded me.

"I'm leading up to that."

"Just let him tell it," Tobe said.

I continued: "I had been in prison just a couple of days when they sent me out with a chain gang to work in the hay fields of some farmer who was subleasing a bunch of prisoners. I spent all day in the sun, forking hay into a bailing machine. I didn't have these calluses then, so by the end of the day my hands were bloody. They locked us up in a little shack that night and had a few men there to guard us. I started to tell one of the guards that I needed medical attention for my hands, but there was a black prisoner there by the name of Reuben who sat me down and told me I had better not mention any of my problems to the guards or things would go rough for me. I took his advice that night."

"What did you have to eat that night?" Tobe asked.

"What the hell difference does it make?" Boone said. "Don't start him to branchin' out or he'll really take the bridle off."

"Everything I've said is true, Boone. But if you don't believe it so far, I warn you that you'll never believe the parts I haven't told yet."

Boone snorted again.

"I don't remember what they had for us to eat that night, Tobe, because I was too cramped up from the work and the sun to keep anything down.

"Anyway, the next day they worked us just as hard and I figured about noon that I wasn't going to live if I had to keep working like that. Old Reuben knew what I had on my mind, though, and he whispered to me not to try getting out of any hay bailing. He stuck with me all day and made it look like I was getting my share done, when really it was him doing his work and mine, too.

"My palms were two big blood blisters that night when they locked us back up in the shack. I managed to eat that night, some kind of gruel. At least they gave us all the water we wanted."

"Is that the water you had to pump to save your life?"

"Shut up, Boone, and let the boy tell his story," old Eli suggested.

Boone heaved a sigh of disgust and settled back against a small oak.

"It was the next day that I had to do the pumping. The black man, Reuben, tried to keep me from complaining to the guards, but the blood from my hands was running all the way down the handle of my pitchfork. I just knew I couldn't live if I had to work that way and I figured it was high time I said so.

"I went to the guard who looked the friendliest and said, 'Sir, I need another kind of job. This work is ruining my hands.' The guard looked at them and, with the most sincere expression of concern on his face, asked me what kind of work it was that I had in mind. I told him I didn't know, but that I was college educated and was not used to working out in the sun.

" 'Would you like a cooler place to work?' he asked.

" 'Yes, sir,' I said, 'I would be grateful to have a cooler place to work,' and it didn't seem to me that the guards were going to be unreasonable at all.

"Then the guard said, 'Men, this prisoner is college educated and wants someplace cool to work. Let's oblige him.' Well, they left just one guard to watch the hay pitching and the rest of them came at me laughing and dragged me back to the shack and locked a ball and chain on my leg and told me they were about to put me to work in the coolest place they knew."

"Where did they put you?" Tobe said.

"They threw me down an old well."

"Oh, my foot," Boone said.

"I said you wouldn't believe it, Boone, but I'm telling you the truth. What was to stop them? Nobody was around who gave a damn about any convicts."

"How deep a well was it?" Tobe asked.

"Yes, and how long a yarn is this?" Boone wanted to know.

I ignored the second question. "It wasn't too deep. About twenty feet or thereabouts and there was only about three feet of water in the bottom. And it *was* cool. The leg iron cut my ankle a little falling in and I got scraped up some on the rocks lining the inside of the well. But I didn't break any bones, and overall, I was happy to be out of the sun and I figured I might get some rest. I thought it was a kind of solitary confinement they were putting me in. I figured they would throw me some food down that evening and then take me out the next morning."

"That what happened?" Tobe asked.

"Nope. About ten minutes after they threw me in the well they lowered a pump down to me. It had a pipe attached to it that ran all the way up and out of the well. And they had sawed the handle off shorter than usual."

"What was they about?" old Eli asked quietly.

"Well, sir, I soon found out. Before they threw me into the well, I had noticed that there was a windmill right nearby and a water tank up on stilts. And they began letting water gush out of the tank and into the old well I was in. It took me about thirty seconds to figure out that I was going to drown if I didn't start pumping."

"I'd have swum," Boone said.

"He had a ball and chain on his leg," Tobe reminded his half brother with a tone of superiority in his voice.

"Pay closer attention, Boone," the old man said.

"They had figured out every way possible to make it tough on me. The pump stood on a pedestal that put it about a foot too high to make pumping easy. And they had sawed that handle off to reduce the leverage."

"I'd have clumb that pipe sticking out of the well," Boone said, "and I'd have dragged that ball and chain right up with me."

"Maybe you could have made it," I said. "You might be strong enough. But I wasn't. Besides, I figured those guards would be on the top, waiting for me. No, I just had to pump and I mean I had to pump quick to keep the water going out as fast as it came in. Even then, I was losing ground. The water level climbed steadily up my chest."

"And with them sore hands, too," Tobe said.

"That was the worst of it, even after I used my shirt to wrap them up in, they still hurt something terrible. But I learned pretty quick not to think about that and I figured I would survive because I estimated about how much water was in that tank on stilts and I knew it would run out sooner or later and I could quit pumping. And I figured out ways to use different muscles. I would squat up and down for a while and use my legs to do the work . . ."

The moon had risen and there was enough light for the Flatt men to watch me as I demonstrated my method of squat-pumping. It was worth a laugh to Boone.

". . . and to give my hands a break, I could catch that pump handle in the crook of my elbow on the way down. Then I would go to using my back muscles, bending over and straightening up. But that well was narrow and I kept bumping my head against the other side. So then I would pump with my arms again and then start over with the squatting method."

"How long did it take for that water tank to empty out?" Tobe asked.

"It never did," I said.

"I knew it!" Boone shouted, laughing. "I knew it was a windy and ol' Royal hooked you good on it, Tobe!"

"No, it's the truth," I said quickly. "The tank didn't run out of water because I was pumping it right back in. I was pumping water in circles."

Two hoot owls called to each other during a brief silence.

"How'd you come out alive, then?" Boone asked skeptically.

"I almost didn't. I gave it all of what I had. I was

pumping for my life. But a man has just so much and I was getting used up. I made it until after dark sometime, but the water was climbing higher up on me all the time. Then strange things began to happen to me."

"Explain that better," Eli ordered.

"Well, I don't know if I can. You see it got pitch-dark in that well and there was that constant noise of the water falling in on me. And I had gotten so cold from standing in the water that I had gone numb all over. I was completely worn out from the work and I couldn't feel or hear or see a thing and my head started to play tricks on me. I saw things I couldn't explain—things that didn't make sense."

"Haints?"

"Yeah, something like that, Tobe. Just strange lights and things. Visions. I guess I kept pumping, though. I guess my body worked longer than my mind."

"Well, did they shut the water off or what?" Boone asked. "How come you didn't drown?"

"The next thing I remember, I could feel something warm in the water with me."

"You mean you pissed yourself again?"

That one even made Tobe laugh, and he was right with me in the story.

"No, it was another man in there with me. That black man, Reuben, had taken all his clothes off and climbed down into the well."

"What do you mean to say, boy?" old Eli growled.

"He took his uniform off because he didn't want to be caught and the guards would figure out that he had come to help me if his clothes were wet the next morning. He had a handful of that gruel and he shoved some in my mouth and made me swallow it. He started doing the pumping for me, too. I told him to shut the water off, but he said he couldn't do that because the guards would wake up if they didn't keep hearing that noise of it flowing.

"The way Reuben pumped that water was something.

He got it down below our knees, then told me he would have to climb up the pipe and go back to the shack. He told me to rest until the water got up to my waist and then to start pumping again. He said they would let me out at dawn."

"Did they?"

"Yes, they did. It was the sweetest silence I ever heard when that water quit falling in on me. They hauled the pump out, then lowered a rope for me to loop under my arms. I thought that ball was going to pull my leg off, but I stayed in one piece until they dragged me out."

"You sure that's all true?" Boone asked.

"I swear by everything holy that it's true."

We sat in the dim silence for a while, the embers in Eli's pipe pulsing orange.

"Was that the worst they ever done you in jail?" Tobe asked.

"Nope," I said. "The worst came right after they pulled me out of the well."

The Flatt men didn't have the heart to ask what more the guards could have done to me, so I had to tell them on my own initiative.

"They forced me to watch as they whipped the life out of poor old Reuben for climbing down in the well to help me out. They stripped all his clothes off him and made five convicts hold him facedown by the arms, legs, and head. Then they used the bat on him."

"What's the bat?" asked Tobe with a touch of dread in his voice.

"It's a handle attached to two straps of leather as thick as the soles of your boots, about four inches wide and up to six feet long. It can turn a man's flesh to jelly. They must have lashed him fifty times with it until he was limp as a rope. The screams he made will never let me be as long as I live. I wake up hearing them sometimes."

"They whipped him to death?" Eli asked.

"I suppose so. At least I never saw him again after that. They just dragged him off and I figured they buried him somewhere. I probably saw or heard a thousand others get beaten with the bat the next three years. It killed a good many of them."

I stretched out under my blanket and put my hat over my face to block the moonlight from my eyes. "But you men are tougher than I was," I said. "When those rangers show up here to break up this feud between y'all and the Standards, if they happen to want to send any of you to prison to make an example of you to the rest of the county, I suspect you'll fare better than I did that first few days."

I had worked hard enough that day to make my body crave rest, and mercifully I soon fell asleep.

THIRTEEN

The next day Eli, Boone, and Tobe made a sweep through the Standard spread, looking for cattle. They wanted to round up a small herd to drive to Austin. Topsy tried to talk them out of cow hunting on the Standards' property, but Eli was adamant. He said some crick in his shin bones told him a hard winter was coming and he needed to cut some cattle from the range. They passed through the cedar brakes on the way back that afternoon.

"We got us six head of cows, four of calves, and nine of yearlin' steers," Tobe reported.

"But not a single head of land grabbers," Boone added.

They moved a herd of about a hundred out that day, planning three days to get the beeves to Austin and one day for their return ride.

Eli and his sons had loosened their guard on me and given me their trust by now, although Boone didn't like to admit it. It's difficult to mistrust a hard worker. I moved my overnight headquarters to the barn. There were beds in the house, of course, but it wouldn't be proper for Topsy to sleep alone under the same roof with the hired man.

She seemed relieved to see her father and brothers ride away from Double Horn Creek for a few days. And I much preferred her company that evening on the gallery of the Flatt home to that of Eli, Boone, and Tobe out on the hard ground in the hills. We got to talking and I told her how the Colorado seemed an entirely different river where I came from, where it snaked through the level clay prairies.

"Do you ever miss your home?" she asked.

"Some things I miss."

"Like what?"

"I miss the colored folks."

Topsy glared at me with her wild green eyes. "Why? You don't mean the colored girls, do you?"

I laughed. "No, I mean the whole lot of them."

"How come?"

"Lots of reasons. I used to go down to their settlements for an evening with a black boy I grew up with named Rafe. Things were usually dull around the white folks' homes, but down there the colored folks always had something going. They had more fun."

"What do you mean?"

"Well, for example, some of my family were violinists but Rafe's people were fiddlers. Us white patties—that's what they called us—we may have passed as storytellers, but the colored folks were raconteurs."

"Raccoon what?"

"A raconteur is somebody who can just flat naturally *tell* a story. Old Uncle Pie was the best yarn spinner of the bunch."

"What kind of stories did he tell?"

"Oh, about any subject you could name. Huntin' stories, fishin' stories, tall tales. But he especially liked to talk about buried treasure."

"Oh."

"You know—those old legends about pirates or lost

gold or abandoned mines. I guess y'all have those kind of stories around here, too."

"Yeah, some," Topsy said.

"Like what?"

"Oh, I ain't no raccoon-teer, but I've heard stories. Some folks say that old Gail Borden found gold on his place down along the Sandy before he invented that Eagle-Brand milk-in-a-can and got rich."

"Oh, really? What else?"

"Well, let me think. Some of the old-timers say that a fellow named Harp Perry buried twelve hundred pounds of silver somewhere on Packsaddle Mountain."

I was trying to find a level place on the warped porch to make my chair sit flush on all four legs. "Twelve hundred?" I asked.

"Yeah. They say he melted it and poured it inside pieces of cane. And then there's an old Indian cave between the Marble Falls and Burnett where they say Sam Bass hid some gold he stole from a bank, but nobody can find it because the cave branches out underground and you can get lost in it. Then there's all them stories about Dead Man's Hole."

"What's Dead Man's Hole?"

"It's a cave right across the river from the town at the Marble Falls. It goes about three hundred feet straight down."

"Why do they call it Dead Man's Hole?"

"Some fellers tried to climb down it a long time ago but they never came out. I've heard you can lower a chicken down on a rope and pull it up dead in a minute or so. The air's poison. Well, naturally, that would make a fine place to put your treasure if you didn't want nobody to get at it."

"Yes, it would," I replied. "That's how most of those old treasure stories end up. There's always something to keep you from getting at the gold."

"Back during the war," Topsy said, "there was a lot of trouble around here with bushwhackers. They killed a bunch of Union men, like Pa. Some of their bodies were never found and everybody says they were throwed down into Dead Man's Hole. There was some talk that Pa's carcass would be the next one down there, but he was too sneaky for the bushwhackers. He stayed hid out like he's been doing here lately and they never got him."

I didn't care about old bushwhackings. I was interested in treasure. "I don't suppose you've ever heard of any treasure buried along the Double Horn," I said.

Topsy laughed. "If we had, Pa'd have dug for it to build his town."

I let the conversation branch into other subjects then, not wanting to seem unusually interested in buried loot. I was hoping for some talk about Annie Standard, but I was too bashful to initiate it. I knew Topsy would have been pleased to talk about certain members of the Standard clan herself, but she didn't have the nerve for it, either.

We did talk about the Standards in general, though, and speculated on when the rangers were likely to show up.

"I heard the rangers were scattered out dealing with the fence wars. I don't guess we'll see them until they get some of that mess under control."

"Is it true that you killed that ranger down in Matagorda County?" she asked abruptly, caressing a tin cup of coffee.

"No," I said, "I never killed him and I never killed anybody on purpose. I feel responsible for getting some other men killed." I turned to look her in the eye. I needed her to trust me. "But I don't think I could have done anything to prevent any of their deaths. I just didn't know enough to be able to see what was coming."

"What about now? What do you see comin' for us and the Standards?"

I tried to come up with some shred of optimism. "I hope to see the rangers coming one day soon. If they can't stop your feud, nobody can." That was the most hope I could hold out to her that evening.

I spent the next three days dealing death to cedar trees. By the end of the third day the cool front that had blown my hat off on Shovel Mountain wore out and the wind shifted back around to the south. The heat made the work tougher, but I managed to keep the production rate up to roughly that of my first day.

About midmorning on the fourth day I finally found a stand of cedar trees tall and straight enough to use as corner posts. I could see their dark green tops sticking up above the rest of the scrubby evergreens in the brakes. I was so anxious to tie into one that I passed through about fifty yards of smaller trees to reach the biggest of the big ones.

It stood every bit of thirty feet tall and rose in one perfectly straight trunk that would have served just as well for a rafter beam as a corner post. The trunk was probably too big for me to reach my arms all the way around, although I didn't intend to embrace it before killing it. The limbs that branched off from the main trunk would provide as many as thirty regular fence posts and an incalculable number of smaller pickets for hog pens, staves, and garden fences. I spit on my palms, wrapped them around the hickory handle of my double-bladed ax, and took my first swing at the granddaddy of all Double Horn Creek cedars.

There was a small bush of some kind at the base of the trunk where I aimed my first blow. The ax scattered its little branches and lodged firmly in the trunk of the big cedar. Instantly I heard a familiar sound that struck a tremor through the entire length of my spine and caused the hairs to stand on the back of my neck like the pikes of an ancient army.

A diamondback rattler of no less than five feet in length writhed wickedly from the bush at the base of the big cedar, its dozen or more rattles blurring in wild vibrations. It looked as big around as the fence posts I had been chopping. It coiled almost at my feet and prepared to strike. I jumped straight up, using the handle of my ax as a springboard and breaking it off in the process. Catching hold of the lower limbs, I pulled myself up into the tree and stuck the crown of my hat smack into the biggest nest of red hornets in the Texas hills.

In a second the buzz of wings accompanied that of snake rattles as the first of many wasps stung me on the right earlobe. I flinched so hard that I lost my toehold and my legs swung pendulum-like in front of the singing rattler, causing it to strike. Luckily the viper failed to lead my legs, as they swooped by quickly, and it completely missed its target. But I didn't care to test its aim again so I swung my feet back up into the tree, hooked one leg over a branch, hung there in a horizontal attitude, and thereby exposed my face to the nest of hornets.

Poisonous pinpricks peppered my neck, face, hands, and even my body through my thick shirt. The world was red with hornets. The only merit I could see to them was that the humming of their wings in my ears almost drowned out the chilling hiss of the rattler's tail. When one wasp stung me on the eyelid I quickly concluded that a giant hornet nest was no proper matter for point-blank scrutiny. I let my legs swing down again so I could expose the crown of my hat rather than my face to the hornet nest.

I must have forgotten that the rattler would strike at my flailing legs again. One look at its scaly shaft of a body lunging arrow-quick at my boots made me hook my legs back around the limb and turn my face to the hornet nest once more. Hanging on with one hand I pulled my hat down over my face to protect it from the marauding insects. The maneuver cost my hand three or four shots of hornet venom.

I had heard somewhere that a wasp would sting only once, then die. I decided to ride out the hornet attack until all the malicious little bugs had spent their single shots on me. I hung horizontal in the tree with my hat on my face, flinching like a worm in an ant bed until I simply could not take it any longer. Certainly two snake fangs could hold no more venom than a hundred wasp stings! I dropped from the tree and landed flat-footed in front of the coiled rattler.

The snake struck at my left shin. It was not a direct blow, so the fangs did not penetrate my jeans and boot tops. Instead they got snagged on my trouser cuffs. I don't know how long I danced the jig of a crazy man, trying to sling that reptile from my leg while swatting at the last two dozen red hornets who had yet to give their lives for their nest, but finally the fangs broke loose and the rattler sailed through the air as if someone had hurled the letter S into the cedar brakes.

I was dizzy either from doing the snake dance or from absorbing wasp poison, and once the danger had passed, the pain increased by degrees until I reached the Flatt home. Topsy was splitting wood when I staggered up to her. "What are you doin' back this time of day?" she asked.

I took off my hat. She gasped. I could feel the skin tightening around my neck and knew I must have swollen up like a poisoned pup. Topsy ordered me to sit on the front porch. She went to the kitchen and came back with a box of baking soda and a pan of water.

"Take off your shirt," she said.

"I will not," I replied.

"Oh, for Pete's sake, take off your shirt, Mr. Huckaby, before I have to take it off of you myself!"

I knew she would do it, too, and I couldn't stand the thought of someone else pulling my shirt off over all those wasp stings so I removed it myself. It didn't really matter. Blushing couldn't have made me any redder than the wasps already had. "I'll have you know that not one of them stung me below the belt," I insisted.

As I told Topsy what had happened, she made a cool paste from the baking soda and water and put a glob of it on each of the stung places, starting with my face. My eye had almost swollen shut where the hornet had stung me on the eyelid. When she worked around to the back of my neck, she stopped for a few seconds, then continued to smear the paste on.

"What caused them scars?" she asked.

"The prison guards whipped me for falling behind in my work one time when I was sick."

She continued to put the cool paste on the stung spots across my shoulders and down my back. Despite the pain, it was pleasant to feel the touch of her slender fingers. I knew then that if I hadn't already met Annie, I would have given Clay Standard some competition for the affections of Topsy Flatt.

"Who gives them guards the right to treat prisoners that way?" she asked.

"They do whatever they want. Some of them used to be convicts themselves. Hey, don't poke at those stings so hard. They're getting sore."

"I'm barely touching you."

I was almost drunk with pain, but the baking-soda paste felt like ice on burns.

"You landed in prison on account of a feud," she said. "What if that happens to Tobe or Boone. Or . . ."

"Or Clay Standard? Ouch! Son of a gun, that hurts!"

"Well, don't wiggle so much. You'd think a man who could take a whippin' on his back like that could stand to get stung some."

I squinted but that made my stung eye hurt, so I just gritted my teeth.

"Ain't you scared of going back to prison?" she asked.

"Not right now."

"Well, you ought to be. You're in the middle of another feud. How do you aim to get out of it?"

"Pray," I grunted.

"Pray for what?"

"Pray for rangers. They know how to stop a feud."

I looked like a spotted mule by the time Topsy finished

daubing me with baking-soda paste. "Leave that paste on till it dries," she said. "It'll cool them bites and draw the poison out. Then you can rinse it off."

About the time I got my shirt back on, Speck came running up to the house panting. In the next minute or two, Eli and his boys had returned from Austin. "How come you ain't choppin'?" the old man asked.

I looked up at him through my one open eye and smirked. Boone and Tobe started laughing.

"Why you wearin' polky dots?" Tobe asked. "What'd you tangle with?"

Topsy told them the story.

"Treed by a rattlesnake!" Boone said. "That beats all the dumb-assed stunts I ever heard of."

"Here are the fangs," I said, remembering the snake teeth stuck in my trouser cuffs.

"Go bury 'em," Eli said. "Don't prick yourself on 'em or they'll kill you just as sure as a bite from a live snake. Bury 'em deep and put rocks on 'em."

I got up to get a shovel so I could satisfy Eli's superstitions. Topsy said I shouldn't be made to work in my condition, but I told her not to worry. I got a shovel from the barn and made a good show of burying the fangs, though I didn't bury them very deep and I didn't put very many rocks over them. When I got back to the front porch, there was an argument going on.

"Don't go," Topsy was saying. "You'll have to drive right through their land. It's too dangerous."

"Go where?" I asked.

"Pa wants to take the money from the herd he sold and stock the house with supplies," Topsy explained, rolling her green eyes.

"Damn right," Boone said. "I'm tired of beddin' on the ground."

"But it's too dangerous to cross the Standard spread," Topsy said.

"That's right," I agreed. "They might be laying for you over there."

"We ain't scared of them," Boone said. "We can fight 'em off any day. Me and Tobe had no trouble with Virgil and Cal in a fair fight."

"That's exactly why they won't fight fair anymore," I said. "They'll shoot you in the back from the bushes as you ride by. They think that's what y'all did to Virgil and Cal so they'll do the same to you."

"Yeah, but you ain't been sleepin' on the ground as long as we have, Royal," Tobe reminded me. "That's no way to live. We're ready to risk it."

"No need to," I said. "Let me go for you. They have no reason to kill me. I'll drive the wagon to town and get the supplies. Besides, I need to get a new ax handle to replace that one I broke."

"You ain't got but one eye to see with," Eli said. "And who will help you load all them supplies? You don't look up to heftin' much, swol' up like you are with them hornet stings."

"I'll go with him," Topsy said. "They won't shoot me neither."

"Oh, hell, Pa, we don't need girls and no-'count drifters to do our work for us," Boone said. "It's just a trip to town."

"Could be your last trip," I argued. "There's no way to defend yourself against an ambush. It's not a question of bravery, it's a question of strategy. Let Topsy and me get the supplies and you all can get some water barrels filled up in the house for a long siege if it comes to that."

"Makes sense," Tobe said.

Eli agreed. He ordered Tobe to help me hitch two mules to the wagon. Tobe had to laugh every time he looked up at me. Soon Topsy and I were pulling away from the Flatt home with a list of supplies and a wad of cash to buy them with. Boone scowled at me as we left.

"Come on, Speck," Topsy said in a singsong voice, and the dog bounced off a spool of barbed wire and jumped to the bed of the moving buckboard, wagging his stump of a tail for glory.

We passed through the Standard spread without seeing a single one of its clan. Of course, we didn't take the road that led by their house. We crossed the Colorado at a sandy ford on the Standard Ranch, and when we reached the other side of the river I got out to rinse the dried baking soda from my face and neck. It had helped some, but my skin was still taut and felt feverish, especially in the places where several hornets had conspired to make their attacks close together.

A good road led to the Marble Falls settlement along the north bank of the Colorado. Topsy and I stopped at a road ranch to have a dinner of roast beef served to us. She said Eli wouldn't miss the cost of one dinner and she wanted to eat something for once that she didn't have to cook herself. I didn't eat very much. I saved my scraps for Speck. The wasp stings seemed to have affected my appetite.

After Topsy ate some apple pie and drank some coffee, we went on toward Lynn's Store. As we approached, I saw three guards from the Granite Mountain quarry sitting on the boardwalk in front of the store, passing around a bottle of Annie Standard's peach brandy. I forgot all about being stung by hornets or treed by rattlesnakes. One of the guards was the sergeant I had spoken to the day I went to the quarry.

Topsy and I ignored them as we stopped the mules in front of Lynn's Store, but we had just put our feet on the ground when the sergeant recognized me and spoke up.

"Well, look who's here. It's ol' Royal." He passed the bottle to one of his cohorts and picked up the sawed-off shotgun resting across his lap. "I don't see no bone meal on your clothes today, Royal. In fact, it looks like something got the better of you."

I stopped and glared at the sergeant through my one open eye. "How do you know my name?"

"That storekeeper told me all about you and your fight with the flour barrel," he said. "We asked around about you after you come to the quarry smart-mouthing me that day. We thought maybe you were trouble. Turns out you're just a convict yourself."

"How would you know?"

"A couple of them prisoners recognized your name. Said they knowed you when you wore stripes at Huntsville."

Topsy was standing at the door of Lynn's Store, waiting for me to go in with her, wondering what kind of previous acquaintance I had forged with the guards. I handed her the wad of money Eli had given me and told her to go on in the store for the supplies.

"What the hell bloated your neck up so bad?" asked one of the other guards.

"Oh, leave it alone," the sergeant said. "You'll embarrass that little redheaded thing. Can't you see that Royal has been lifting her skirt and she's been biting him to keep him off."

I could ignore just so much in my attempts to avoid trouble. I did not intend to stand by and listen to a sergeant of prison guards dishonor feminine virtue. I had listened to such men slander my mother and sisters often enough when I was in chains and helpless to defend womanhood. Now I meant to make the sergeant with the scattergun pay for every foul word I had ever heard cross the lips of a prison guard.

"Don't pay them no mind," Topsy said, but I was already stalking toward the trio of guards. The one with the shotgun laughed as I approached, assuming I was bluffing. When he saw the angry glint in my eye it was too late.

I wrestled the shotgun from his hands and applied the butt of it to his stomach. Then I used it like a club to strike him over the shoulders. The other two guards grabbed me, took the gun away, and pinned me against Eli's wagon. My swollen neck smarted terribly when one of them hooked the crook of his elbow under my chin to hold me still. I heard Topsy yelling and Speck growling low from the far corner of the wagon bed.

The sergeant threw a couple of punches into my mid-section, but they hurt me less than the blows I had given him with his own gun. Then he hit me hard in my good eye. When he backed off and prepared to kick me between the legs, Topsy rushed in to stop him, but he grabbed a handful of her blood-red hair and threw her down on the boardwalk.

Suddenly I felt fur leaping over my shoulder and knew Speck was lunging for the sergeant. The dog sank his fangs into the back of the sergeant's thigh and wrenched his head as if shaking a snake to pieces. Topsy scrambled for the nearest weapon—the brandy bottle—and had just reared it back to throw when a rifle shot went off.

Speck ran to hide behind Topsy's skirt. I saw Lynn standing at the door with a brand-new brass-bellied Winchester smoking from the muzzle. The two guards turned me loose immediately and when they did I kicked the sergeant where he had intended all along to kick me. Then Speck tore into the thigh again and Topsy had to call him off.

"That's enough, Roy," Lynn said. "Topsy, kick the shells out of that shotgun and give it back to them."

When Topsy had done so Lynn said, "You two pick him up and get on out of here. And don't you ever suppose to harm another one of my customers."

"What the hell are we?" asked one of the guards as they helped the sergeant onto his mule. "We buy our supplies for them prisoners here."

"You spend more on liquor than you do on food for them convicts. Now, git!"

Lynn never took his sights off the guards until they had ridden completely out of sight.

"Mr. Huckaby," he said, turning to me, "every time I see your face, you are fresh from some form of calamity. Your luck must run over some pretty rugged country."

"My soul craves trouble," I admitted. "I can't seem to avoid it."

"Have you been robbing bee hives?"

"No, I've been chopping cedar posts. I got into a big nest of hornets."

"I'd say you're in a nest of something worse than that. What have you joined up with the Flatt family for?"

I had to explain how I had been captured while hunting on the Double Horn.

"Oh, I see," Lynn said. "If only someone had warned you about hunting there, I suppose you'd be living elsewhere under much healthier circumstances right now."

I shrugged sheepishly.

Lynn helped us load rations of bacon, beans, coffee, salt, sugar, pepper, and flour. We also bought ammunition for the rifles of the Flatt men.

When I went to look at the ax handles I found a collection of tools nearby including a pickax. It looked like just the implement to use in excavating buried treasure from the rocks. I picked it up and tested its balance in my hand. I found myself longing to bury its point somewhere 49 degrees northwest of the zero stone.

Why wouldn't the rangers come to locate that marker for me? Where were they? I touched the steel point of the pick and imagined the sound it would make when it poked into the buried treasure chest. I was hearing that sound. I was digging for treasure. I was clawing back the dirt and throwing gold, silver, and jewels over my shoulders.

"What do you want with that pickax?" Topsy asked.

"What? Oh. I was thinking this might come in handy for digging post holes in the rocky places."

"We already got us a pickax," she said. "Don't forget to git you that ax handle, though."

When we settled our account, Lynn told us to be careful on the way home and he stepped out on the boardwalk with his slightly used, brass-bellied rifle to make sure no one was waiting for us with shotguns.

"Oh," he said as I took up the reins. "I almost forgot to mention it. Those guards aren't the only ones who have been asking questions about you around here."

My neck was so swollen and sore that I couldn't turn my head to look at Lynn. I had to shift sideways in the seat to face him.

"Another fellow came by a couple of days ago. Said he was an old acquaintance of yours. Called himself Little Jimmy Fitzhugh. I told him you had gone back to Johnson City."

The throbbing in my head doubled and my heart flopped over once or twice in my rib cage. I turned to the mules and stared over their backs. Someone at my bank in Matagorda County had let it slip that Royal Huckaby had wired for money to pay a fine in San Antonio. Little Jimmy Fitzhugh had trailed me from there to Burnet County and had come to resurrect the Williams-Fitzhugh feud, three years dead.

Where had it all gone wrong? At what moment had my plans for a trouble-free existence become unworkable? No matter which way I traced it, it all came down to the exact instant I saw the old Mexican. That wicked old mapmaker had caused me to stray from my formula. It was his fault and none of my own. He had started me on the trail to senseless greed and self-destruction.

If I could just find that zero stone without getting killed by Flatts or Standards or Fitzhughs or prison guards. If I could just satisfy my lust for the unnamed treasure. If only I could break the spell of singing doves, I swore I would never seek riches again as long as I drew breath.

If only the rangers would come. Where in hell were the Texas Rangers?

"Thanks, Lynn," I said, and whistled at the mules to get them moving. The eye that the sergeant had punched was beginning to get puffy.

FOURTEEN

W ho's Little Jimmy Fitzhugh?" Topsy asked on the way home.

"A fellow who's waited three years to kill me."

She didn't say anything for a half mile or so, but her curiosity finally got the better of her. "I guess he was part of that Williams-Fitzhugh feud you got mixed up in."

"Yep."

"What started all that trouble, anyway?"

"A calf."

"A calf?"

"Yeah, a couple of Williams brothers accidentally put their brand on a Fitzhugh calf."

"And they started a feud over one little bitty ol' calf?"

"Well," I said, turning painfully in the seat to make sure the load was riding alright in the wagon, "that was what touched it off. But it really started with my sister, Chastity."

She shook her head. "You Huckabys have the funniest names."

"That's exactly what Chastity always said. My father's name is Champion and he named my two older sisters Opal and Spirit. Then he named me Royal and then came Chastity."

"What's Opal mean?" Topsy asked.

"That's a kind of precious stone they use in jewelry."

"That's a pretty name," she said, scratching behind Speck's ear who was perched right behind the seat atop the highest barrel in the wagon bed. "What's Chastity mean?"

"What's Topsy mean?" I asked evasively.

"Short for topsy-turvy. I used to romp and roll around a lot when I was a sprout so they took to calling me Topsy-Turvy, then just Topsy. My real name's Jane, but I suspect most everybody has forgotten that by now."

"Well, nobody is likely to forget Topsy," I said. "That's a memorable name."

"You didn't say what Chastity means."

"Oh, yeah. Well, let me explain it the way Chastity herself always did. She said all of us Huckabys had horse names and hers apparently meant she was supposed to stay a filly all of her life."

Topsy thought for a moment. "What kind of a name is that to give a girl?"

"It was my father's idea. Chastity hated it. She always made me call her Chaz. She hated her name so much that she just set out to let everybody know it didn't fit her. She used to slip out at all hours with her beaus and she ran with some pretty wild young bucks."

"Oh, goodness, gracious. Pa would tan my hide if I acted like that."

"Old Champ did tan her hide on a regular schedule, but she kept at it. She finally settled down with one fellow, though. A fellow my mother used to call 'that reckless cowboy.' His name was Joe David Williams."

"Was that one of the Williamses from the Williams-Fitzhugh feud?"

"None other," I said. I was riding the brake against the

wheel because we were dropping down to the river. Speck was clawing wildly on the barrel, trying to keep from falling in our laps. "You see, the day Chaz married Joe David, one of her old beaus, Sloan Fitzhugh, showed up at the wedding drunk and wanted to fight the groom. Well, some Williams men dragged him off and roughed him up a little and he never forgot it."

"But what about the branding of that calf you were talking about?"

"Well, back in Matagorda County," I said, "the cowboys of the neighboring ranches used to carry each other's branding irons and they'd brand one another's calves. It was just sort of a favor you could do for your neighbor and everybody did it for each other so it saved a lot of work. Well, for a wedding present old Champ gave Chaz and Joe David a spread of twenty thousand acres right next to the Fitzhugh League. And Joe David put two of his brothers to work on his new ranch."

"Get to the branding part," Topsy said. "And give me those reins. Your eye has swollen up so bad that you can barely see out of half your face."

I passed the leather to Topsy and sat back in the seat to enjoy the ride as much as I could, being covered with hornet stings and hunted by an enemy in an old feud. "I *am* getting to the branding part. See, one day these two Williams brothers, Tom and Milam, were branding calves—some of their own and some of the Fitzhughs—and they roped a Fitzhugh calf and just happened to pick up the wrong iron out of the fire and put a Williams brand on it."

"Uh-oh," Topsy said.

"Yeah. The worst of it was that they didn't even catch their mistake. And Sloan Fitzhugh just happened to see the smoke from the branding fire and rode over to see what was going on. Well, he noticed one of his cows nursing a calf with a Williams brand and right away he accused Milam and Tom of rustling. They called him a liar, so Sloan pulled out a gun and started shooting. There was already all that bad blood between the Williamses and the Fitzhughs because of what had happened at the wedding."

"Did he kill them?"

"He killed Milam but Tom got away. Those were the first shots fired in the Williams-Fitzhugh feud, but they wouldn't be the last."

"What happened then?"

"Well, Joe David and Tom Williams wanted to get even right away for Milam's murder and they were going to do it, too. But I heard what had happened from Chaz and caught the Williams brothers and talked them out of taking revenge. I told them they would get more pleasure and less trouble out of seeing Sloan hang. So we took Milam's body to the sheriff and did everything legally."

"And that Fitzhugh boy went to trial?"

"He certainly did," I said. We were nearing the ford that would cross us over onto the Standard Ranch. "But he got off."

"How? Didn't you say that the Williams boy named Tom saw the murder?"

"Yes, but here's what happened. They put Sloan on trial at the county seat in Matagorda. That's right down at the mouth of the Colorado River. The day he went on trial the town was packed with spectators who wanted to watch the proceedings. Then the storm hit us. Maybe you remember hearing about it. It was the big storm that swept about half of the town into the bay."

"Yes, I do remember that from a few years ago," Topsy said. She was just easing the wagon into the river for the crossing. The ford was a little sandy, but the mules were strong and could pull the wagon across easily. The river wasn't up enough to get the supplies wet in the bed.

"Well, when the storm really started blowing the judge had to adjourn court and everybody took refuge in the houses around town. Except for Sloan. They locked him up in the jail. Stop right here," I said, once we had reached the middle of the river.

"What for?" Topsy asked.

"I want to show you something."

She pulled the mules up and made them stand in the rushing current.

"You see how fast this water is flowing by us?"

"Of course I see it. I ain't the one whose eyes are swollen shut."

"Well, this is about how fast the water was flowing through the town of Matagorda the night of that hurricane. Except it was about three times as deep."

"My Lord!" she said, quickly urging the mules toward the south bank.

"Houses were swept clear into the bay. Dozens of people drowned. And Tom Williams, the only witness to the murder of his brother, was one of the ones who was never found. The courthouse was flooded and a lot of the evidence against Sloan was destroyed, including Tom's written statement and the shirt with the bullet holes that Milam had been wearing when Sloan shot him."

"What happened to the murderer?"

"Sloan? They let him out when the jail flooded. He survived the storm and went free. There wasn't enough evidence left to convict him. The charges were dropped."

"Were you there?"

"Oh, yes. I was in one of the houses that didn't get swept away, thank God. My brother-in-law, Joe David, was there with me. We both survived. But Joe David went crazy with hatred because both of his brothers had died on account of Sloan Fitzhugh and Sloan was free."

"And Sloan was your sister's old beau, too, right?"

"That's right. That was at the heart of it. Sloan Fitzhugh was probably the biggest mistake Chaz ever made, though she hadn't courted him very long."

"It don't take long to give a feller ideas. When did you git mixed up in it all?"

"I was already in it to a certain degree, just because Joe David was my sister's husband. But there was more to it than that. I had a hunting lodge down on the river and Joe David and I used to hunt together a lot. And that black boy I told you about, Rafe, the one that I grew up with, he used to serve as our guide and cook. He had the best pack of hunting dogs in the county."

At my mention of dogs, Topsy started scratching Speck behind the ear again.

"Joe David asked me one day after the hurricane if he could use the lodge. I told him of course he could. He didn't say what he wanted to use it for, but, naturally, I figured he wanted to go hunting. I got to thinking about it and decided I would meet him there and hunt some with him. So Rafe got his dogs together, and I brought some of my best jumping horses because I wanted to run a wolf or two. We went to the lodge to wait for Joe David to show up."

We were on Standard land now and it made me balk to be talking about how I had entered one feud knowing I was now stuck in the middle of another one.

"Well?" Topsy prodded. "What did your brother-in-law want to hunt for? Fitzhughs?"

"Exactly. Joe David showed up at the lodge after dark and told me he had just shot Sloan Fitzhugh dead. He said he had waited up under an old rose hedge fence by the cow pens where Sloan came every evening with a colored man to feed a big bremmer bull they had penned there."

"Did he shoot the colored man, too?"

"No. He had no reason to. Anyway, while Joe David was telling me what he had done, Rafe's dogs took to growling at something in the pecan bottoms by the hunting lodge. Rafe said it was probably coyotes prowling around out there so Joe David grabbed his rifle. Just as soon as he reached for that rifle, the shooting started."

"Shootin'? Who was shootin'?"

"The rangers. Poor Rafe got hit in the head and I dragged him into the lodge, but he was already dead. Joe David was hit in the leg, but he kept on fighting. I swear, though, it didn't take those rangers any longer than a minute to kill Joe David and bust the door down on the lodge. They wanted to kill me, too, because Joe David had managed to kill one of the rangers and they were thirsty for blood."

"Is that the ranger they said you killed?"

"Yeah, the other rangers said so, but I never picked up a gun during the whole fight."

"How did they catch up to your brother-in-law so quick after he killed that Fitzhugh feller?"

"That was just luck. That colored man who was with Sloan when Joe David shot him went to tell the sheriff. There just happened to be four rangers in town staying with the sheriff that night. Sloan's hired colored man also happened to be coonhunting partners with my friend Rafe. Rafe had told him many a time how Joe David hunted at the lodge so he figured Joe David might be going there to hide out and he was right."

"How come they sent you to jail if you never picked up a gun?"

"I guess the county just wanted to make an example of somebody so feuding wouldn't get too common. Everybody figured Little Jimmy Fitzhugh would come after me next because some people said I had helped my brother-in-law murder Sloan. You know how gossip goes. My lawyer got me off of all the murder charges, but they convicted me as an accomplice to Sloan's murder. They said I had brought fresh horses to the lodge to help Joe David escape."

We were easing the wagon over the rocks in the crossing at Double Horn Creek. We hadn't seen any sign of life on the Standards' ranch. It seemed they had forted up and were waiting for the rangers.

"Is that what you brought the horses for?"

"No, of course not. They were just hunting horses, but nobody believed that other than my family. Us Huckabys were not real well liked by everybody in Matagorda

County because we had bought up so much farm and ranch land and run the old owners off."

"So they gave you three years for something you never did?"

"I don't know whether I deserved those three years or not. I'd like to think I served them for something. I guess Little Jimmy Fitzhugh might have killed me by now if I hadn't gone to prison. I thought I had spent those years learning my lesson to stay out of family fights, but here I am in the middle of all your troubles with the Standards. I guess maybe it's just my fate to get mixed up in these things."

"My foot," Topsy snapped. "I can't believe the Good Lord would make it anybody's fate to kill their neighbors."

"I wish you could explain that to Little Jimmy Fitzhugh. He's Sloan's brother, you know. He probably believes I had something to do with Joe David killing Sloan. He's the main reason I didn't go back to Matagorda County after I got out of prison. I figured he'd be gunning for me as soon as I got home. Now he's come after me anyway. I guess Lynn's right about the way my luck runs."

The mules were quickening their steps because they knew the barn was nearby and they wanted their oats. The drab Flatt home came into view around the next bend and I saw Eli and sons carrying buckets of water from the springhouse to the back door and knew they had moved their rain barrels into the house and were brimming them. None of them seemed particularly pleased to have Topsy and me back, but they were glad to see the supplies, and Tobe condescended to pat Speck on the head once or twice.

"Git out of the wagon," Boone growled, and the dog bounded down.

Tobe came over to check on the progress of my face. "Let's see how them sores look. Oh, my word, his other eye has nearly bloated shut now."

Topsy explained what had happened at the store as we unloaded the supplies. Eli thanked me for taking up for his daughter and Tobe mentioned that I had some kind of gumption to take on a man with a shotgun.

"Sounds like the damn dog got the most licks in," Boone said.

Eli ordered us to carry the goods inside and stack most of the kegs and crates in front of the windows so the Standards couldn't shoot in. "We still can't rest easy," he said. "We'll have to take turns standing guard so they don't sneak up and set fire to the place. This old house would go up like fatwood."

I was informed that I could continue to sleep in the barn and wouldn't be expected to stand guard. Boone added that I wouldn't be trusted to stand guard as far as he was concerned.

"There's somebody you might want to keep an eye out for besides the Standards when you're standing guard," I mentioned.

"Who's that?" Boone asked.

I explained about Little Jimmy Fitzhugh coming to Burnet County for my hide.

"Hear that, Pa?" Boone said. "Now we've got the damned Fitzhughs comin' after us and we don't even know 'em. Let's get shed of this saddle bum. We can't trust nobody but our own till we win this fight and he ain't one of our own."

Tobe looked me over as if trying to make up his mind whether or not to agree with his half brother. Topsy held her breath. She would never say so, but she felt some comfort in having me around to help keep the old man from causing trouble. I was wondering just how Boone planned to get shed of me.

But Eli didn't give Boone's suggestion much consideration. The old man had the misconception in his mind that if it came to shooting I would fight with the Flatts. He said, "No, Royal's handy to have around the place with us spending so much time watching them Standards.

He can help us keep this place runnin' and he don't eat much, anyway."

Boone grabbed a rifle and went to patrol the perimeters. Eli sat down on the gallery to smoke his pipe. Topsy went to the log kitchen to fix something for supper. I went to take care of the mules and Tobe came along to ask me how it felt to get treed, stung, and ganged up on all in one day.

FIFTEEN

Before I approached the tree the rattler had chased me into, I threw about two dozen rocks into the remains of the bush at its base to make sure no other snakes were hiding there. I got the ax head loose from the trunk, then knocked the hornet nest out with the new ax handle. There were still a good many hornets on it and they swarmed but I was too quick for them and got away without getting stung.

I started a small fire and burned the old handle out of the ax head and wedged the new one in while the wasps settled down. Then I made that tree pay with its life for all the pain and embarrassment it had caused me. I took pleasure in chopping off each and every one of its limbs.

I spent the next several days chopping and stacking cedar posts and still there was no word of the Texas Rangers. I was getting nervous. I had so many posts cut that I knew Eli would order me to start building fences any day. I had conflicting feelings about building fences. On the one hand I feared stretching wire would rile certain members of the Standard family and cause them to put a stop to the practice.

On the other hand, digging the post holes interested me considerably. It seemed like a perfect way to test a lot of ground for treasure. Maybe I would get lucky and find the trove without having to wait for the Land Office investigator to come and locate the zero stone.

Finally, Eli indeed told me to start building fences. To my relief, he decided to start by patching up the corrals and picket pens around the barn. "Tomorrow I want you to use the wagon," he said as we looked at the dilapidated enclosures, "and haul as many pickets and posts as you'll need to fix up these pens. You can stack 'em over there by the bob wire. And hitch the mules to some of them big corner posts you chopped and drag 'em up here. These old ones have plum rotted out."

The next morning I harnessed the mules and drove them to the cedar brakes. I intended to drag the big corner posts first while the mules were still fresh. The first one I hitched up to was all that remained of the old cedar the snake had chased me into. I had kept it singled out because I wanted to plant it deep on a prominent corner and let it stand as a memorial to the great hornet and rattler war.

I dragged it and a dozen more big cedar trunks to the house without interference from any of the Flatts. They had gone to find some wild hogs they had trapped and castrated in the spring and then turned loose again. It was time to kill some bacon to smoke for the winter. Topsy went along to keep the old man from wandering onto Standard land.

After dragging the corner posts, I hitched the mules to the wagon and drove back to the brakes to start loading pickets and posts and rails.

It was almost noon when I thought I heard a voice call my name. It came in a whisper. I stopped and glanced around, but saw no one, so decided I must have misinterpreted some natural sound. I had been working too hard.

Then it came again: "Royal."

I turned all the way around and still saw no one. I was alone.

"Royal," it said again. It was the ghost of the old Mexican, leading me to treasure!

I took a step in the direction I thought the voice had come from.

"Over here, Royal."

I looked into the shadows of the brush along Double Horn Creek and saw the vague shape of a man crouched behind the bushes.

"Who is that?" I asked. Maybe it was Little Jimmy Fitzhugh. Maybe it was one of the Standards. It could have been Tobe playing a trick on me. But I still hoped it was the ghost of the old Mexican, he having acquired English in the great beyond.

"Come here. I don't want to git out in the open."

I neared the dark place in the undergrowth and saw that the man hiding there was just as dark as the shadows—a black man in the soiled uniform of a convict. "Who are you?" I asked.

"You know me. You ain't forgot me, I know."

I walked cautiously into the shadows of the underbrush and the man stood part of the way up, looking nervously all around. "My God," I said. "I can't believe it's you."

"I knowed you'd remember me. I knowed you'd remember ol' Reuben."

I suddenly realized that Reuben was standing as straight as he was going to stand. Years of forced labor had bent his body. His frame had wasted to bone and sinew and his hair had taken on a frosting of white. I wondered if he still had the strength to crawl down a dark well shaft and cheat death for a stranger.

"I don't believe it." I put my hand out and he shook it. "How did you get here?"

"I got away last night. Been walkin' in the river all night to find you."

"How did you know where?"

"I listen. I always listen. I heard them guards talkin' about you and that redheaded white girl they said lived down here. That bull-driver was plenty mad about you grabbin' his shotgun and hittin' him with it. He stayed mad a long time. He didn't go easy on us."

I looked at the ground between my feet. "I'm sorry. I should have known he would take it out on y'all."

"Don't worry no more about him. He won't never beat no more convicts. He got drunk last night, come around and told me to go with him outside. When I saw him pick up that bat, I choked him to death, Royal. I squeezed him so hard around the neck his eyeballs stuck out." Reuben wrapped his hands around an imaginary neck and choked the guard all over again in his thoughts.

I sank back against the trunk of a tree and drew in a breath of dread. "Did they come after you? How did you get away?"

"They was all drunk. They didn't know ol' Reuben was gone till this mornin'. I just need a little help. I need clothes to wear. I need a hoss."

"But, where do you expect to go? How long do you think you'll last before they catch you?"

He grinned, teeth missing. "Last time I was out three months. This time I won't never go back. Give me a hoss, Royal. I swear they'll never know you give it to me."

"You know better than that. You know they'll beat the truth out of you if they catch you."

Reuben grabbed me by the arm and squeezed with all the strength he had once used to save my life in the flooded well. "Ain't nobody ever gonna beat ol' Reuben again. They got to kill me. They won't never chain me again."

I pried his fingers from my arm as he glared at me. "Okay," I said. "Okay. Wait here." I couldn't get over the shame I felt for not wanting to help him. I knew I would help him, of course, because I owed my life to him. But I didn't really *want* to help him. I only agreed to aid him in his escape to repay a debt. Reuben hadn't owed me a thing the night he descended the well shaft for the sake of my wretched life.

I drove the wagon back to the Flatt house, took Liberty out of the corral, bridled her, and tied her to lead behind the wagon. Then I went into the barn to get my saddle and the suit of clothes I had worn the day I left the state penitentiary at Huntsville. I turned the wagon around and ran the mules back to the creek.

"Give me your clothes," I told Reuben when I got back to the brakes. "I'll burn them over here. I already had a fire going this morning so nobody will question the ashes."

"What about the hoss? What are you gonna tell 'em about the hoss?" he said, stripping down.

"I'll tell them she must have wandered off," I said. I tossed him the freedom suit.

The old convict turned his back for a moment to pull on the pants and I saw a horrible mass of scars stretching from his heels to his neck—great welts of deformed flesh. I heard the sickening screams and the wasted pleas for mercy.

He caught me gaping. "They give me the bat whenever I escape. But I won't take it again."

When Reuben got dressed, he came to stand by the wagon as I stirred the ashes of his striped uniform to make sure it had all burned, just as I had stirred the ashes of the old Mexican's map. My coat hung awkwardly from his shoulders and we had to cut a piece of rope to keep the pants up. "It looks good on you," I said.

"Yeah, feels good, too," he said, keeping his eyes trained for pursuers.

"Where will you go?"

"Don't know."

"Here, take this." I pulled the page marker from Sam Jessom's Bible out of my shirt pocket. "Go south to Johnson City. There's a blacksmith there called Deacon Sam. Show him this card and tell him I gave it to you. He'll help you with some food and anything else you want."

Reuben took the card and looked at it. "What's it say?" he asked.

"Never mind. Just take it and give it to Deacon Sam."

He nodded and put the card in his pocket. "I don't want your saddle. Don't want your bridle neither," he said, picking up a length of rope from the wagon bed. "Take it off that mare. I'll make a hackamore."

I did as he said because it would make my story about Liberty wandering off sound better. She didn't usually put her bridle and saddle on before wandering.

"You like this job?" Reuben asked, glancing around at the cedar posts.

"I guess."

"Good," he said, tying another knot in the hackamore. "Stay with it. Don't worry about them rich men with all that money. You don't need that. Just work here and keep what you make. You'll be alright. Just be glad you're free, that's all. That's all you need."

"Good advice."

"You know why they put me in prison, Royal? I wanted me a Christmas ham. I tried to sneak me a pig out of a white man's pen, but he caught me. I was a boy. Didn't know better."

"That's all you did to get all those years?"

"No, not all," he said, grinning at me under Liberty's neck as he slipped the hackamore on. "I escaped when I thought I learned my lesson not to steal no more pigs. Then I escaped again when I thought I learned my lesson not to escape no more. Five times I been out. This here's the last time. They got to kill me before they chain me this time." He flopped across Liberty's bare back and threw his leg over.

"Stay well on the west side of this creek," I said, "or you're liable to run into some of the Flatts. If they see you riding my horse, they'll shoot." I was praying that

Topsy was holding Eli on his own side of the Double Horn. "And stay off the road on the way to Johnson City. They'll be looking everywhere for you."

He laughed down at me from the back of my mare. "Don't tell me nothin'. I know where they're gonna be. Who kept you alive in that well?"

I half smiled and nodded. "Good luck."

"We're even, now, you and me." He looked across the cedar stumps. "You best start loadin' them posts again. You got to earn your honest way." He nudged Liberty in the flanks and turned toward Johnson City, and I picked up another post and threw it in the wagon bed as if nothing peculiar had happened.

I was piling cedar posts by the spools of barbed wire when the Flatts came back. Boone and Tobe were dragging hog carcasses behind their horses. I was relieved to see that Reuben's carcass was not being dragged along with them. Topsy put her horse away and started gathering wood to build a fire under the big kettle in front of the kitchen.

It didn't take long for Eli to miss my mare and ask where she had gone. I had already put my saddle and bridle away and had taken a couple of old cedar rails down from the corral. "I guess she jumped the corral where I took those rotten rails down," I said. "I wouldn't worry about her. She never wanders far. I'll go hunt her up in the morning."

"That fat old mare jumps?" Eli asked.

"I reckon she does," I said.

"I'll go find her," Tobe said.

"The hell you will," Boone said. "You ain't slippin' off while there's work to be done." Boone was preparing to slip off himself, though. It was his turn to patrol the perimeters for Standards.

"Get your ax and cut us some gambrels," Eli said to me.

I found a couple of stout green cedar pickets in the wagon and chopped sharp points on both ends of each one. Tobe and Eli dragged the hogs up under the big live oak behind the kitchen and poked holes through the skin at the hocks so we could shove the gambrels through to hold the back legs apart. Then we tied ropes to the gambrels and hoisted the hogs up to hang head-down from a tree limb. They weighed about three hundred pounds each, so we had to grunt some to get them hung.

"I'll go see how the water is coming along," I said as Eli and Tobe tied the ropes. I walked around to the front of the kitchen and asked Topsy if the water was hot enough yet.

She dipped her hand quickly into the big cauldron with the wood burning under it. "No, it will take a few more minutes."

"Where did y'all find the hogs?"

"I saw sign of them the other day over by Sandy Point when I was checking the bogs for cattle, so I got Pa to go there and look first. We hunted all morning and finally came on them. Just in time, too. Pa was wanting to go over across the Double Horn."

Reuben had been lucky to avoid the old man, I thought, and he was probably almost to Johnson City by now. "Who shot them? Looks like both of them were hit clean in the head."

"I shot one and Pa shot the other."

"You're a good shot."

Topsy shrugged, but smiled a little. "He was only a hundred yards off." She leaned toward me and whispered. "Listen, you better watch out for Pa because . . ."

Eli came around the corner of the log kitchen and Topsy moved quickly away from me. "How hot is it?" the old man asked. "Don't make it boil or it'll set the hair. Make it just shy of boiling."

When the water got just hot enough, I carried a bucket of it around behind the kitchen and poured it slowly over the carcass of one of the hogs. Topsy carried a bucket for the other one. Eli and Tobe scraped the hogs with their knives as we poured the hot water on them.

"That's just right," Eli said. "The hair's slippin' good." As we applied pail after pail of hot water, Eli and Tobe scraped every hair off right down to the knuckles and the snouts until the carcasses looked as smooth and clean as porcelain. They seemed out of place in their rough surroundings. Eli cut their throats to let them bleed.

I gutted one hog and Tobe did the other. We let the entrails fall into tubs positioned under the carcasses.

"Take the hearts and lights and let the dog eat 'em," Eli told Topsy. She plunged her knife into the tubs of viscera and cut away the morsels for Speck. Tobe and I then carried the rest of the guts away to throw in the woods. By the time we got back, Topsy had rinsed the blood out of the body cavities and we were ready to take the carcasses down and butcher them on an old plank table built against the side of the kitchen.

We cut the heads off first and I carried one for Topsy and we put them into the now boiling water in the cauldron. "I guess we're going to have headcheese for supper," I said.

"What?"

"Headcheese."

"Is that what you call it? We call it hog head souse. Have you et it before?"

"Only with the colored folks." I lowered my voice. "Say, what was that you tried to tell me a while ago about watching out for your pa?"

"Oh, that. He's got him an idea that he can get you . . ."

Topsy clammed up again when Tobe brought some pig feet around and threw them in with the heads. "Pa wants you to help with the butchering," he said to me.

I winked at Topsy and went back around the kitchen where Eli was chopping along the backbone of a hog carcass with a hatchet, separating the ribs from the spine. "What do you want me to do?" I asked.

"You can handle this backbone soon as I get it loose. You know how to do it, don't you?"

"Yes, sir. We did a hundred hogs a day sometimes on the prison farms."

Eli grunted and shoved a side of pork out of his way as I picked up my ax. "Somethin' I want to talk to you about," he said. "I've come to trust you, Royal. Me and the boys have been talkin' about it. It's plain to us you're on our side now. I guess Topsy's told you that we plan to build us a town on the river as soon as we get over this trouble with them Standards. We'd like you to have an equal share in it. It's sure to mean a fair profit for us all once the steamboats start running up the river."

So this was what Topsy had tried to warn me about. Eli had plans to draw me into his fight and make me one of his own. He needed another gun on his side. Lon Standard had one more son still among the living than Eli. Eli probably even had plans of making me a son-in-law. "What would you expect in return?" I asked.

He had chopped the backbone loose and tossed it in front of me on the table. "Expect? Nothin'. Oh, I'd expect you'd want to be up on a level with the rest of us, take your turn standin' guard and all, and we're willin' to allow that. But we don't expect nothin' particular out of you."

He was willing to let me get shot at by Standards for a share in a town that would never be built! I almost had to bite my lip to hold back the sardonic laughter. I was using my ax to chop the backbone into lengths of about six inches and I figured my proposed stock in Flatt, Texas, would be worth about as much as a couple of those chunks of backbone out of a wild pig. "That's a generous offer, Mr. Flatt. But I'm not the sort to bother with investments and such."

The yellow tips of Eli's beard had dragged through some pig blood. "I ain't after money. You're a hard worker. I could use your help. Think about it for a while. It'll grow on you. You could have streets and parks named after you. How would that sound?" he asked, elbowing me. "Royal Avenue and Huckaby Park."

"That sounds fine, but I'm not so sure about the government being able to clear the raft out of the Colorado to let the steamers in. I used to live alongside of that raft, you know, and they haven't been able to clear it yet."

"Uncle Sam's cherry picker cleared the one on the Red River, didn't it? I ain't goin' into nothin' half cocked, boy. I've studied it. That raft can be moved."

"I know they have the machinery to do it," I said. "But I'm not so sure they have the funds. The government tends to run out of money every time it just gets to work on removing that raft."

"They'll git the job done, boy. I have connections in the gov'ment, you know. They'll clear the damned raft this time."

The old man tossed the other backbone in front of me and I let my ax rive another section of spine.

"Even if they do clear it," I said, "I'm not so sure those steamboats will come this high up."

"What the hell do you mean? We already had one come plum up to the Marble Falls!"

"Yes, but that was a wet year, wasn't it? Do you think the river will be deep enough for steamers year to year?"

"When I was a boy, before I come to Texas," Eli said, "I took a ride on a steamer up the Missouri, clean up into the plains. Don't tell me a steamer can't come up this river. Them pilots don't need but two feet of water for them stern-wheelers."

"The Missouri's wider," I said. "More room to navigate."

Eli buried the blade of his butcher knife in the wooden table and glared at me. "We're gonna' have us a town here, boy. Now, I'm offerin' you a chance to be a part of it. You best think about it real serious. It's the smartest thing for all of us to throw in together. With that Fitzhugh feller after your scalp, you could stand to make some friends about now. You can take the first watch tomorrow evenin'."

I didn't answer. Tobe had come out of the house with

a twenty-five-pound keg of salt to cure the knuckle joints, square shoulders, and hams. "What do you want me to do with these ribs?" he asked the old man.

"Put 'em in the springhouse to keep 'em cool. We'll have 'em for dinner tomorrow."

I helped Tobe salt the quarters and hang them in the smokehouse to cure for a couple of weeks before the actual smoking would start.

By the time we finished the butchering and salting Topsy had boiled all the meat off of the heads and feet and mashed it up and mixed in some peppers and salt and sage. When the souse cooled and jelled we ate it on the table against the side of the kitchen. Topsy took some out to Boone. I wondered what Boone had said that afternoon about taking me into the Flatt gang.

I also found myself wondering about other individuals—where they were and what they were doing. Where was Marion Harkey? Was he selling a lot of barbed wire? Where were the Standard men—Lon, Lum, Nat, and Clay? And what was Annie doing? Working in her garden? Where was the old Mexican? Heaven or hell? How far had Reuben gotten? Was he eating better fare at Deacon Sam's? Where was Liberty? Where was Little Jimmy Fitzhugh? And where were the cotton-pickin' Texas Rangers when you needed them the most?

SIXTEEN

The morning came on cool and wet. The mist fell so fine I couldn't feel the drops, but I still got soaked after staying out only a few minutes. Boone and I were tearing down the old corral and I looked forward to burning the pile of rotten posts and rails. It was a good day for burning. No chance of starting a wildfire in that mist.

We had been at work a few hours when Tobe came running to the house from his guard post. "Get Pa," he said to Topsy, then turned to watch the road that led toward the Double Horn and the Standard Ranch.

Boone and I trotted over to the house to see what had upset Tobe. He was breathing too hard to tell us. Eli came out with Topsy, pulling his suspenders up and rubbing his eyes. He had been catching up on sleep lost during his midnight watch. "What is it?"

"Two strangers coming," Tobe gasped. "A big feller on a big horse and a little one on a Spanish pony. And they're leading a pack mule and Royal's mare."

I felt the clammy grip of the wet day seize me like death

and knew some ill fortune had befallen poor old Reuben.

"They armed?" Boone asked.

"The little one's got guns all over him. The big one has a rifle, but I think that's all."

Eli turned to me. "You think it's that Fitzhugh feller?"

I shrugged. "I can't tell until I see them."

Eli rubbed the sleep out of his face. "Get your rifle and hide behind that pile of old rails," he said to me. "If it's Fitzhugh, blast him out of the saddle and we'll get the other one."

"Hold on a minute," I said, but Eli was already giving other orders:

"Tobe, get up in the loft. Boone, you and me in the house. Topsy, you get a pistol and hide in the kitchen. If one of them comes in, shoot him."

The Flatts scattered to their posts.

"If it's not Little Jimmy, I'll talk to them," I said. But I couldn't be sure whether any of them had heard me except Topsy, who paused to look at me, wild-eyed, before she ducked into the kitchen.

I took my place behind the rotten timbers and waited. Speck came to stand beside me, looking alert, sensing my fear. I soon saw the horses appear through the mist, turning the bend in the road. I didn't recognize either of the riders. The little man on the mustang was leading Liberty and the big man on the big horse had the pack mule in tow. When they got almost within rifle range, the little one stopped and yelled in a high-pitched voice: "Eli Flatt!"

The dog ran out from behind the pile of rotten timbers and started barking. "Shut up, Speck," I said. The dog obeyed, but continued to growl and glower at the men on his road.

I stepped out from behind the pile of old corral rails, holding my rifle muzzle down. I waved for the men to approach. The little fellow waved for me to approach him instead. The big man shook his head and said something to the little one. I made Speck stay and started walking out to see what the men wanted. I hoped they were not prison guards. I hoped Reuben's body was not tied to the pack mule.

I got close enough to see rainwater dripping from their brims and beading up on their slickers. The big man tipped his hat at me and, with a graceful stroke of his hand, sculpted the handles of his salt-and-pepper mustache into an elegant curve. He straddled a beautiful smokey black horse fitted with a silver bridle. A couple of poles of some sort stuck out of the tarp-covered pack his mule was carrying. He appeared to fall in somewhere between the ages of Boone and Eli. He slouched casually in the saddle.

The little man on the silver buckskin mustang had a big Sharps repeater in his hands, cocked. His slicker was tucked inside the grips of his Colt revolvers. A shotgun hung from his saddle horn by a thong. I could see a shaggy bit of pale yellow hair sticking out from under his black hat and his eyes were glaring spots of lucid blue. He had the build of a jackrabbit: narrow across the shoulders, weak-chinned, and scrawny. He seemed to be about equal to Tobe or me in age. "Who are you?" he asked in a throaty little voice.

"Who are *you?*" I asked. "And what are you doing with my mare?"

"Shut your mouth, mister. I'll ask the questions."

"Oh, settle down, Cotton," the big man said. "We've been here thirty seconds and you've already made us an enemy." He smiled at me. "I'm Dub Coe of the General Land Office. And this little firebrand is Cotton Anderson of the Texas Rangers. We're here to talk with the Flatts."

"And serve them with subpoenas to appear at an inquest concerning . . ."

"When the time comes, Captain," Coe said, interrupting the little ranger. "Take your spurs off for once, will you?"

"Why do you have my mare?" I asked again.

"We'll explain everything if we could get out of the

rain and have a cup of coffee," Coe said. "You must be
Roy Huckaby if this is your mount."

"A convict and a ranger-killer," Anderson said with
disgust. "You must like prison. You're liable to go back."

Coe sighed and rolled his eyes. "Don't mind him," he
said, jerking his head at the ranger. "Cotton's mammy
weaned him young on a sour pickle and he's been ran-
kled over it ever since." He returned Anderson's scowl
with a smirk, then looked at me again. "How about that
coffee?"

"Stay here a minute," I suggested. "I'll go tell them
who you are, then wave you in. You have to be careful
with these Flatts. They're expecting to go to war with the
Standard family."

Cotton Anderson didn't wait for me to wave. He trotted his mustang past the house and into the barn before
I could tell anyone what was going on. "It's alright,
Tobe," I yelled. "He's a ranger." Speck barked and
growled like a rabid wolf.

Topsy came out of the kitchen to call the dog off. The
old man and Boone stalked out of the house about the
time the boundary investigator got down from the saddle.

"Howdy. I'm Dub Coe of the General Land Office.
Would it be alright if I put my stock in your barn?"

Eli's eyes lit up like lanterns and he instantly put on a
cheerful face I hadn't seen him wear. "Land Office! Why
didn't you say so? Help him with his animals, Royal.
Topsy, put some coffee on for the gentlemen. We've been
waitin' on you, Mr. Coe."

Dub tipped his hat and turned to lead his horse and
mule into the barn. The ranger had already availed himself of the facilities without asking. He had unsaddled his
mustang and was using one of Eli's saddle blankets to
dry the little horse off. When I entered the barn with Coe,
Tobe began to come down from the loft. His rifle butt
bumped against the ladder.

In a snap, Cotton Anderson had dropped to one knee,
whirled, pulled both of his Colts from their holsters,

cocked them, and aligned their sights on the loft ladder. Tobe's eyes bulged and he dropped his rifle onto the hay below.

"Who are you?" the ranger asked.

"Tobe Flatt."

"Where're the others?"

Eli and Boone walked into the barn behind Coe.

"They're all right here," Coe said. "Now, put those Peacemakers away. These men don't aim to bushwhack you."

Anderson jammed his pistols back into their holsters and pulled some folded papers out from under his slicker. "Tobe Flatt, Eli Flatt, Boone Flatt," he said, handing out the summonses, "you are ordered to be at an inquest the twenty-first of next month in the county courthouse to answer some questions about the way you murdered those two Standard brothers. Then you'll be put on trial and most likely hung."

Tobe felt insulted enough to pick up his rifle while Eli and Boone glowered and trembled with anger. Boone took a step toward the ranger.

"Mind your authority, Captain!" Coe shouted. "Just serve the papers and keep your mouth shut."

"Damn it, Coe, stop calling me that," Anderson said. "You know I ain't no captain."

"Maybe not yet. But you intend to make a captain, don't you?"

"I intend to see that you find that damned boundary marker and then I intend to bust up this feud."

"In the short run, yes," Coe said. "But on the long haul you intend to make a captain, don't you?"

"I don't reckon it's any of your damned business what I intend."

"None of my . . . !" Coe pulled the saddle from his smokey black stallion. "You are a servant of the public trust, Cotton, and I am a taxpayer and a representative of the popular vote. It concerns me a great deal what you intend."

Anderson swore and stalked into the mist.

Coe chuckled. "That boy wouldn't back down from a whole nation of armed outlaws, but he can't last two minutes in a good debate."

Eli watched the little ranger walk away and then told Boone and Tobe to help Coe with the pack mule.

"Now," Coe said to me, "I promised to explain how we came across your mare. I imagine you thought her lost."

"She got out yesterday," I said. "I didn't think she'd wander far, but she looks spent. Where did you find her?"

"Me and Cotton got to Johnson City yesterday about evening time. Just as we trotted into town, a bunch of men came galloping by, and of course Cotton just had to find out what they were up to. Turned out they were prison guards from the granite quarry over at the Marble Falls and had chased an escaped convict into town. It seems the convict was riding your mare."

"What?" I said.

"Don't act so dumb," said Anderson's grating tenor voice. He had snuck around and come in the other end of the barn and now stepped from the shadows to glare at me. "You brought horses to help your murderin' brother-in-law escape Matagorda County, didn't you? It's plain you gave that horse to that convict yesterday, too."

"How the hell would you know who I give horses to," I said.

"When somebody kills a ranger, I make it my business to know what they do."

"He didn't give no horse to no convict yesterday," Tobe said in my defense. "He was here all day haulin' fence rails in the wagon. He must have hauled five hundred or more. That don't leave no time to mess with convicts."

Anderson simply walked out of the barn again when Tobe started talking. I saw him prowling around the house, peeking into the kitchen where Topsy was, reading the tombstones in the family plot.

"How did y'all come to get my mare away from that escapee?" I asked Coe. Boone and Tobe were helping him unpack a strange cargo from his mule.

"Well," he said, "the fugitive jumped off your mare and holed up in the blacksmith shop and was yelling at the guards that he had a gun and would shoot the first man that came after him. Cotton had to be the first man, of course. When he charged the shop, the convict ran out with what looked like a pistol in his hand and pointed it at Cotton and Cotton shot him dead. Turned out it was just a piece of pipe that convict was holding."

"He must have wanted to get shot," I said. "Can't say that I blame him. I've seen what they do to escapees when they catch them."

Coe nodded. "It did appear that's what he wanted. The blacksmith recognized your horse and so did the prison guards. The guards said you were working out here with the Flatts, so I volunteered to return your mare for you. The blacksmith vouched for you. Said you were a fine individual. The guards didn't agree, but I tend to believe that blacksmith over those guards."

"Not me," Anderson said. He had appeared in the doorway again. "I think he's just a murderin' convict joined up with a gang of outlaws."

Eli, Boone, and Tobe turned their eyes together to stab the little ranger.

"Damn it, Cotton, quit poppin' up like a mud duck," Coe said. "Stand in here among us if you want to auger."

But Cotton was already gone again.

Coe reached into his pocket and pulled out a sealed envelope. "The blacksmith asked me to deliver this to you," he said.

I took the envelope and saw it addressed to me, from Deacon Sam Jessom. "Thanks," I said.

"My pleasure."

Topsy shouted to us, saying the coffee was ready.

"Royal, see that Mr. Coe's animals get some feed," Eli said. "Come on, Mr. Coe, have some coffee and get that slicker off."

After I fed the horses I stopped to look over the equipment Coe had taken from his mule's packsaddle. It included an old surveyor's compass almost as big around as a dinner plate, a staff for mounting the compass, and two poles with a chain running between them. I imagined it was the same type of chain the old Mexican had used to measure the distance between the zero stone and the treasure. In fact, every tool I would need to locate the wealth was lying on the barn floor in front of me. And Dub Coe was the man who would find the zero stone for me.

The tremor of greed I felt filled me with shame. I should have been mourning Reuben, but all I could think of was treasure. A strange truth came to me. I didn't want to buy anything. I didn't want to spend my treasure. I only wanted to find it. I owned a gentle horse and a good hunting rifle and I desired no other possessions. The treasure had come to possess *me*. It was hunting for *me*. It was getting closer and closer to claiming *me*!

I stood by Liberty and scratched her on the withers as she ate her oats. She seemed destined to carry convicts to their fates. Reuben had found his. The fate he preferred to imprisonment. When would Liberty carry me to mine?

I remembered the letter Coe had given me and went to stand by the door to read it in the dull light that came through the drizzle.

Dear Roy,
The prison guards tell some bad stories about you, but they are a sorry lot and I don't trust what they say. Why are you mixed up in that business with the Flatts and the Standards? Leave immediately and come to work with me. An old acquaintance of yours who called himself Little Jimmy Fitzhugh stopped by

here to find you. I sent him to the Marble Falls, but he came back having failed to locate you and went on to San Antonio yesterday. Now that I know where to find you, I shall send a messenger to catch Mr. Fitzhugh and tell him you have been located. He is quite anxious to see you.

Samuel Jessom

Quite anxious to see me, indeed, I said to myself. And more anxious to see me dead. But Deacon Sam had no way of knowing that. That was the trouble with John Wesley's rule. When you do all the good you can, to all the people you can, in all the ways you can, you sometimes commit well-intentioned debacles. It is better to let people do good for themselves.

I walked through the mist toward the house and found Topsy making more coffee in the kitchen. "That Land Office man wants to stay and talk to Pa today," she said. "Then he's going to talk to the Standards tomorrow, then he says he's going to find the zero stone."

"Good," I said. "Maybe he can end this trouble before it goes any further."

"I hope so," she said. "Where do you reckon the rest of the rangers are?"

"I was wondering the same thing. They must be coming. Surely they'll be here before Coe goes to hunt for the zero stone."

"I hope so," she repeated. "I have to cook something. Pa says to put out the best we got. Would you go get those spareribs out of the springhouse for me? I guess I'll cook them up with some fixin's."

I fetched the ribs for Topsy, then carried a fresh pot of coffee into the house. The men had pulled every chair in the house into the front room. The fireplace was burning for the first time since I had lived among the Flatts. Eli's clothes were dry, so he sat back from the fire. Boone and Tobe and Dub Coe were drying themselves right in front of the hearth. Cotton Anderson was as wet as any of them, but he sat apart from the rest, in the shadows of a corner.

"Oh, 'investigator' is a fancy handle," Coe was saying as I came in with the coffee. He had taken his hat off to reveal an unexpected bald spot in the middle of his graying head. "I'm just an old surveyor is all I am. My pappy was a surveyor, too, and he taught me the profession. He surveyed for the Republic of Texas and knew all the methods they used to locate lands back then. I learned about all that from him and so the Land Office likes to send me out to find the lost boundary markers because I know a thing or two about how they were probably located in the first place."

"You won't find ours," Eli said. "I'm sure you know your business, but you won't find no boundary markers between us and them Standards."

"Why do you say that?" Coe asked.

"Because if there ever was a zero stone, I'm sure old Lon Standard has taken and destroyed the thing."

"The Bible says something about that," Coe said.

" 'Cursed be he who removeth his neighbor's landmark.' That's in Deuteronomy, chapter twenty-seven, verse seventeen. That's about all the Gospel I can quote, however, so don't ask me to preach come Sunday." Coe laughed and thanked me for refilling his coffee cup. "But, you see, Mr. Flatt, even if your neighbor has removed your landmark, that don't mean I can't find where it was."

"How's that?" Eli asked, stroking his beard.

"Them old-time surveyors left more than just corner stones behind. They left all kinds of sign. You just have to know what to look for."

"Like what?" Eli asked.

"Oh, they built little stone mounds, drove stakes, blazed trees. That sort of thing."

Eli laughed. "This place was surveyed forty-seven years ago. The stones have been scattered, the stakes have rotted, and the blazes have growed over if the trees ain't burnt down altogether."

"You'd think so, wouldn't you?" Coe said. "But I think we'll find some sign of that old survey party. You'd be surprised how long some of those marks can last. I have even found that if you rub a stone with your hand you can sometimes find marks left by a chaining pin where the old surveyors ran their original lines. Even if it was fifty years ago."

Eli looked worried for several seconds, and Coe glanced at him and read the expression on his face. Then the old man put on his false laughter again. "Look if you want to, Coe, but I don't think you'll find anything. You'll have to go by my testimony on where the boundary was because I'm the only man alive who was here when the surveyors were. They showed me my land, and though I don't remember exactly where the boundary ran, I can swear the west line was on the other side of the Double Horn. That creek is mine. But you won't find no zero stone. No, Lon Standard has destroyed it."

"Won't hurt to look some," Coe said.

Cotton Anderson jumped up from his chair and walked out of the room and out of the house.

"That boy squirms more than a wormy pup," Coe said. "Can't stay put no longer than a cricket in a chicken yard."

I took the ranger's chair from the corner and pulled it up to the fire to warm myself. "How will you know where to start looking for the zero stone?" I asked.

"I'll have to start by going on Mr. Flatt's word. And, to be fair, I'll have to go by what Major Standard says, too. I have the field notes from the old survey, but they don't help much."

"Why not?"

"Oh, them old-timers, they did things sort of slipshod. Didn't have much choice in it, though. Not everybody wanted to go and survey among Comanches and Apaches. You know what the Indians called the surveyor's compass? They called it 'the thing that steals the land.' Them Indians knew what a survey party meant and generally didn't hold to it. So them old surveyors were mostly rough frontiersmen. Some of them didn't even learn how to figure magnetic variation of a compass needle. They just ran the lines the best they knew how and took field notes and put up markers. And when Indians were around, like they were when this place was surveyed, why them surveyors didn't mess around and run the whole boundary. They'd just locate a couple of corners and move on.

"The field notes didn't have much to say in a survey like that." Coe took a folded piece of paper from his pocket. "I've got a copy of the field notes for the old survey done in '38 on this place. You can see what I mean. These were written up the day before the survey party was massacred."

Coe unfolded the paper, held it to catch the light from the fireplace, and recited: " 'Beginning at inscribed rock.' That's the zero stone. 'Thence north 4,433 varas to Colorado River.' So the zero stone should be about 4,433 varas from the river, depending on how high the river was that day in '38 and assuming the river hasn't changed course too much since then. 'Thence 5,702 varas downstream.' I guess that means as the crow flies and not on the meander, but you can't be sure with these old field notes. 'Thence south 4,433 varas to stake about 45 varas southeast of a bunch of bushes. Thence west to the place of beginnings.' "

"That's it?" Eli asked.

"Yep."

Eli started chuckling and his laughter, of a genuine type this time, built until he was guffawing and slapping his knee. "It's been so long since I read them notes, I forgot what a worthless mess of writin' it was!" he finally said.

"I agree," Coe said. "It doesn't make any mention of any creeks, hills, canyons, trees, or any other landmark except for that clump of bushes, and God knows there must be enough clumps of bushes around here to shelter a million head of jackrabbits. The only information of any help these notes have is the reference to 4,433 varas from the river. That's between two and three miles."

"What is a vara?" I asked.

"A vara is thirty-three and a third inches. It's an old leftover from the Spanish and Mexican days. This is the only state in the Union that uses the vara for surveys. Texas never adopted the system of township, section, and range used everywhere else in the States. I've got my chains set for ten varas, just like they did during the Republic of Texas days when this place was surveyed. So the zero stone should be about 443 chains from the river."

Everything before my eyes suddenly turned golden in the firelight. In one breath Dub Coe had told me the last two mysteries surrounding the interpretation of the old Mexican's map: the length of the chain and the length of a vara. My mood took an instant swing toward improvement. It became suddenly clear that Reuben's death was not my fault. I had done everything expected of me to help him. The first of the rangers had arrived. The zero stone would be found within days. The feud would end and I would dig for buried treasure. Maybe, just maybe, it had all been worth the trouble. If only I could dig up my reward and scat before Little Jimmy Fitzhugh caught me.

"Those field notes," I said, thinking of the old Mexican. "How did they get to the Land Office if the surveyors were attacked by Indians?"

"Looks like somebody survived the massacre and brought the notes in," Coe said. "The Indians understood about field notes and generally tried to find them and burn them when they raided a surveyors' camp. That and bust up the compass. But somebody got away from the Indians here in '38 and brought the field notes in to the land commissioner. That's the only way Mr. Flatt here was able to patent his land. At least those field notes had some use to somebody. They're dang near worthless as horse apples to me.

"Yes, I'm afraid the only way we're going to settle this dispute is to find the zero stone itself. Or what's left of it if it's been destroyed. Even if somebody up and carried it away, we should find some chips of stone left over from the chiseling of the inscription on the thing. That and a blazed tree or a stone mound or two will be enough to settle the case. That much will stand up in court. I've seen it happen before."

"Shit," Eli said. "You won't find no zero stone. I guarantee that. That stone is long gone and the only thing that can settle this fight is my testimony. I'm telling you, Coe, I was here in '38, the day before the Indians wiped out that survey party. The surveyors showed me my land. Double Horn Creek was a part of it. That's what you'll have to go by to settle your case. You'll never find no zero stone."

Coe shrugged and changed the subject.

SEVENTEEN

When Topsy finished cooking, she called us into the dim dining room in the back of the house that faced the log kitchen outside.

She had done her best. She had fried the spareribs and cooked turnips and greens seasoned with one of the lengths of backbone I had chopped with my ax. She had also made biscuits and gravy and had put out all the milk, buttermilk, and butter she found in the springhouse.

Cotton Anderson came in as the rest of us pulled our chairs up to the table. "What's all these boxes and barrels in front of the windows for?" he asked in his accusing whine.

"Them is our supplies and that's where we like to put 'em," Boone said.

Cotton pulled a length of ribs loose and sat on one of the kegs against the wall to eat. "A Sharps rifle will shoot right through it," he mentioned, to Boone's chagrin.

"Miss Flatt," Coe said, taking a couple of biscuits and handing the platter to me, "this is the finest spread of feed I have witnessed in many a day. Pass the gravy, please."

As we ate, Dub declared how unfair it was for him and Cotton to put the Flatts out of all that grub.

"Don't mention it," Eli said.

"No, I want to make it up to you. Maybe I'll go huntin' if the weather breaks and bring in some game for supper."

"I'll go with you," I said.

Though I didn't look up from my plate, I could tell Eli was glaring at me. The room became silent except for the chink of tarnished silver utensils against chipped bone china.

"Where are the rest of the rangers?" Topsy suddenly asked in a small voice. Everyone turned to look at her, surprised to hear her speak.

"Beg pardon, miss?" Dub Coe said.

"They said a whole company of rangers. I ain't seen but this single little one."

Boone chuckled with his mouth full.

Cotton Anderson flushed and scowled. "There won't be a company. Just me. The rest got to stay down on the border and fight rustlers and I had to come up here to clean up this damned feud."

The Flatt men glanced at one another quickly and almost gloated. But Topsy sank breathlessly back from her plate.

"Just one ranger to stand against two feuding families?" I asked, to the deep resentment of Cotton Anderson.

"You know what they say," Coe said. "If you ain't got but one riot, you don't need but one ranger. Same goes for feuds, I guess. And don't slight Cotton. He ain't much of a diplomat, but when it comes to war, he's got him a reputation."

Reputation or not, the puny ranger looked mighty insignificant perched on his keg against the wall when I thought about all the Flatts and all the Standards and all their guns coming together in one place.

To Topsy he looked worse than insignificant. He looked invisible. Dub Coe might just as well have come alone. She knew one ranger could never overcome the treachery of Eli Flatt.

After dinner the men sat on the front gallery to smoke while Topsy cleared the table—except for Cotton, who was prowling around somewhere. The mist had died down to almost nil and the clouds were getting thinner.

"Roy, I believe it will stop raining and turn out to be a good day for hunting," Coe said.

"I think so, too."

"I sure would like to leave the Flatt family with some game hanging to make up for all their hospitality. Let's load up and go kill something."

Eli followed us out to the barn where our weapons were.

"I'll just need to make a trip to the privy, first," Coe said, "then we'll go."

When he left for the outhouse, Eli pulled me aside. "What are you up to?" he asked.

"Just going hunting."

"Be careful of what you say. Don't give that surveyor no ideas."

"Ideas on what?"

"On where he ought to find that zero stone."

I scoffed. "What interest do I have in the zero stone?"

"An interest worth your share in our town."

"I never agreed to help you build that town. Besides, if the zero stone lies where you claim it does, your town site is secure."

"It don't matter what I claim. Only what Coe claims."

"Huh?" I grunted.

"Use your head, boy. That surveyor is fishin' for profit like everybody else. You heard what he said. He claims he can find marks of chainin' pins fifty years old on rocks where nobody else can see 'em. Says a few chips of rock'll stand up in court as evidence where the marker was chiseled. Hell, he can place that damned zero stone wherever he pleases. He'll favor whoever makes him the best offer."

"You mean, you think he's after bribes?"

"Works for the gov'ment, don't he? Just don't let on that I'm broke. When he asks, tell him far as you know Eli Flatt is flush with money and has got it to spare. Here he comes."

Coe came into the barn, picked up his rifle, and began meticulously filling it with cartridges. "When it rains all day the game likes to crawl up under the brush and loaf," he said. "But when you get a break in the weather like this, they're liable to get up and move around. That's why I like to hunt this kind of weather."

We were just about to step out of the barn when Coe noticed an old set of deer antlers, covered with dust and cobwebs, tacked up in the barn above the door. The ten-point antlers were connected by a strip of skull that a hunter had sawed from the buck's head after killing it.

"Say, Mr. Flatt," the surveyor said, "would you object to my using those deer horns?"

Eli's eyes squinted. "Use 'em for what?"

"For me and Roy to rattle up some bucks. I'll have to break that piece of skull in two, but I could tie them back together whenever I get through with them and tack them back up on your wall."

"What do you mean rattle up some bucks?" Eli asked.

"Well, some vaqueros that ran my chains for me down in the chaparral showed me how to rattle up the big bucks and bring them runnin' right at you like you never saw."

"How do you do it?" I asked.

"Well, you just rear back and rattle a couple of old horns together to make it sound like two big ol' bucks fightin'. If there's any big bucks around, they'll come to join in on the fight."

Eli looked skeptical, then glanced at the antlers and grinned. "Oh! Rattle 'em up! I see, you want to show Royal how to rattle 'em up." He snickered and pulled at the antlers above the door.

"Yes," Coe said. "It only works two or three weeks out of the year, when the bucks are ruttin' and lookin' to fight each other for does. But I think the rut is on right now in these hills. Me and Cotton saw a buck running a doe in the rain this morning."

Eli put the piece of deer skull in the vise beside the door and broke the antlers apart by pulling on one of them. "Oh, sure. The time is right to rattle up some bucks," he said, winking at Coe.

Coe took the antlers from the old man and held one in each hand as if testing the weight of a new pair of revolvers. Suddenly he spread his arms like the wings of an eagle and banged the antlers together, twisting them, grinding them, gnashing the tines. He struck them together like a plowboy trying to knock cakes of dirt from a pair of boots. A cymbal player in a military marching band wouldn't have hit his instruments together as hard at the height of the "Star Spangled Banner."

"They've got a pretty good sound to them, don't you think?" he asked.

"Loud," I said.

Eli laughed. "Open the gates and we'll rattle 'em right into the stalls!"

We left the old man slapping his knees and walked eastward to look for game. Coe stopped at the water trough to rinse the dust and cobwebs from his rattling horns. "Old Flatt thinks I'm taking you on a snipe hunt," he said. "But this rattlin' business is genuine. I've seen it work many a time. On a day like this I'd say we have half a chance to rattle one up. Could be colder and clearer. But the bucks are runnin' the does and that's the main thing. You do believe me, don't you?"

"I'll believe you when I see the bucks running at us," I said.

The big surveyor who had lumbered through the Flatt house clopping his boots against the floorboards now became the epitome of stealth. Every step I took crunched or scraped something, but Coe's strides fell silently under him. Finally he turned to frown at me. "Walk quiet," he said.

I shrugged.

"Put your heel down soft and then roll onto the rest of your foot."

I tried it, with better success, but I stepped into a circle of dried bunch grass and the stalks collapsed and crackled under my soles.

"Step on the grass like this." Coe used the side of his boot to sweep the dry stalks of grass down flat against the ground and then put his weight on them. The maneuver was almost perfectly silent and he performed it with the grace of a waltzer.

I mimicked his moves, concentrating hard on walking in silence. To Coe the gait was natural and he poured his concentration into studying the sign around us. He pointed his rifle barrel at a shed snakeskin lying crooked over a low mesquite branch. He stooped to pluck a square-ended turkey feather from the ground and tucked it into a buttonhole on his shirt. He picked up a shiny pellet of deer dung and smashed it between his fingers. "Fresh," he said. "Not even cool yet."

I must have turned my nose up.

"What's the matter?" he asked, amused at me. "It washes off. They just eat leaves and stuff."

I spotted a few full tracks of deer and turkey feet pressed into the damp ground, but Coe found tiny pairs of dents made by the cloven toes of deer on hard ground. He recognized the depression of a single toe of a turkey in the gravel. "Fox," he said, pointing to a mound of dung perched on top of a rotten log. Then he showed me a small cedar tree whose branches had been mangled and whose skinny trunk had been stripped of bark by some force unknown to me.

"Buck rub," he said quietly. "Some big old boy has used this place to polish the velvet from his horns. This rub marks his territory and he'll fight to keep it. As soon as we find a clearing we'll try to rattle him out into it."

I had spent many days hunting and had swapped yarns with many a hunter and never had I heard of things like buck rubs and horn rattling. But, not presuming to know everything under the sun about deer hunting, I went along with Coe's strategy.

We pressed on through the oak motts. Coe showed me places where deer had browsed on their favorite shrubs and he knew the names of all the plants. At last we came to a clearing about eighty yards wide on the side of a hill.

"You set against this tree," Coe suggested. "That will give you a full view of the place. I'll hunker down beside you behind these agarita bushes. I'll do the rattlin' and you do the shootin'." He squatted behind the agarita, put his rifle down, and took an antler in each hand.

"We're upwind," I said. "Shouldn't we hunt on the other side of this clearing?"

"Not when you're rattlin'. The bucks usually come in downwind to get the smell for what's going on, so you want a clear spot downwind where you can get a clean shot at 'em. Even if they wind us, I can bring 'em back with the horns."

I smirked and sat down against the tree. "Alright, if you say so. But I've never been on a hunt like this before."

"Just keep your eyes open. They might come galloping right out in the open or sneaking in cautious through the woods."

I drew my knees up and put my rifle across them. Coe took a firm grip on the old antlers and raked the tines together for about fifteen seconds, but not with the same ferocity he had used in the barn. He settled back against the tree with me to watch.

After five minutes we had seen nothing move so Coe took the antlers in hand and bashed them together again, louder than before. They clacked and scraped and rang with the dull timbre of a padded tuning fork. I frowned my disbelief.

"Just wait," he said. "It sometimes takes a while."

A while went by and still no bucks had charged, fighting mad, into the meadow. Coe started gathering sticks around him. "Here," he said with a perfectly straight face, "break these while I rattle this time. And rustle that agarita some with your foot."

I rolled my eyes as I took the sticks from him. "What in hell for?"

"It sounds like two fightin' bucks stamping down the bushes. If this don't bring 'em runnin', we'll move to another spot."

He crashed the antlers together. I sat idle. He looked at the sticks in my hands, urging me to break them. He gestured toward the agarita bush. I sighed and kicked halfheartedly at the bush and snapped some of the smaller twigs in my hands. I could already hear him telling the story to the Flatts: *I had ol' Roy hunting upwind of the clearing, breaking limbs across his knee and stomping hell out of an acre of agarita bushes!*

Two minutes after Coe allowed me to stop the foolishness with the sticks and bushes, he nudged me with his elbow. "See him?" he whispered.

I looked into the empty clearing. "I don't see anything."

"Keep watching. To the right. There's a pretty good buck coming in through the shadows." Coe kept his eyes fixed on a spot across the clearing.

I followed his stare and saw nothing. "Look here, Coe. You better not be pulling my leg."

"Watch, Roy. You'll see him directly."

I leered casually toward the phantom buck. There was absolutely nothing there. Then a movement came to me and the buck materialized as if suddenly carved from the trees around him. He came strolling toward the clearing, his head held low, the great curve of his antlers bobbing among the branches.

My heart rhythm doubled in one beat. I eased my shaking rifle into shooting position.

"Eight-pointer," Coe whispered. "A good one. Wait till he gets in the open."

The buck stopped two steps shy of the clearing and looked our way. His horns swept wildly through the air as he craned to glimpse the struggle he had heard.

The horn rattler touched his instruments together, locking the tines and grinding them. The eight-pointer quivered with excitement and sniffed the moist air. Still he avoided the clearing. He stayed among the trees and moved farther to our left, intending to use the wind to scent us.

"He's a smart one," Coe said in the lowest whisper. "Get ready to break some more sticks."

When the buck got just downwind of us, he whirled with his nose in the air, leapt, and vanished in the shadows. I dropped my rifle and wrenched a handful of sticks to flinders. Coe smashed the rattling horns together. He attacked the agarita bush, whipping it violently with the antlers as he rattled them. He thrashed his cover to shreds as he banged the old bones together. He produced the most astounding spectacle I had ever seen until the buck went him one better.

I dropped the sticks and groped for my rifle. The eight-pointer was galloping headlong at us across the clearing. He stopped so close I could see his nostrils quiver. A single shot through his neck reduced him to a carcass.

"Good shot!" Coe hollered, springing to his feet.

I rose and followed him to the dead deer. Coe put his hand around the base of the antler and hefted the lifeless head. "Damn, we did alright together!"

The smell of burnt powder was in my nostrils and the ring of the rifle shot was still in my ears. I stared dumbly at the dead buck. "He knew we were here," I said. "He smelled us. Why did he come back?"

Coe pulled a folding knife from his pocket and stropped the blade against his boot top. "They can't help theirselves. They get a craziness for the sound of rattlin' and they'll charge into sure danger to find it. They lose all their good sense, I guess."

I understood such insanity better than Dub Coe. He had seen it work on rutting bucks, but I had felt it in myself every time I heard mention of the zero stone. For an instant I saw myself in the eight-pointer's place, my eyes clouded in death, a bullet hole between them. The slain buck's death knell was the rattle of old horns; mine was the jingle of ancient specie.

We hung the buck by the antlers in the fork of a tree to gut him. The branches showered us with rainwater as we shook them with the dead weight of the deer. Dub told me more about horn rattling as we worked. Then he showed me another way to call animals, putting two fingers across his pursed lips, sucking air in and making the most pitiful squeaks and squeals imaginable.

"What does that attract?" I asked.

"That's the wounded rabbit call. It'll bring all sorts of carnivores down on you. Coyotes, foxes, bobcats. Even wolves and bears and mountain lions. You should learn how to call your game, Roy. It saves a world of footwork.

"I surveyed some in the caprock country in the fifties and I had some Delaware braves scouting for me who used a folded leaf or a blade of grass to call antelopes. Tried it once myself. Spotted some pronghorns away off and crawled up through the grass, I guess three hundred yards from them. Then I took a wide blade of grass and made it squeal like the Delawares had showed me. It sounds like a fawn bleating for his mammy, you see."

"Did you call one in for a shot?"

"No, I worked on that blade of grass for fifteen minutes or so, then I heard something rushing me off to the left. It was the biggest old panther you ever saw in your life coming to kill that fawn he had heard bawling. I whirled my old muzzle loader, pulled the trigger, and broke his neck with the ball. He was in the air on his last jump to get me and he fell across me and knocked me down."

We finished field-dressing the buck and headed for the

Flatt house to get a mule. With the hunt over, Coe turned his eyes to things other than game sign. Picking up a stone he said, "Looks like there's some iron ore in some of this rock."

He found a trail of ants carrying tiny leaves to their underground den. He called them "umbrella ants" and was not satisfied until he had back-trailed them to find the bush they were cutting the leaves from. "Wonder why they picked this one?" he asked.

About a half mile from the house, he pointed out some little plants on the ground and asked if I knew what they were. "Bluebonnets," he said, laying his rifle down beside him. "It amazes me that just about nobody recognizes them when they ain't bloomin'." He knelt and picked up a handful of tiny pebbles that he poured into my palm.

"Thanks," I said. "What am I supposed to do with gravel?"

"Now, that's what leads men into trouble—jumping to conclusions. Those are bluebonnet seeds. They just look like gravel so the birds won't eat them all up. Give those to your gal and tell her to plant them shallow in a sunny spot and next spring she'll have bluebonnets blooming."

"I don't have a gal," I said.

"What about that redheaded one back there?"

"She's not interested in me," I said. "Just between us two, she's sweet on one of the Standard boys."

"Do tell? Maybe she can keep her old man from killin' off all the Standards if she's pining for one of them."

"Maybe," I said.

"It's not my habit to give advice, Roy, but I'd urge you to help her keep that clan of hers out of trouble if you can. And don't let them talk you into fighting on their side by any means. Cotton won't hesitate to shoot any one of them or you either. I know how little he frets over spilt blood."

"I don't plan to be anywhere near when the shooting starts," I said.

"Good. I'd hate to see you get into hot water." He

raised his hat above his scalp. "See what happens when you can't stay out of hot water? Your hair starts slippin'!" He grinned and dropped the hat back over his bald spot. "Anyway, just hold on to those bluebonnet seeds and give them to your gal once you find her. No hurry. They'll keep a couple of years or more. You see, that's what happens to them in nature when a drought sets in, they have to keep until it starts to rain again and then . . ."

Coe continued the lesson in natural history as we approached the Flatt home to brag on our kill. We failed to convince Eli that bucks could truly be rattled up.

That night, after eating fresh venison, Coe got to rambling and started telling a story about a survey line he had run in the pines of east Texas: "The line ran right near a log cabin and I was sighting through the telescope on the transit when a woman came out of the cabin with a broom and beat me well nigh to death with it. Turns out she thought I was a Peeping Tom . . ."

As I listened and laughed, Topsy brought me a cup of coffee.

"I reckon Mr. Coe is what you'd call a raccoonteer," she said quietly.

"Yes," I answered. "He rivals old Uncle Pie."

EIGHTEEN

C otton Anderson probably weighed little more than
Topsy but he had more fight in him than a pit dog
and he seemed always eager to engage it. When he and
Coe got ready to leave for the Standard Ranch after
breakfast, while the rest of us stood out in front of the
house, he stepped up onto the gallery and began to lecture us from his makeshift lyceum.

"I got somethin' to say," he declared in his peculiar
tone. We all looked as he started pacing the gallery, his
thumbs hitched over the hammers of his revolvers. "And
make sure you listen good because I ain't gonna say it
but once. It's my duty to see that Coe finds the boundary
between here and that other ranch and you can be
damned sure of one thing. I don't need your help and I
won't stand for your interference. While we're huntin'
the marker, you all best stay clear. If I see a hair of any
one of your murderin' heads, the whole lot of you will
soon be joining your kin." With that, he pointed a bony
finger at the fresh graves in the family plot.

"Why, you little runt," Boone said, cracking his knuckles and mounting the bottom step of the porch.

Coe stepped quickly in front of him, grabbed Anderson by the collar, and led him down from his platform. "Shut up and mount your mustang. Don't you know better than to threaten men from their own front porch? You'll have to pardon Cotton," he said to the Flatts, "he was raised by mad coyotes and still thinks frothin' at the mouth is good manners." Coe made sure Cotton got on his horse and then mounted his smokey black stallion. "We thank you for your hospitality, Mr. Flatt." He tipped his hat at Topsy. "And good day to you, miss."

Coe turned, driving the ranger in front of him like a stray jackass. But he had gone no farther than thirty yards when he stopped his stallion to look at the pile of cedar posts I had stacked near the corral. He leaned from the saddle to look closer. Then he got down and knelt beside the pile of big corner posts. He reached down to stroke one of them. It was the big one. The one I had climbed to escape the rattler.

Cotton turned to see what was holding Coe back while the Flatts and I approached the pile of posts. As usual, Eli, Boone, and Tobe picked up their rifles before wandering that far from the house.

"Now what's he lookin' at?" Tobe said.

"Who chopped these posts?" Coe asked when we came close.

"I did," I said.

Eli glared at me and nervously stroked his beard. "What difference does it make to you?"

The surveyor stood and faced me. "Can you tell me where you chopped this post? I mean the exact spot. For this big one right here." He kicked the cedar log.

"Yes," I said.

"Are you sure?"

"Positive."

"What difference does it make to you where we chop our posts?" Eli repeated.

Coe knelt beside the big corner post again. "Look right here." He ran his fingers over an indentation in the face of the cedar trunk. "This tree was blazed. It's been a long time. Decades. The bark has healed over. But I've seen old blazes and that's what this is, I'm sure. This is a witness tree from the boundary. If you remember where you chopped it, Roy, I'll have to ask you to come with us and show me. It will most likely lead us right to the zero stone."

"He won't go with you to show nothin'," Eli said. "He works for me."

"He'll come with us if I say so," Cotton said from the back of his silver buckskin.

"The hell," Boone said.

"Now, go easy, men," Coe said. He stood up and sighed. "Roy, we can't make you go with us without a court order of some kind. But you're a free man. If you think it's best that you come with us, I'd be obliged. If you don't want to, you can stay until we get the order. The choice is yours."

The ranger and the three Flatt men glared at me as if they would kill me no matter what I said. Topsy wrung her hands. Coe waited patiently for me to make up my mind. But there was no choice for me to make. I possessed information that would lead to the zero stone and it looked as though the old cedar, having come from the east side of the creek, would place the survey marker on that same side—the wrong side for Eli. I could imagine all kinds of fatal accidents happening to me if I chose to stay among the Flatts with that kind of knowledge in my head.

Besides, it was my destiny to locate the zero stone. That fact became suddenly clear. How else could I have stumbled across the old Mexican, Marion Harkey, Dub Coe, and the blazed cedar tree in one lifetime? I had no choice to make. "I'll get my mare," I said.

"Damn you, boy, I trusted you!" Eli shouted. He trembled with an animal ire so deep that his words came out in an unnatural quake. "If you help these bastards steal my land you'll get just what you deserve. You go with them now and I'll . . ."

"You'll what?" Cotton said, jumping down from the mustang. "You'll kill him? Do it now, then. Go on, point your rifle at him and kill him dead right here. But you better reckon on dealing with me next. I won't just stand by and watch a murder."

"Put a scabbard on it, Captain," Coe said.

The ranger ignored him. "Go ahead. One of you can shoot Huckaby and the others can try me. This is your best chance. There's three of you against just the one of me. I can't kill all of you. I'm not *that* fast. One of you will get me. You've got the odds. I'm a dead man if you'll just go ahead and kill me right here. Of course, I'll get one, maybe two of you, and you don't know which ones I'll shoot at first, do you? What's the matter? Why don't you shoot?"

Tobe licked his lips and glanced at his father. Boone and Eli stood silent, but rumbled with anger within.

"I know what it is," Cotton said. "You damned bushwhackers are used to shooting men in the back. You hide safe in the bushes and shoot when they ain't lookin'. But I'm standing right in front of you and lookin' you dead in the eyes. No, you don't have the guts for this kind of fight."

Eli shook as if he had taken the palsy and I knew he would raise his rifle to shoot any second. Suddenly Topsy was shoving her way through the men. She pushed her brothers aside and marched straight at Cotton Anderson, her red hair bouncing after her. She balled up her little fist and punched the ranger right on the chin, staggering him back a step or two.

Speck appeared at Topsy's ankles, growling and popping his teeth at the ranger.

"The Flatts ain't no bushwhackers," Topsy said. "And you. You come here to keep people from killin' one another and all you can think about is killin' us yourself. You call yourself a lawman but you ain't no better than a hired killer." She turned to me. "Well, go git your mare. You can't stay here now, that's for sure."

I saddled Liberty in short time, got my few belongings together, and joined Dub Coe. I didn't bother to ask for my wages. Anderson was still eyeing the Flatt gang, but he was on his mustang now and Topsy had taken a good deal of the fire out of him. As we rode away, I heard Boone say to Eli, "I knew we should have killed him the first day we seen him."

The relief I felt at riding beyond rifle range was something akin to the feeling I had experienced during my first hour out of prison. Cotton became even more surly than usual, but I was almost cheerful to be free of the Flatts and so was Dub Coe. Then a welcome thought came to me. We were going to the Standard Ranch. I was going to see Annie.

I asked Dub if he didn't think it would be a good idea to bathe in the Double Horn before arriving at the Standard place. He said the same thought had possessed him and that he had spotted a fine swimming hole from the road the day before. The weather had cleared somewhat and the sun was coming through the clouds.

We stopped by a pool of clear water with a canyon bluff against one side and a gentle slope against the other. It was ten feet deep or more and there were fishes swimming around in it. Coe and I began shucking our clothes, but Anderson had no intention of divesting himself of guns much less clothing.

"I've been wondering about something," I said to the surveyor. "Where does the name Dub come from?"

"He won't tell you," Cotton squeaked.

"I will so tell him. It's a short way of saying my real name."

"What is your real name?" I asked.

"William Westfall Coe."

"I told you he wouldn't tell you," the ranger said.

"I just have told him, Cotton. The difference between Roy and you is that Roy is smart enough to figure it out."

I'm afraid I disappointed Dub on the capacity of my intelligence. I couldn't think of any way Dub could be short for William Westfall.

"It'll come to you," he said, wading into the cold swimming hole, his big white body glowing like a full moon underwater.

Cotton climbed the bluff on the other side of the creek and stood guard. I kept my back turned away from both of them. I didn't want them inquiring about the scars.

My clothes were still a bit clammy when I put them back on, but they were clean and that made me feel more at ease about facing Annie.

"That was some shot that little redhead give Cotton, wasn't it?" Coe asked as we pulled our boots on.

I chuckled and looked up for the ranger only to find that he had vanished. Then I heard his sharp voice right behind us in the bushes.

"She packs a good punch for a gal," he said.

Coe turned around. "Why, Cotton, that's the first respectful thing I ever heard you say about a woman."

The ranger shrugged. "I still think there'd be a bounty on 'em if you couldn't breed 'em."

Coe frowned and shook his head. "I swear you must have never had a mammy."

Cotton rode in front as we took the fork leading to the Standard house. We were listening to Dub tell how a survey party of his had once gotten caught in a buffalo stampede when another voice interrupted.

"Stop," it said. "Put your hands up."

We obeyed.

A young man in buckskins stepped out of the bushes aiming a rifle at us. The skins he wore were not of the greasy, blackened variety seen on frontiersmen. His were still new and golden. He was clean shaven and had his hair cropped so short that barely any stuck out from under his hat. "Identify yourselves," he said.

"Identify your own damn self." Cotton refused to hold

his hands up any longer. "And point that gun at something else or I'll take it and jam it . . ."

Dub interrupted and made the necessary introductions and the young man in deer skins lowered his rifle. But he looked at me with particular enmity even though I hadn't smarted off the way Cotton had.

"Sorry about the gun," he said to the ranger. "We've been keeping a watch out for bushwhackers. I'm Clay Standard. The house is this way. I better walk in with you."

As we turned the next crook in the road, the plantation home of the Lon Standard family came into view. It stood in the middle of about ten acres that had been cleared of growth except for the largest oak and pecan trees. Blooded horses cavorted behind whitewashed fences on either side of the road that led to the front door of the house. Rows of pecan trees had been planted to flank the road, but were only half-grown.

The two-story limestone house stood in front of all the barns and outbuildings, rising high among the boughs of centuries-old live oaks. On both floors, galleries ran all the way around the house, lending space here and there to rocking chairs and porch swings. Trimmed shrubs grew in front and a flagstone walk led to the broad steps.

As we rode between the rows of young pecans the pastured horses followed along behind their fences. Coe's stallion was particularly excited about them and pranced sideways down the drive, making Coe beam with pride.

Clay had a hunting horn looped around his neck and he blew it to announce our arrival. Half a dozen hounds answered the call and came loping around the corner in a pack, baying and barking. They swarmed around Clay, wagging their tails, jumping and nipping at his elbows.

Major Lon Standard came around the house then, walking ramrod straight, suspenders bulging around the barrel of his chest, sleeves rolled up above his hairy forearms. He wore a wide-brimmed panama and striped trousers. He had the kind of legs that buckled inward a little at the knees, but otherwise looked as sound as an ox.

"They're here, Daddy," shouted Clay. "It's the man from the Land Office and the first of the rangers."

Lon walked out to meet us at the hitching rail and Dub made the introductions followed by the initial explanations. Up close, the old major looked more haggard than he had from afar. The mask of mourning was still on his face. There were gray hairs in his thick pork-chop sideburns and black circles under his eyes. But when he shook my hand, I knew he had plenty of life left to fight with.

"What did *you* come for?" he asked me.

"I think I can help find the boundary marker. I happened to stumble upon a blazed tree on the other side of the creek."

"And he's volunteered to help us at risk to his own skin," Coe said.

Cotton scoffed, hitched his mustang, and began prowling. Clay still looked at me with some distaste.

Mrs. Standard appeared at the front door about that time. She wore an apron around her waist and had her hair tied back in a bun that seemed to pull the rest of her features smooth and taut across her cheekbones. I could easily see the resemblance between her and Annie. She invited Coe and me into the house for some arrack punch.

"Arrack punch!" I exclaimed involuntarily. "That's a specialty of my mother's. I haven't tasted any in years."

"You should go see your mother more often," she said.

"Yes, ma'am," I admitted.

"Son, ride down to the pens and tell your brothers we've got company," the major said to Clay. "Then go by Annie's garden and ask her if it wouldn't inconvenience her too much to come, too. Your mother could use her help."

Clay trotted for the stables with his dogs as the rest of us went inside.

The Standard home could have served equally as well

as palace or fortress. It didn't quite rate with the house I had grown up in on the Huckaby estates and it probably stood a notch or two below the Standard home the Yankees had burned in Virginia, but it was a house that would stand for generations and one to take pride in.

Charlotte Standard led us to the kitchen table where we would drink our punch. Dub downed an entire glass in two or three gulps and asked for more. Cotton glanced at us through the window from outside and then passed by.

"What is that ranger doing out there?" Charlotte asked.

"He's avoiding us," Coe said. "Cotton doesn't get on real good with people."

Lon slipped his hand around his wife's arm. "Mother, Mr. Huckaby here says he found the old boundary across the creek and is going to lead Mr. Coe there tomorrow."

Charlotte studied my face. "God bless you for that. The sooner we can end this trouble the better."

Charlotte's kitchen included a fireplace, a wood stove, an icebox, and an indoor pitcher pump with a basin that drained somewhere to the outside. She chipped some more ice for Dub's drink, and we made small talk until we saw Lum and Nat returning to the house. Lon suggested that we go out to meet them in the stables and he would show us around the place.

"You have a string of nice-looking horses," I mentioned as we walked to the stables.

"Thank you," the major said. "We used to breed racing horses in Virginia before the war. Now we deal mainly in cow ponies. Quarter horses, mostly, although we have kept a couple of Spanish ponies before."

Dub was surprised to learn that I had already made the acquaintance of the two newly arrived Standard brothers. They had a fine time telling him how the flour barrel had turned my mare from a seal brown to a roan.

Cotton Anderson interrupted the laughter. "Is this all

the men of the family here?" he asked, appearing suddenly at the door to the stables.

"Except for Clay," Lon said. "He's gone to get Annie."

"Well, I have something to say so I'll just tell y'all now and talk to him later." He began his pacing motion in the broad doorway. "It's my duty to see that the boundary marker gets found between you all and that other ranch. Tomorrow morning Coe and Huckaby and me are going out to hunt it. We don't need no help and we won't stand for no . . ."

"What he means to say is this," Dub said. He gave the Standards their orders to stay clear of our party with more diplomacy than Cotton could have mustered on his happiest day.

"We'll keep out of your investigation," Lon promised.

"I appreciate that," Coe said, giving Cotton a smirk. "But I do want to hear your side of the story. If you can tell me where you think the marker is, I'll check for sign of it there."

"I can show you exactly where I always figured it to be," Lon said. "Come on around front."

We all followed Lon around to the hitching rails where our horses were tied. Lon stepped up on the porch and pointed to the hills. "The land patent I had before the courthouse burned seemed to indicate that the marker was on top of that hill. You can just see the crest of it up the creek valley."

"Which hill?" Cotton demanded. "I can't tell which one you're pointin' at."

Lon asked to borrow a rifle, so I pulled mine from the saddle scabbard and handed it to him. He pushed an armchair sideways against the rail on the porch. He knelt and rested the barrel of the rifle across the porch rail and the stock across the arm of the chair, looking down the sights from his kneeling position. He took a pair of leather gloves from his back pocket and put them under the barrel, doubling them over until they had become thick enough to prop the rifle barrel at the correct angle. Then he stepped away.

"That hill," he said. "Look down the sights and you'll see the peak of it."

We all took turns kneeling behind the rifle to sight down the barrel like astronomy students taking turns at a telescope. I recognized the hill in the gun sights as the one from which Eli Flatt had shot my canteen just before I made his acquaintance.

"The first time Eli claimed my land, I went up on that hill to find the corner," Lon said. "I didn't see a trace of it. Of course, I didn't really know what to look for, either. I don't know what kinds of marks those old surveyors used. But the patent I had when I bought this place indicated that the hill you're looking at is the one with the zero stone on it."

"We think old man Flatt dug it up and moved it," Nat said.

"Who thinks that?" Lum asked.

"Well, I do."

"Nobody asked you what you thought."

"Hush, boys," Lon said. He gave my rifle back to me and I returned it to the scabbard. Clay came trotting up on his horse then and I heard the rattle of a buggy coming from behind the house and knew Annie was returning from her garden. I asked Clay if I could put my mare in the stables, and he looked disgusted but said he guessed it would be alright.

As I led Liberty into the stables I saw Annie jump down from the spring seat of her buggy. Her eyes grew wide when she recognized me, and she quickly tossed her hair over her shoulders and straightened the fabric of her dress. "Roy!" she said. "Clay didn't say *you* were here."

"It's a pleasure to see you again," I said.

Instantly her bright eyes narrowed and she looked as though she would scold me for something. "How are you getting along with the Flatt family?"

"Not well. Not since I refused to cover up the location of the boundary for old Eli."

One of Annie's eyebrows peaked, but she continued to glower at me. Even her anger was beautiful.

"How's Topsy?" she asked with an accusatory tone in her voice.

I shrugged. "Fine," I said. Then I reached a wonderful understanding. Annie was jealous of Topsy for the days I had spent with her at the Flatts' house. I rejoiced and panicked all at once. "Except that she's worried sick over your brother Clay," I added, pleased with my own quick thinking.

Annie gasped. "Is she still sweet on him?"

"I should say so."

"Well, I swunny! I told Clay she wouldn't have him for a pet after everything that's happened. It was hard on us all when those Flatt boys murdered Virgil and Cal. But Clay took it harder than any of us because he figured he had lost his girl along with two brothers. I bet he hasn't done a lick of work since we buried them. He started wearing those buckskins and spending all his time spying on the road to the Flatts' house. Says he's watching in case they want to come shoot some more of us, but I think he wants to get a glimpse of Topsy. He saw you and her go to town in the wagon one day and it sure made him jealous."

"I'll have to set him at ease, then," I said. "She's got her mind on no other fellow but him."

Annie beamed again and I saw an opportunity.

"I brought you something," I said, reaching into my pocket. I pulled out a little bundle of cloth in which I had wrapped the bluebonnet seeds Coe had found for me. Annie knew exactly what they were.

"I've heard a lot about your garden and thought you might want to grow some wildflowers there."

"Thank you," she said. "That was nice of you to think of it."

She put the seeds away and asked if I would like to

help unload the cargo in her buggy. She had several tow sacks filled with pecans that we put away in a feed room. One of the sacks contained nothing but the paper-shelled variety, she told me. We kept it separate from the others because it was worth more.

We stripped the gear from our horses and gave them some feed. I also helped her carry baskets of fall vegetables to the kitchen. But then I was chased out of the house so the women could cook.

I decided to hunt up Clay and tell him that he had occupied a lot of Topsy's thinking of late. When I convinced him of the fact, he started treating me like his oldest pal instead of his vilest enemy. I had to keep scratching dogs as I sat on the front steps and talked to him, for they followed him everywhere, and it seemed that any pal of Clay Standard's was good enough company to set their tails wagging.

NINETEEN

When Major Lon Standard said grace, I couldn't help peeking at Annie. I figured all the eyes around the dining-room table would be closed, and the heads bowed in prayer. They were, except for Annie's, who risked a glance at me, too, making us both blush.

I noticed something else unexpected as Lon blessed the food. Cotton Anderson had his hands clasped as tight as anyone. He even quivered with the Spirit of the Lord and when Lon finished, he said amen louder than anybody.

We had chicken-fried steaks, mashed potatoes, gravy, corn, and mustang wine from Annie's native vineyard. Coe asked where all the vegetables and wine had come from and Lon told him about Annie's garden.

"I love a garden," the surveyor said. "When we finish our job tomorrow, I'd like a chance to look at it."

"Me, too," I said. "I'd like to see how you graft the pecan limbs from the mother tree to the other ones."

The Standards stopped and stared at me.

"The storekeeper at the Marble Falls told me about it," I explained.

Cotton was sitting at the corner of the table, his arm wrapped around his plate as though he thought one of us would try to take it away from him.

As the conversation evolved over dinner, I learned that the feud with the Flatts had caused Lon to postpone his political aspirations. He had intended to run for a seat in the state house of representatives.

"What'll your platform be?" Coe asked.

"Oh, Lord," Charlotte said, "now you've done it."

"Don't get him started on politics," Lum said. "You'll hear nothing else all day long."

"Don't worry, I'll be brief," the major said. "I wouldn't want to bore the ladies."

Annie started to say something, but her mother elbowed her.

The major dabbed his chin with a napkin. "Transportation's my main objective. We need more railroads in Texas and we still have plenty of public land to trade for them. Not the school lands, of course. We need to protect them so we can educate our upcoming young men."

"And women," Annie said.

"Now, Annie, don't start," Charlotte said. "Not while we have company."

The major ignored Annie and went on with his stump speech. "And I think it's high time we stopped letting every saddle bum in the state carry a revolver on his hip. Side arms should be for lawmen only."

"Amen," Cotton said.

"I have nothing against a man carrying a rifle to hunt and shoot varmints, but a pistol is for combat. Now that the Indians are all on the reservations, there's no need for men to carry revolvers everywhere they go. We need legislation against them."

"You'd get my vote, Major," the ranger squeaked.

"Then there's the fencing controversy. I know the free-range days are drawing to a close, but, by golly, those big-pasture men don't have the right to fence everything under the sun. We need laws requiring gates at three-mile intervals on the fences so other cattlemen can drive their herds to market. And no one should be allowed to fence a public road. And there should be penalties for those who fence in public range before they acquire legal ownership."

"I agree," Coe said. "We can't jump from free range to private ownership overnight. We should ease into it."

"Exactly," the major said.

"What about that other idea of yours, Daddy?" Nat said, sidling his eyes toward me.

"Oh, yes. I've been observing the operations at the Granite Mountain quarry. I think it's an abomination the way those convicts are treated. I don't care if they are criminals. We need prison reform."

Before I could contain myself I snorted rather mockingly. Everyone at the table gawked at me.

"Do you find that amusing, Mr. Huckaby?" Lon asked.

"On the contrary, there's nothing funny at all about the need for reform in the prison system. It's just that I've heard it all before and know how the politicians are misled to think reforms are being enacted, when actually the abuses just continue or get even worse."

Lon tapped his knife against his plate. "Not to pry into your past, but I've heard you have some firsthand knowledge of the system. Perhaps you could tell us about some of the abuses you are talking about."

"I'll be glad to. But not now. The dinner table is not the place for it."

We had biscuits and butter and peach preserves for dessert and then retired to the parlor for a smoke. Cotton ordered Nat to show him around the grounds, expressing particular interest in seeing the family burial plot and the fresh graves of Cal and Virgil.

"I can't figure that ranger, Dub," I said after Cotton

left. "He thinks more about killing than anybody I ever knew and yet I saw him praying like a parson over dinner."

"Cotton belongs to that religion where they think the Good Lord has everybody's time to cross over marked on his calendar and nothing nobody can do will change it."

"You mean he's a fatalist?" the major asked.

"Yes, that's what they call it. It's a convenient way of thinking for lawmen because then they don't have to fret about whether or not they'll get shot. They know all the frettin' in the world will do them no good."

"But he was praying at dinner," I said. "He said amen and everything. What's the use of praying if it won't change anything?"

"Cotton only prays to give thanks. He never asks the Lord for nothin'."

When we had exhausted the topic of fatalism, Lon asked me if I didn't think the time appropriate to tell him about the problems within the prison system. I said it was as good a time as any and started by decrying the use of the bat.

"But there must be discipline," the major said.

"The bat is seldom used for discipline. It's used as an instrument of torture and intimidation and nothing else. I'll wager that in all your years as a slave owner and a Confederate officer you never saw a human being or even a dog treated the way those convicts are by their guards."

"Wasn't there a chaplain installed in the prison system a few years ago? The chaplain should be the man the prisoners go to to report abuses."

"Any chaplain who reports an abuse soon finds himself looking for another congregation," I explained. "The system works him out right quick."

The major puffed broodingly on his pipe. "Did they ever use the bat on you?"

"Just once," I said. "I was lucky. Except for that once I managed to stay healthy enough to keep up with the work expected of me. And my skin was white. That helped some, too."

"How severe are the beatings?"

"In my case I was unable to sit or lie down on my back for eight days. One fellow I know of was paralyzed below the waist. Many men have been beaten to death."

"What?"

"Yes," I said. "Once I worked with another convict in a sawmill. He took sick and couldn't finish the day's work. The guards took him for a slacker and whipped him without mercy. The next day he was sicker. He knew he couldn't last for sixteen hours and that's what they expected of us. So he cut his own hand off with the saw blade so the guards would send him to the infirmary back at the walls. He knew he wouldn't be beaten there."

Major Lon sat stone quiet across the parlor, the smoke from his pipe swirling around him like a storm cloud. Wordlessly he rose from his chair and went to a writing table near me. He opened the ink well, took up the quill, and made a note or two on a sheet of stationery. "What else?" he asked.

I told him that the contract system should be abolished and that prisoners should no longer be hired out to work for private farmers and businesses.

"But I have read the reports of the commission," he argued. "I was led to believe that the prisoners enjoyed getting out of their cells for the exercise and work. And I know for a fact that the disease and death rates are lower on the farms."

"That's because the sick and injured men are sent back to the walls to recuperate or die. The healthy ones are sent out to the farms and kept there until they are too sick or worn down to work. And they beat the weakest ones as examples of what will happen to those who don't work hard enough. It would be easier for them to do the work expected of them if they were fed enough."

"How can they be fed too little?" the major asked.

"The legislature appropriates a set amount for food. Where does it go?"

"The guards take it. They openly take the food from the commissary and use it to feed their families."

The major scribbled on his stationery. "Go on," he said.

As I preached the evils of the Texas penal system, the men in the parlor left one at a time until only Lon was there to listen to me. "I don't understand how it could happen," he said. He shook his head and scratched one of his bushy sideburns. "The commission inspects the prison units and the farms and has never reported any of these crimes to my knowledge."

"The guards know the commission's schedule," I explained. "Before the inspectors arrive at a farm, all the sick or injured convicts are sent somewhere else and the ones that remain are told to keep their mouths shut. We used to look forward to the inspections, actually, because the guards had to feed us properly when the inspectors were there."

"The solution, then," the major said, "would be to conduct unannounced inspections. Then the guards would have to treat the prisoners properly all the time or risk getting caught and charged for the abuses."

"And the contract system must be done away with."

"Yes, that, too."

"And standards should be set when hiring guards."

"Standards, yes. References required. Bonds put forward." The major stood and ran his fingers through his hair, paced the floor, rubbed his brow. He looked ready to sway the entire congressional delegation. "So much to be done," he said. "It won't be easy." Then he asked me what on earth a man of my temperament and training had done to get thrown into prison in the first place.

When I told him, he looked through the window at Nat who was trotting a colt in circles on a long lead rope. "It could just as well have happened to one of my boys," he said. "It could just as well have happened to me."

"It could just as well happen yet," I said.

Lon nodded. Then he clapped me on the shoulder. "We've been cooped up in here long enough. Come on, let's get some air."

Dub took a nap that afternoon, beneath the shade of a huge live oak in the Standards' yard. Cotton cleaned and oiled his armory. The Standard men worked with some horses, except for Clay. Mrs. Standard sent him and me to the watering tank to net some catfish Clay had caught and thrown in for safekeeping some time before.

The whisker fish, skinned and filleted, became supper, fried along with some of Annie's fresh okra and accompanied by sweet potatoes, green beans, and peach brandy.

After supper we all sat on the front gallery to watch the stars appear. It was a pleasant evening. A portent of something seemed to hang in the air. The conversation naturally turned to the subject on everyone's mind and Lon began telling Dub Coe his side of the dispute with Eli Flatt.

"When we moved here after the war," he said, "the fellow I bought this land from told me the patent was at the county courthouse. For some reason it was never sent in to the General Land Office."

"That's common," Dub said. "My pappy used to gripe about how unorganized the Land Office was in them days. Patents were scattered out all over the state."

"Well, this one had been drawn up in 1842," Lon continued, "after this plot was surveyed. At that time, the location of the zero stone was still known. The surveyors of '42 found it and connected their survey to Eli's land and drew up the patent."

"Where is the patent now?" Dub asked.

"Blown away to the four corners. It was still in the courthouse when it burned in '74. I regret that I never had it sent to the Land Office or made a copy of it. It had a plat drawn on it that seemed to place the zero stone on that hill I showed you this morning in the rifle sights.

I have no proof, of course. Only my word."

"Old man Flatt was the one who burned the court-house down," Nat said.

"No, he wasn't," Lum said. "It was rustlers trying to burn up all the brand records."

"Old man Flatt was probably a rustler on top of every-thing else," Nat argued.

"Now, Nat," the major said. "Let's stop speculating and just tell what we know as fact. The point is that the patent was the only document in existence to show the location of the zero stone. Now that it's gone, it's just my word against Eli's. He says the zero stone is on this side of the Double Horn and that the creek belongs to him. I say otherwise."

"How come it took the two of your families so long to go to war over the land?" Cotton asked. "The courthouse burned in '74 and you've just now got around to killin' one another."

Coe grimaced at the ranger's phrasing.

"Eli's family and mine got along fine at first," Lon said. "He welcomed us here when we first arrived and he and his boys helped us build the log house we lived in before we got this place built."

"Yeah, the Indians were still bad when we came here," Lum added, "and we chased 'em with the Flatt brothers whenever they came around to steal stock or hunt scalps."

"That's right, we were good neighbors to one an-other," continued Lon. "We never even discussed exactly where the boundary ran at first. It wasn't necessary. Even though most of the land was privately owned around here, we used it like free range. Our cattle ran together and we rounded them up and branded them just like they do on the government ranges. Eli and I were the only landowners to actually live on our places. All the others were waiting for the Indians to get cleared out, I suppose. It wasn't until after the last fight at Packsaddle Mountain that the valley began to settle up.

206 / Mike Blakely

"Even after the courthouse burned, Eli didn't try to claim my land right away. In fact, it wasn't until that stern-wheeler came up to the Marble Falls that year that he told me he was going to build a town at the mouth of the Double Horn."

"And that's when the shootin' started?" Cotton asked.

"No, not then. I simply told Eli the mouth of the Double Horn was on my land and I didn't see much future in building a town there and if he wanted to build one, he should put it farther downstream on his own land. He told me then that he had always considered the Double Horn his. We argued about it, but we weren't mad enough to shoot each other. After that argument I realized that I didn't have any proof to back up my claim since my patent had burned up. I hunted some for boundary markers, but didn't know what I was looking for. Anyway, Eli didn't mention the subject again for a while and I just forgot about the whole thing."

Lon sighed and reached for Charlotte's hand and squeezed it. "If I had known that damned strip of land would cost me two sons, I'd have given it to him in the first place. But, damn it, I swore when I left Virginia that I would never let another man take my land again. The carpetbaggers had taxed my plantation out from under me back there. I just wanted to leave my children something. The last thing I wanted was for them to die because of it."

We all sat silent on the gallery for a long moment. Cotton shoved his chair back and walked into the dark.

"You know why I never liked old Mr. Flatt?" Annie said.

"Why is that, miss?" Coe asked.

"He always looks in his handkerchief after he blows his nose."

"Oh, Annie!" Charlotte said.

"It's true, Mother. You can't a trust a man who does things like that."

Dub laughed, then asked the Standard men what had

happened between them and the Flatts after the steamboat came upriver. Lon seemed unwilling to tell about it, so Lum did. "Well, nothing happened for a long time," he said. "Then, a few months ago, old Eli told us he was going to string a fence on this side of the Double Horn. The newspapers had run a story about clearing the raft at the mouth of the river so steamers could come in and old man Flatt figured he would make a fortune in the steamboat trade if he could just put his town at the mouth of the Double Horn. Daddy took him to court over it."

"Yeah," Nat said, eager to get in on the story, "and old man Flatt tried to tell the judge that he was the only one who knew where the boundary was because he was here with the first survey party in '38 and that Daddy had torn the old marker down. The judge didn't believe him, of course. He sent out an order for you to come, Mr. Coe. That made old Eli mad and those Flatt brothers pulled guns on us on the way home."

"Dang sure did," Lum said. "Shot at us, too. Put a bullet through my hat. We just started shootin' back and killed Reed and Bass."

"We didn't have no choice," Nat said. "It was kill them or get killed ourselves. Then Virgil and Cal got bush-whacked on their way to town one day . . ."

Dub interrupted. "The shootin' part is for the courts to look into. All I need to know about is the zero stone."

The Standard brothers looked at the sky. Lon stared at the porch floor. I saw something move away in the dark and knew it was Cotton.

"I've always wondered," Annie said. She sat at the far end of the gallery from me. I could barely hear her voice and could not see enough of her face in the starlight. "Why do they call it the 'zero' stone?"

Dub threw a cheerful twang into his voice as if he had decided to single-handedly take the gloom out of the con-versation. "It's called that because it stands on top of the first corner ever surveyed in this part of the territory," he explained. "It was supposed to be the starting point for all surveys to follow for years to come. And, as any-body knows, if you start somewhere, you start at zero. Of course, it didn't work out that way because the Indians killed the survey crew after they had platted just one square.

"A lot of old lines were lost in ways like that. Why, I remember the first lost boundary I ever had to find. It was up in the Cross Timbers between two families that was feuding over the land. Well, I was a young man back then, green as a red blackberry . . ."

Dub slipped into his story, but I had trouble keeping my mind on it. I strained to catch Annie's eyes at the other end of the gallery, but it had grown too dark. I turned my gaze to the sky. The stars began to twinkle and I let them play tricks with my eyes. I let them sparkle like jewels, like sunlight glinting on the face of a polished bar of silver. I invented my own constellations: the dou-bloon, the ingot, the chain of jewels, the pieces of eight.

In the morning I would find the zero stone, the place the old Mexican's map had told me to begin in my search for *el tesoro*. One hundred eighty-nine lengths of Dub Coe's survey chain, 49 degrees northwest—by that for-mula I would come to stand on the most valuable point of land in Texas. Stand? No, I would drop and kiss it!

And then? After I found the loot? Oh, why not? Why be greedy? Of course I would share it with the Standard clan. There would be enough for Annie and I to build our own limestone mansion, raise our children, send them to college.

Only one hitch could keep me from it. Eli would be watching tomorrow. So would Boone and Tobe. Little Jimmy Fitzhugh might even have joined them by now. Their guns would be loaded and leveled on the boundary hunters. But Topsy would try to stop them. And if she didn't, Cotton Anderson would take them all on by him-self. And I had my rifle and Dub had one, too. The Flatt gang would not deny me my reward.

Think like a ranger, Roy. Your day is marked on God's circle of time. You have no cause to worry. Your fretting changes nothing. You are a fatalist, Roy. You fear no one. It is your destiny to follow this path to the zero stone and you have no control over it. It's above you, Roy, it's beyond your grasp or understanding. You must let the hand of One greater than you will you where He would.

". . . and the other clan was a freckle-faced race of people and every one of them had the brains of a, oh, I guess a razorback hog or so—which is not all that ignorant, by the way. Both clans were so poor they left five-toed tracks on the way to Sunday school. They both wanted that land bad."

Dub's tale was coming through to me again.

"They had been feudin' for fifteen years. They had already fought over women, whiskey, horses, religion, politics, and then land. I had a dozen rangers with me the day I went out to find the boundary between them. It was a case just like yours because it was an Initial Monument—a zero stone—that determined the line. When I went out that morning to find it, those rangers had more guns on them than a battalion could carry . . ."

"What?"

"I say, more than a whole battalion, Roy, really."

"No, what did you say before that? You went to find what?"

"The zero stone."

"The zero stone?"

"Yes, that's what I said. I went to find the zero stone."

"But the zero stone is here," I said, pointing into the darkness.

"One of them is. 'Zero stone' is just an old-fashioned term for an Initial Monument. A starting point for one of the frontier surveys."

A paralysis seized my throat. "But . . . How many?" I wheezed. "How many zero stones are there?"

"How many? Heck, I don't know, Roy. Hundreds, I guess, all over the country. Anyway, those rangers had guns to beat an army that morning when I went to hunt the zero stone up there in the Cross Timbers . . ."

TWENTY

The stars died in the night sky. Blackness closed in on me and left me alone with my agony. The grip tightened around my windpipe. The blood pounded against my temples. The bile rose in my guts. I stood and walked but, blinded, knew not where I went.

I had known just one ambition the day the old Mexican gave me the treasure map. There was only one old Mexican. He gave me only one map. There was one Marion Harkey, one Eli Flatt. One Texas, one Burnet County, one Double Horn Creek. There was one Annie Standard and there was only one fool named Royal Strickland Huckaby. But there were hundreds of zero stones.

I staggered like a drunk. I reeled and swooned. Why had I failed to consider the possibilities of multiple zero stones? What had made me think I could see the term once written in Spanish on a worthless Mexican treasure map and then coincidentally hear it spoken from the lips of a complete stranger like Marion Harkey—unless the zero stone existed in a thousand manifestations across the entire country?

I had staked everything on a zero stone. My freedom, my future, my very life. In the morning I was expected to run a gauntlet of guns leveled by the sure hands of the Flatt gang to help Dub Coe find a zero stone. If I survived, what would be my reward? A one-in-one-thousand chance of digging up a buried treasure trove? I had never bet against those kinds of odds and I had no intention of starting now.

There was just one thing to do. Run. Turn my back on the Flatt-Standard feud and flee to some kinder destiny. When all the Standards had gone to bed, when Dub Coe and Cotton Anderson had kicked off their boots and pulled up their covers, I would sneak out to the stables, saddle Liberty, and ride like a lost soul in limbo.

"Roy," I heard the voice say.

I shook my head to clear it and found myself leaning against the doorway of the stables behind the house.

"Roy, what are you doing?"

It was Annie, her tawny hair collecting the sparse starlight.

"Oh, I just . . . I needed to check on my mare before turning in." Thank God it was dark. Perhaps she hadn't seen me weave and stagger. Or perhaps only my thoughts had tripped and my legs had swung true.

"Mother asked me to tell you that you'll be staying in the guest room tonight. At the top of the stairs. Mr. Coe and the ranger will get Virgil and Cal's old room. Mother hasn't opened it until tonight."

She moved closer to me. I heard the rustle of her clothing. "I'm glad that you came here, Roy. It helps to know this trouble may be ended soon. I think you're very brave to help us."

"Annie," I said.

"No, let me tell you. I know you're modest, but I want you to know how I feel. I knew when you put your horse between that flour barrel and those children that you were a thoughtful man, that you cared about people, and that you would help those unable to help themselves if you could. But I never dreamed you would risk your life to help us."

She came nearer still. I smelled the sweet aroma of her skin. I felt her warmth. She touched my hand. "It could be dangerous tomorrow and you haven't shown the least sign of fear all day. I want to give you something to bring you luck in the morning."

"Annie, there's no need," I began. But then I felt her body press against mine and I felt her breath on my chin. Her lips touched below my jaw and then found my mouth. The darkness overwhelmed me again and I reeled and swooned in a whole new way.

"Who is that?" Dub said.

Annie bit my lower lip and pulled away from me. "Damn it, mister! Don't you respect privacy?"

"Oh, I, uh, sorry, miss," the startled surveyor said. "I just came to look after, uh . . . ." He started chuckling. "Well, how was I to know?"

Annie slid away from me. "Excuse my language, Roy, but . . . oh, never mind!" She stomped back to the house.

"Sorry, Roy, if I busted in on anything. The major was telling me how hard he had found it to raise a southern belle on the Texas frontier. Now I see what he means. He said he got his older daughter married off and sent back to Virginia. But that Annie, she's a hellion."

"Huh?" I said.

"Say, listen! Did you hear that?"

"What?"

"Listen."

I heard the faintest yelps somewhere in the sky. Scores of them.

"Geese," Dub said. "You know what that means?"

"Means?"

"Norther coming tonight. Those honkers are ridin' it down from Canada. It'll be cold in the morning. Mark my words."

* * *

We rose before dawn and it *was* cold. The windows were patterned with frost. I found occasion to wear my long handles for the first time since I had purchased them in Fredericksburg. The entire Standard family got up with us to eat breakfast and see us off on our quest for the troublesome zero stone—one of hundreds.

The peculiar thing was that I had dreamed of the old Mexican again overnight. He had implored me, pointing his gnarled fingers at the ground under his feet. *"El tesoro,"* he said again and again. But folly lingers in dreams.

Before we left the house, Annie caught my eye and ran her finger across her lower lip, wordlessly asking me what kind of damage she had done to me the night before. I smiled and winked to let her know the pain had been worth the pleasure. Major Standard caught us glancing at each other and narrowed his eyes at me.

We rode at first light, Dub trailing the mule loaded with his surveying equipment.

"I think I've figured it out, Dub," I said to the surveyor as we left the stables.

"What's that?" he asked.

"Your name. Did you ever go by your initials? W. W.?"

"Yes, in fact I did," he said, grinning.

"And when folks got tired of calling you W. W., I guess they just shortened it to 'Dub.' "

"See there," he said to the little ranger, "I told you he was smarter than you."

"If he's so damn smart, what's he doing here?" Cotton said.

The animals puffed white clouds of vapor. It mingled with the fog that rose from the river and drifted south on the breezes, clouding our movements.

"This fog'll help us," Cotton said. "They'll have to git in close to shoot us in this stuff."

The misty air gave me some comfort, too. I felt as if I could hide in it.

"Cold north air on that warm river water," Coe said. "That's where this fog's coming from."

We went back to the Double Horn, crossed it, and turned south off the road. Cotton rode with a hand on one revolver. "How come you remember where you chopped that particular tree with the blaze on it?" he asked as I led us through the cedar stumps.

"It was the biggest one. It made an impression on me."

Even in the fog, I had no trouble finding the place. I saw the furrows the big corner posts had dug when the mules dragged them to the Flatt house. Then I saw the circle of ashes where I had burned Reuben's convict uniform. I knew exactly where to find the stump from there.

"Here it is."

"Look's big enough," Dub said. "Are you sure this is the one?"

"There's no doubt."

Dub tried to count the number of growth rings in the rough ax marks on the cedar stump. "Must be almost a hundred," he said. "Look how much this tree grew during these three years right here, Roy. Must have rained a lot then. Looks like, oh, in the fifties sometime. That's funny. I don't remember the fifties being that wet."

"God Almighty," Cotton said. "Forget the weather and find the damned boundary marker."

"It'll wait on us, Cotton. It's been there well nigh fifty years already."

I helped Dub unload his surveying equipment. He mounted his big, dinner-plate compass on something he called a Jacob staff. It was a hardwood pole with a sharpened steel spike on the bottom. On the top, where the compass was clamped, it had a ball-and-socket joint that allowed for leveling the instrument. The compass had two bubble levels beside its face that enabled the surveyor to get it exactly horizontal.

"Why don't you use that telescope thing you were telling us about when the lady thought you were a Peeping Tom?" I asked.

"I'm using the same type of equipment they used when they surveyed this place in '38. That will give us the best chance of duplicating the original lines. This old peep-sight compass is an antique. Nobody uses them anymore."

Dub fastened a bracket to either side of the compass. The brackets had vertical slots that the surveyor looked through as if sighting along the irons of a rifle.

"I'll need you boys to move the chains for me while I line you up with the compass. The zero stone should lie 190 chains due south of this stump."

"How do you know that?" I asked.

"The blaze on that witness tree you chopped was a section mark. That means it was one mile from the zero stone. That's about 1,900 varas or 190 chains. Shouldn't take us but a couple of hours to run it."

"At this rate?" Cotton complained.

The ranger took one chaining pin and I grabbed the other. Like the Jacob staff on which the compass was mounted, the chaining pins had steel spikes on them that allowed them to be planted firmly in the ground. We stretched the chain and lined the pins up on a north-south course as indicated through the slots in Dub's compass brackets.

As we moved the pins south for the second chain length, Cotton refused to leave the horses behind. His Sharps rifle and scattergun were attached to his saddle and he would not stray from them. In fact, he kept the reins to his silver buckskin looped around his elbow, which slowed down the chaining process considerably.

By the time we had stretched several chain lengths to the south, a disturbing trend became evident to me. I noticed that I could see over a hundred yards through the fog. It seemed to be lifting and leaving us unprotected. But on the next ten varas, it thickened so much that I could barely see Cotton at the other end of the chain. It was coming across us in waves.

When the fog was thin, the little ranger ceaselessly

swept his pale blue eyes across the cedar brakes and brush around us. But when a finger of mist shrouded us, he relied more on his ears, cocking his head at every sound like some hard-hunted game bird.

We rattled the links through the moist litter of cedar needles and hardwood leaves. We laboriously moved the horses southward with us, chain by chain. Dub lined up the pins, holding us dead on course, keeping a running tally of the number of chains we had stretched.

It was tedious work pulling the chain through the brush. We found many trees and bushes growing along the line we were running. If practical, Dub would chop them away with a hatchet he had packed on his mule. But some trees were too big and we just had to stretch our chain around them and estimate the number of inches taken off the length of chain due to the variation from the straight line.

"Runnin' around all these trees," Cotton said, "we ain't gonna come out like them surveyors did in '38. Hell, half these trees probably wasn't even here then. This ain't gonna come out right, Coe."

"No need to be that precise," Dub replied. "The men who left the zero stone didn't stretch their chains perfect, either, you can bet on that. Not with Indians breathin' down their collars. We'll git within spittin' distance and that'll be close enough."

After half an hour of work, we came to a rocky place on a steep grade. The surveyor began brushing away the leaves on either side of our line. He rubbed the rock with his palm in several places.

"What are you lookin' for?" asked the ranger.

"I'm trying to find a place where one of those old surveyors might have stuck their chaining pin."

Cotton scoffed. "Forty-seven years ago?"

Dub kept looking and rubbing the rocks and directly he called me over to look. "See those old scratch marks? Could be their trail."

"Damn cold trail if you ask me," Cotton said. A column of fog had just rolled onto us and he was listening carefully for unnatural noises.

"I *didn't* ask you," Coe said.

"How will we know for sure?" I asked.

"Let's measure due south from these scratches. If we find another set of them at exactly ten varas, we can pretty much bet we're on the old line."

We stretched the chains and found faint marks under the other pin as well. We stretched it again and found more old marks, almost illegible except to the practiced eyes of Dub Coe.

"We've strayed about a foot to the west of their line," he said. "But now we're back on center. There's no doubt in my mind now, Roy. That cedar you chopped was a witness tree. It will lead us dead straight to that zero stone."

"Don't yell it to the whole damned valley," hissed the ranger. The wave of fog had pulled away from us and there was nothing to muffle our voices or cover our movements.

We ran the line southward, moving the horses, chopping the brush, dragging the chain. Dub came to a large sycamore perched on the creek bank and paused for a long moment to study it. Neither Cotton nor I complained about the delay and sat to rest, holding our chaining pins upright in their places. I exhaled into my cupped hands to warm them.

"This looks like an old witness mark, too," Dub said, sighting along the side of the trunk with one eye. He pulled the hatchet from his belt and scraped some bark away. "Yeah, it's a hack. I'll just freshen it up a bit." He chopped a deep horizontal gash in the side of the tree.

"What's the difference between a hack and a blaze?" I asked.

"A hack goes crossways on the trunk. A blaze is like the blaze on a horse's face—up and down. Looks like these surveyors used the blaze for a section mark and the hack just to mark any tree standing on the boundary."

For another hour we worked in and out of fog until we had stretched the chain 180 times by Dub's tally. "Ten chains to go," he said.

We stood halfway up the hill that Major Standard had sighted in his rifle irons the day before. I had already become accustomed to judging distances in increments of ten varas. I could tell that our final stretch of the chain would leave us standing on top of that hill. If the Flatts were going to stop us from finding the zero stone, they would be waiting for us there.

"Makes sense that they would put the corner up there," said Dub. "The old-timers usually tried to pick a rise as a starting point when they could. That made the markers easier to find."

The norther had blown a million doves south. They burst from the trees in flocks as we dragged the chain and led the horses, their wings popping in the cold air and their little voices shrilling in spasms. The day before, I might have recognized one of them as the old Mexican. But today they were just annoying noise-makers.

A dense cloud seemed to have snagged on the ridge of the knoll and I was grateful for its presence. It covered our progress up the rocky slope. Despite the problem of moving the horses with us, we had fallen into a kind of rhythm over the last two hours and we made good time ascending the hill.

Cotton was braced for battle. Coe was eager for discovery. I was scared almost witless. The fight between my late brother-in-law and the Texas Rangers at my hunting lodge in Matagorda County—the only gun battle I had ever been in—had taken me by surprise and had spared me an incalculable amount of worry because of it. But my anticipations of the impending battle of the zero stone were almost too much for me to endure. I might have considered running, but I couldn't stand to think of how Annie would cuss the memory of me if I did. Besides, Cotton Anderson would probably shoot me in the back for deserting.

No, I had to charge up the hill with the surveyor and the ranger. I had to fulfill my wretched destiny. How would posterity remember me? I wondered. Roy Huckaby: bushwhacker, ranger-killer, convict, and whorehouse brawler. Could not stay away from blood feuds. Picked fights with strangers on street corners, broke hardened criminals out of prison, seduced the daughters of fine gentlemen. It was a great day for Texas when the hard-fighting Flatt men killed him at the shootout on Double Horn Creek.

But maybe Topsy would come through. Maybe she could hold off her father and brothers until we could find the marker and git. And the fog would help us, too. It was so thick on our hill that the Flatts would have to crawl closer than thirty varas to find us in their sights and we would hear them coming.

There is hope, Roy. There is always hope. Think like a fatalist.

We lacked only two chains to reach the summit of the hill when, through the fog, I saw a pile of rocks standing on the very crest. It had several scrubby bushes and a yucca plant growing out of it and seemed to be a natural part of the hill. I judged that two more chain lengths would bring the final pin down at the edge of the rock pile.

"We're here," I said, laying my pin down.

"Wait," Dub said, "run the last two chains. We'll have to run the whole line to satisfy the courts. Besides, we're looking for a chiseled stone and I don't see nothin' yet but a pile of rocks."

"Maybe it's buried under them rocks," Cotton said. His voice squeaked higher than ever with the excitement.

"Maybe," Coe said. "Run the last two chains and then we'll see."

The last stretch of the links brought my chaining pin down right on the edge of the five-foot-tall pile of stones. "This pile of rocks ain't natural," Dub said.

"How can you tell?" I asked.

"Did you ever know rocks to pile theirselves up on top of a hill?" he asked. "Rocks roll down, not up. You boys just relax. I'll look around before we move anything."

Cotton squatted down in front of his mustang and strained to listen through the fog. Dub took a little straw hand broom from his pack mule and started brushing away the dirt here and there around the pile of stones, especially in the low spots that carried rainwater downhill. He picked up several tiny objects as he worked.

"What are you looking for now?" I asked.

"These." He showed me a handful of small stone flakes of different colors.

"What are they?"

"I think they're chips left over from chiseling the zero stone. I don't see what else could break off so many little bitty pieces of rock up here. The marker must be under that pile of rocks, like Cotton said. Somebody's buried it, most likely." He poured the stone chips into a small paper envelope that he put in his vest pocket. "Come on, Cotton. Make some use of yourself and help us move these rocks."

We pulled at the bushes in the pile of rocks and they came loose without much effort. Then we started picking up the melon-sized boulders or rolling them aside. A couple of them got away from us and crashed down the hill. There was some dirt mixed in with the rocks and Dub used a small shovel from his packsaddle to scrape it away. With all the noise we were making, the Flatts would have no trouble knowing we were there in the fog, digging up the zero stone, disclaiming Eli's right to Double Horn Creek, smashing his dreams of becoming a town father.

Thank God the fog stayed with us. And the wind was just barely blowing from the north, letting the mist linger over us.

The rocks came away from the pile easily until we reached a point of stone jutting up from the middle of the pile. I pushed it, but it didn't budge. It was the same kind of red brindle stone that the convicts carved out of the

Granite Mountain quarry. "This piece of granite won't move," I said to Dub.

"Of course it won't. It's part of the hill. It's what these flakes came from." He patted his vest pocket and grinned.

"It's the zero stone?"

"Most likely."

We dug more frantically, tossing stones into the fog all around us. My heart pounded—more from a strange, exhilarating sense of discovery than from the exertion or the fear. A layer of dirt covered the piece of pink granite. Dub scraped the soil off with his shovel.

I thought I could see a flat face on the stone but I couldn't be sure until Dub brushed more dirt away with his whisk broom. There were words carved into the granite outcropping, but the letters were still clogged with dirt and we couldn't read them.

"I'd have used this for a marker myself," the surveyor said. "It's perfect. Set high on a hilltop and permanent, too. You'd have to blast this away to move it."

I felt a strange pity for old Eli. His greed and treachery were exposed now. He was naked to the truth. He had buried the zero stone, never imagining anyone would have the skills to find and unearth it.

"Get your canteen," Dub said, "and we'll wash it off and read it. I hope they didn't deface it. I'd like to know what it says."

I poured the water down the flattened west face of the zero stone as Dub brushed it with his hand broom. The mud came away in streaks and the lettering became clearer. When we had the entire marker cleaned we stood back a foot or two to read it:

INITIAL MONUMENT
ORIGINAL SURVEY
1838
REPUBLIC OF TEXAS

Dub stood with his little whisk broom in his hand and his hatchet tucked under his belt. He breathed in a great sigh of satisfaction. "Don't let nobody ever tell you Dub Coe can't run a straight line."

As I smiled at the old surveyor, I realized the protective wall of fog was slipping away from us, bringing the surrounding trees on the hilltop into view. I heard a faint but familiar noise: the sound of a lock tripping in its machinery. Cotton was next to me. I tackled him, pulling him down behind the zero stone.

"Get down!" I yelled. But I was too late. A rifle crack sounded and a bloody hole tore open in Dub's back. The impact threw him and he slid down the hill.

Cotton jumped up cussing, both revolvers blazing, running to get his guns from the mustang. I huddled behind the zero stone, shards of it spraying all over the hilltop. A bullet hit the silver buckskin and the horse fell, almost on top of Cotton. Coe's stallion and Liberty spooked and ran down the hill. His horse kicking in agony, the ranger tried to pull his Sharps rifle out of the scabbard, but the buckskin had fallen on it. Another volley of bullets tore pieces of horse flesh away and the mustang stopped kicking.

I could hear footsteps running toward us from the other side of the zero stone. I had no weapon. I had been unable to carry my rifle while running the survey chain and I had never worn a pistol in my life.

Cotton got the scattergun loose from the saddle horn and threw it to me. "They're trying to flank us," he said. "You watch the south side and don't let them get around us over there. I can't get you any more shells. They're in the saddle pocket and the horse died on them. Make both shots tell."

The cold barrel of the sawed-off shotgun felt good in my hand, but I longed to have a rifle with a full magazine. Buckshot wouldn't carry far with any accuracy.

Cotton reloaded his pistols with cartridges from his belt and tried one last time to get the saddlebags loose from the dead mustang. Then the shots rang out and the ranger rose to return them. He let both his double-action Colts fire as fast as he could pull the triggers and ran to the survey marker, falling in beside me.

"Are you hit?" I asked.

"Not bad." There was blood running down from his right arm. Again, he replaced the spent cartridges.

The fog thickened for a moment and I lost sight of the treeline I was guarding to the south. Then: shots and points of fire and bullets hitting rocks in front of me. I aimed at the gunfire and let one of the barrels loose. I heard a yell and the fog swirled and I saw Boone scampering for cover.

"That's not buckshot!" I yelled at Cotton.

He shrugged. "It's a riot gun. Bird shot."

"How do you expect me . . ."

A twig snapped behind him and the ranger whirled to shoot. His bullet struck Tobe in the knee, taking him down behind a boulder. In a few seconds, he began to moan.

I heard Eli's voice. "Git up and fight," it said.

Tobe continued to moan, but put his pistol over the rock and fired blindly. Then Boone came again from the south side. I let my second load of bird shot fly ineffectually.

"Give me a pistol," I said.

"You can have my guns when I'm dead." Cotton rose above the protection of the zero stone and fired his pistols in two directions as the bullets shattered stone around us. I heard Boone coming behind me and Eli firing from the other side of our chiseled battlement. I saw Tobe rising above the rock he had fallen behind, his bloody hands leveling a rifle on the ranger.

Cotton's revolvers ran dry and clicked against dead cartridges. He started to empty the shells and reload.

"No!" Tobe yelled. His voice told the pain he was feeling. "Drop them pistols!"

"He said drop 'em." Boone's voice came from the other slope, below me.

Cotton let the pistols fall from his hands and stood at attention to face his death.

Boone came up the hill, parting the fog, pointing his rifle. He had a few points of blood on him where the bird shot had gotten under his skin. "Git up, Royal," he said.

I rose beside the ranger, dropped the empty shotgun, and stood in front of the inscribed face of the boundary marker.

"Kill 'em!" Eli's voice yelled from the trees across the zero stone. I saw him walk out into the open. "Land grabbers! Shoot 'em!" He was shoving cartridges into the loading port of his carbine.

But Boone didn't shoot. He came around the crest of the hill to look at Dub Coe's body. His eyes bulged out as if the sight of the dead man horrified him. He looked at Eli. "Pa, this ain't no hammer. It's a hatchet."

Tobe was using his rifle as a crutch, whimpering with every step he took on his shattered leg. He also gawked at the surveyor's body. He stumbled and fell beside the dead man and took the whisk broom out of his hand. "You said he had a chisel, Pa. This ain't nothin' but a broom. He wasn't gonna chisel no stone. Sweet Jesus, we killed him for nothin'."

"Kill them others, too," the old man said, still shoving cartridges into his saddle rifle with trembling hands.

"Sure, go ahead and kill us," Cotton said. "What are you waiting for?"

I backhanded the little ranger in the chest. "Shut up, Cotton. I'm not ready to die just yet." I stepped away from the zero stone. "Coe didn't have to chisel anything," I said to the Flatt brothers. "The chiseling was done forty-seven years ago. See for yourself, Boone. Here's the zero stone, where it's always been."

Boone gaped and lowered his rifle. "Pa," he said. "You were wrong. God in heaven, you were wrong."

"Shut up," Eli said. "This is my land. I was here first. Kill 'em. They're land grabbers."

Boone stared at the stone and Tobe moaned with his head against Dub's lifeless body.

"Kill 'em!" Eli shouted.

Boone set his jaw. "I ain't a murderer. I won't kill in cold blood."

"Now, son. You mind me and kill those land grabbers. We'll drag 'em across the creek and blame it on the Standards. We'll say Lon and them killed 'em to keep that surveyor from finding the boundary. Then we'll bury the marker again and nobody will ever know nothin'."

"I can't do it," Boone said. "You said the land was ours. You sent me and Tobe out to kill Virgil and Cal for nothin'." Boone threw his rifle down. "Goddamn you, Pa, you lied!"

I heard a single set of hoofbeats coming.

"I'll kill 'em myself, then," Eli said. He levered his rifle to work a shell into the chamber, but the action caught the end of his long white beard and he couldn't pull it loose. It was almost comical the way he struggled to get his whiskers free.

Suddenly Cotton rushed the old man, drawing a knife from his belt as he leapt over stones. The old man yanked half his beard out of his face to free the carbine and used it to club the ranger to the ground with one mighty sweep of the barrel.

The hoofbeats had grown louder and now I saw a horse coming through the fog up the east face of the hill.

Eli worked the action open and started pulling his whiskers out of the breech to make sure the gun would fire so he could shoot me. I glanced back to check Boone's position and found him standing stupidly, unable to act against his father. Before I knew it, I was running at Eli myself, my hands outstretched for his throat. He closed the breech, swung the carbine up, aimed it at my head. I closed my eyes and lunged and heard the shot and fell on top of the old man.

I heard Eli gasping. I was choking him. A powerful hand pulled me away. Boone threw me to the side and fell across his father, weeping. The old man was blinking at the foggy sky. Then I saw Topsy astride the big gray gelding, staring wildly at her father, the smoking rifle in her hands. Her skirt had blown up over the knees of her buckskin britches. Her red hair looked like a plume of blood against the gray mist.

Eli rolled his eyes and spoke: "My God, girl, you've shot me."

Topsy dismounted slowly and let the heaving gray gelding wander away. She dropped her rifle and stood over her father. She covered her face and began to cry.

I heard more hoofbeats coming and knew the Standard men were riding to join the fight. I ran to an open spot against the north face of the zero stone's hill and waved at the Standard gang. They saw me and came running, flailing their guns, but I held my hands high and told them not to shoot. I told them it was over.

They gathered on top of the hill to look at the dead and the wounded. They read the zero stone silently. Cotton Anderson moaned and pulled himself up on all fours. Boone was trying to stop the bleeding from Eli's chest. Topsy had shot him through both sets of ribs. Boone looked around at us all. "Help me," he pleaded. "Help me get him to a bed."

Eli's broad old hand grabbed Boone around the elbow and squeezed. He shook his head. "I'm killed, son."

Lon got down and knelt beside Eli. "You knew it was there all along. Why did you want this damned strip of dirt so bad?"

"My land," Eli said, wincing. "I come here first. I told them surveyors I wanted to patent this piece of land east of the creek. And I wanted the creek, too. Good runnin' water. I wanted to put up a mill. I told them to put the corner on that hill across the creek. But they had to put the son of a bitch here." He lifted his head to look at the stone. "Just because a good piece of rock stuck up on it for the marker. What kind of fool reason . . ."

Eli squinted and let his head fall back against the ground. "Somethin' you never knew about me, Lon. I was tradin' with the Indians for hides back then. I knew 'em good, chiefs and all. So I told 'em about the surveyors stealin' their land here. I knew they'd kill 'em, then I could hire me a new survey party. Put the damn boundary wherever I wanted it."

"You *let* the Indians massacre all those men?" Lon asked.

Eli nodded, grimacing. "Hell, I told 'em to, more or less. Then I come back to burn up the field notes. Couldn't find 'em. I found the chief surveyor, dead and scalped. The chain men, the flag men, the cook, the guards. All dead. The corner builder, too. Everybody dead and scalped but one. Mexican wrangler. Couldn't find him. Son of a bitch got away, I guess. Took the notes in."

As Eli paused, I collapsed and sat on a pile of rocks Dub Coe and I had thrown aside from the zero stone.

"So I had to bury the zero stone. Couldn't dig it up. Couldn't move it. Rooted too deep. Now you know how hard I worked to get ahold of this land," Eli said. "My land." His eyes stared blankly at the sky. "My land." He muttered about his land until he bled to death.

TWENTY-ONE

We carried the dead to the Marble Falls in the Standards' buckboard wagon. Cotton arrested Tobe and Boone for the murders of Cal Standard, Virgil Standard, and William Westfall Coe. He sat in the bed of the wagon with them and guarded them all the way to town, pouring water over his wounded head about every mile or so to keep himself alert. Neither of the prisoners offered any resistance. Clay drove the wagon and Topsy rode beside him.

Annie took her buggy and insisted that I drive it so I could tell her the story of the zero stone fight on the way. Everyone else rode saddle horses.

The sun had burned off the fog by the time we pulled up in front of Lynn's Store. We began attracting a crowd almost immediately. Miss Teeter somehow heard about our arrival and let her class out so the students could see the dead and wounded.

Tobe, Boone, and Topsy sat in the wagon like statues, refusing to acknowledge any of the conversation that went on around them. The shame they felt for their father's treachery seemed surpassed only by their will to sustain some measure of personal dignity. They lowered their eyes to no one, but looked through all comers. Even Tobe, who was pallid from loss of blood, sat upright and unwavering.

Lynn came out of his store when we stopped the wagons. Cotton climbed down, keeping his eyes on his prisoners. He raked the wet yellow hair back over his bleeding scalp and put his hat on. "I mean to hire a wagon to take these prisoners and these dead men to the county seat," he said to the store-keeper.

"Don't look at me," Lynn said. "I don't run no livery."

"Who does?"

"This town ain't got one yet."

Cotton turned to Lon. "Major, I hereby appropriate this wagon to take these prisoners to the county jail. I have the authority of the State of Texas behind me, so don't go refusing to . . ."

"Didn't any of Dub Coe rub off on you?" I said. "Just ask the gentleman and he'll no doubt lend you the damned wagon."

"Yes, go ahead and take the trifling wagon," the major said with a wave of his hand.

"I'm going, too," Clay said. "Somebody will have to bring Topsy and the buckboard back."

Lon nodded, tight-lipped.

"Then let's go," Cotton said. He sat between the dead men in the wagon bed to guard Tobe and Boone. "Don't go skippin' the county," he said to me as if I were a common fugitive. "You'll be wanted to testify sooner or later." He didn't bother to bid farewell to any of us as the wagon rolled out of town.

The crowd dispersed after the bodies and the prisoners left. I stood in front of the store with the Standards and J. L. Lynn and told what had happened half a dozen times until everyone was satisfied he had the story straight. Finally, Lon suggested taking a drink at the saloon catty-corner across the street from Lynn's Store.

"No, thank you," I said. "I made a vow to stay out of saloons and I intend to keep it."

Lum and Nat looked at each other and shrugged, but the major seemed impressed by my show of temperance. "Would you be so kind as to escort my daughter home, then?" he asked.

"I would consider it my pleasure," I said.

Annie put her hand around my arm as the Standard men walked across the street to the saloon. I started to help her into the buggy.

"Don't go just yet," Lynn said. "There's a letter for you here."

"A letter for me? Are you sure?"

"You know somebody else called Royal Huckaby?"

The merchant rummaged around in his pigeonholes for a couple of minutes and finally turned up the envelope. It had my name on it. I opened it to find a brief missive scrawled in an almost illegible hand:

Royal Huckaby, Esq.,
God help me if this letter doesn't find you alive and in good health. I have promised the XIT Ranch to supply 5,000 cedar fence posts before Christmas. Ten times that many after the first of the year. The ranch paid up front for the posts and I assured them the first shipment of cedar would get here on time. I opened an account in your name at my bank in Austin. Get the money, hire a crew, freight the posts. Hustle, man! More orders pending.

Marion Harkey

Annie read the letter after me and glowed with pride for my new venture. "You can clear the brakes from our place. Daddy said he wanted to. There's wolves up in those cedars and they come out to get our foals and calves."

"I have a few thousand posts ready to ship on the Flatt place already. I guess I can claim them since I never got paid for chopping them."

"Sure you can," Annie said. "Topsy will let you have them."

I thanked Lynn for holding the letter and escorted Annie to the door.

The storekeeper held me back as Annie went to jump in the buggy. "It amazes me that you came out of it alive," he said. "And you got the prettiest gal in the valley on top of it all. I've changed my mind about your luck, Roy. You ought to get on alright in this country."

I shook Lynn's hand and walked around in front of the buggy horse to climb in beside Annie and enjoy her company on the ride back to the ranch. I got one foot on the step when I heard a voice that rang with a familiar timbre.

"There he is right now," it said. "Hey, Roy!" The voice belonged to Deacon Sam.

I turned to greet the blacksmith and saw five men in front of the saloon—the deacon, the three Standards, and a goliath that stood a full head taller than any of them and carried more bulk than half of them. He wore a hat the size of a butter churn and a sheepskin vest that had required the sacrifice of more than one sheep. Though I hadn't seen the face in three years, I immediately recognized it as that of Little Jimmy Fitzhugh.

I had grown up contesting the Fitzhugh boys at everything from wrestling to horse racing to target shooting and I knew how well Little Jimmy could use that iron holstered on his right hip. It seemed God had marked this day as my last on his calendar, and one way or the other, I was going to cross.

I stepped away from the buggy so Annie wouldn't get shot, though I didn't think Little Jimmy would miss me by that much. I held my hands away from my body and turned my palms up to show that I had no weapon with which to defend myself, though I didn't expect that to stop him from killing me.

Little Jimmy, who had been grinning like a sunning alligator, began laughing wickedly, and to my horror, the Standards grinned and laughed with him. What lies had Little Jimmy told them? They obviously thought he had come in friendship. They knew nothing of the giant's intention to see my blood wash the streets. They wouldn't know to help me until it was too late. I couldn't even attempt to explain. I would be dead before I got a single syllable out of my mouth.

More than death, I feared that Annie would have to see another dead man, and she had witnessed enough of such for one day.

Little Jimmy took a thunderous step down from the boardwalk, laughing, shaking the ground below him as his strapping frame lumbered toward me. His eyes gleamed with wickedness, his hulking shoulders shook with the homicidal mirth rumbling from his lungs.

Then he mocked me! Oh, the insult of it! He held his hands away, palms upward, like mine, as if to suggest he had no weapon with which to shoot me dead. Then I understood. He wouldn't shoot me unarmed. He wouldn't have to. He would take me hand-to-hand. He wanted by blood under his finger-nails as well as my scalp on his belt. For three years he had waited, and now he would have his day. I saw a Bowie knife on his left hip. My God, it would run me clean through!

The human behemoth bore down on me, leering, rejoicing, savoring his moment of vengeance. His shadow engulfed me but still the knife stayed in its scabbard. When would he reach for it? Then the arms opened wider. Great God in heaven! He was going to squeeze the life out of me with his arms alone. I knew those arms—elephantine limbs, keg-like in girth—arms that could crush an ox.

The huge hands pulled me in against the sheet-iron chest and the arms enwrapped me. My feet left the ground, my lungs collapsed, and my rib cage all but buck-led and still my murderer tightened his hold.

Laughing, he whirled me, my arms pinned against my side, my heels flying out behind me. In terror, I heard the Standard men laughing, too. And Deacon Sam. And Annie! They thought he was hugging me! They couldn't tell I was being killed! They couldn't feel the heart flut-tering in my chest or the blood miring my veins.

There was only one chance. The pistol. I had to reach it. I felt blindly with my left hand. I grasped the belt, felt the cartridges. I used all my strength and pushed my shoulder downward in Fitzhugh's hold. I touched the ivory handle, but couldn't grip it. My fingers clawed like the talons of a dying hawk until I had no strength left. I was limp, breathless, done for. The fog rolled back over me.

Then the ground came up under my feet and fresh, cool air rushed down my windpipe. The murderous laughter was still going, but Little Jimmy had stopped killing me. He gripped me by the shoulders. I could barely see his face through the tears in my eyes. His huge hand patted my cheek like a bear toying with a carcass.

"Thank God I've found you," his baritone said. "Chaz swore if I didn't bring you home, she'd bolt the bedroom door and have me bunk alone on the floor rug." His laughter came like the winds of a cyclone. "A man wants his wife beside him with the winter coming on!"

TWENTY-TWO

Little Jimmy was the only one of Sloan Fitzhugh's next of kin to survive the hurricane that swept half of Matagorda into the bay the day Sloan went on trial. He was the only man who might have wanted to prolong the Williams-Fitzhugh feud by killing me in return for the death of his brother.

Chaz had realized this and made up her mind that she would put an end to the feud herself before I came home. She had spent three years mourning the death of her husband and lamenting the imprisonment of her only brother. She meant to make Matagorda County safe for my return. A month before my release from the penitentiary, she went to call on Little Jimmy.

As Little Jimmy Fitzhugh explained, "One meeting led to another and, well, we wound up meeting all night and decided to hitch up in double harness."

The Williams-Fitzhugh feud was dead. Little Jimmy said he never believed that I had hidden under the rose hedge fence with Joe David to shoot Sloan anyway, because Sloan's black hired man had witnessed the whole thing and named only Joe David Williams as the bushwhacker.

He said he had put some stock in the idea that I had acted as an accomplice by bringing a fresh horse to the lodge to aid in Joe David's escape, until he found out which horses I had brought there.

"If you wanted to help Joe David get away," he said, "you'd have brung that Spanish horse with the blaze on his head. Now, that horse had good bottom. But those were your jumping horses you had at the lodge that night. Good on a wolf hunt, but not made for outridin' the law."

So there had never been any danger at all waiting for me in Matagorda County. Chaz and Little Jimmy had meant to surprise me at the train depot the day I was to come home. When I didn't show, Chaz put her new husband on my trail. "I turned over dang near every rock in Texas trying to find you," he said.

I wouldn't let Little Jimmy take me back to the Gulf Coast, of course, because I had too many things to do in Burnet County. But when we got back to the Standard place, I wrote a long letter to my sister explaining why I could not come home right away and asking her to please let her husband back into the bedroom as a personal favor to me.

That seemed to satisfy my new brother-in-law's concerns and he left for home the very next day.

I spent the day after the battle of the zero stone counting cedar fence posts and making arrangements to fill the incoming orders from Marion Harkey. I would have to go to Austin the next day to hire a crew of cedar choppers and see about the bank account Harkey had established there in my name. That afternoon, after taking inventory of my cedar posts, I went back up to the zero stone to collect Dub Coe's surveying gear. I had decided to take it to the General Land Office while I was in Austin and give it to someone who would know what to do with it.

Wolves or coyotes had already torn the entrails out of

Cotton's dead mustang and eaten off part of a hind quarter. I looked around at the bloodstains on the ground and the bullet holes in trees. I sat down and studied the old corner marker and thought about the men who had located it and the deaths they had suffered because of Eli's greed—except for that one who had escaped—the Mexican horse wrangler.

All the men in the survey crew were faceless personages to me except for that young horse wrangler who had escaped the massacre and returned the field notes. When I thought of him dodging through the brakes with the precious field notes clutched in his hand, I saw the face of the old Mexican.

Yes, the chances were slim. There were hundreds of zero stones mounting hundreds of hillocks all across the country. And hundreds of the old survey crews must have employed Mexican men as well as men of every other nationality and race. But something about the Mexican wrangler Eli had spoken of seemed incongruous to me. For a while I couldn't put my finger on just what.

I sat on the hill of the zero stone and pondered for half the afternoon until I figured out the thing that didn't make sense. Why would a horse wrangler bother to save the field notes with a band of murderous Indians grappling for his scalp? Why? Because he wanted to make sure the location of the zero stone remained known. Why? Because he wanted to return to it. Why? Because it would lead him back to the lost loot the survey party had found before the massacre!

Then I remembered something Dub Coe had said. Texas was the only state in the Union to measure land in varas. The treasure and the zero stone charted on the old Mexican's map had to be in Texas, for the distance between them was measured by chains and varas. How many zero stones were there in the state? How fair were my chances now?

I cradled my head in my hands and almost wept. When would my blood purge itself of the fever? After all that had happened, it still boiled in my veins. I didn't even want the damned treasure anymore. What would Annie think of me if she found out greed had fostered all my bravery? I scorned the tarnished treasure, but I could not turn away from the hunt for it. And despite every morsel of rationality I applied to my situation, I could not help being awed by it. I was, after all, alone beside the zero stone with a surveyor's chain and compass at my feet.

I decided to go ahead and do it. I decided to run that line to the northwest. Perhaps then I could get on with a more ordinary life and put the adventure of the zero stone behind me. It wouldn't be easy moving and aligning the chaining pins by myself, but I resolved to give it a try. One hundred and eighty-nine chains amounted to something less than a mile and I thought I could get through with the job by nightfall. Then I could lay to rest forevermore any oddball notions of digging up filthy lucre.

My first problem was getting the chaining pins to stand upright by themselves. I could stab them into the ground where I crossed deep soil, but in the rocky places I would need something to hold them up so I could align them. I solved the problem with Dub's hatchet that I found lying on the ground. With it, I chopped four cedar poles. With some strips of leather that I cut from my saddle, I tied two cedar poles to each chaining pin, turning them into crude tripods that would stand up on their own.

I planted the first pin at the base of the zero stone. I pulled the chain tight in a general northwesterly direction, then picked up the peep-sight compass mounted on the Jacob staff and sighted exactly 49 degrees northwest. The chain was off several degrees, so I had to move the second chaining pin. When I had it aligned perfectly, I moved ten varas to the northwest.

The line led me down the hill and into the valley of Double Horn Creek. I got my boots wet crossing the stream. I had to chop brush as I went, of course, and the going was slow. I maintained a very strict count of the chain lengths I had measured, repeating the tally under my breath as I worked.

Along the course I looked for old sign. I eyeballed the trunks of the largest trees for witness marks. I almost rubbed the calluses off my hands trying to turn up sign on the rocks. I saw nothing to encourage me and yet I had no doubts that I should continue.

I was working toward a terminus. There was perhaps only a chance in one hundred that I would find treasure, but the odds were much better that I would regain a certain serenity of spirit that had been absent from my life since I had met the old Mexican.

Once I fell into the rhythm of the job, the work entangled all my senses. I was so absorbed with the staffs and compass that, at forty-four chains, I was surprised to look up and find myself standing right in the middle of the wagon road that led from the Flatt and Standard ranches to the Marble Falls. I ran the line as quickly as I could across the road before somebody came along wanting an explanation.

One hundred chains found me ascending a slope, chopping brush, yanking the chain through snags. The novelty of the treasure hunt began to wear off and I still had eighty-nine chains left to run. It looked as though I might not finish before dark. My feet were sore and I was tired. I considered giving up for several chain lengths. Then I reached the crest of the ridge at one hundred and seven chains.

The moment I looked to the northwest from that summit, The Feeling seized me. The serpentine floodplain of the Colorado unfolded below. It stretched level, only partially wooded. There was good bottom land down there. The Feeling told me that. But there was something more than mere fertility of soil. There was a greater wealth awaiting me. Eighty-two chains would land me somewhere shy of the river—on Standard property.

With cheerfulness I hacked the brush from the downward slope and moved my chain ten varas more. I placed the pins precisely. I pulled the links snug against one another. I remained true to the line at 49 degrees northwest.

When I hit the floodplain, the chaining became easier. The sun dipped behind the rim of the valley and took the glare out of the sky. I sank my faculties into surveying with more intensity than ever. I could not tell what kind of terrain or vegetation I passed. All that I saw grew on a thin line, 49 degrees northwest.

I whispered the tally as I worked: ". . . one-fifty, one-fifty, one-fifty; one-fifty-one, one-fifty-one . . ." I found fewer rocks and deeper soil. The Jacob staff and the chaining pins stabbed easily into the silt washed there by centuries of floodwaters. This was the kind of soil that facilitated the burial of things.

Daylight drained from the valley, funneling my senses ever more sharply to the line under my chain. ". . . one-seventy, one-seventy; one-seventy-one . . ." Yes, I would finish before nightfall, mark the final spot with a stake carved by Dub's hatchet, and return in the morning with a pick and shovel.

My heart pounded and mourning doves fluttered in my stomach. When I looked through the peep sight, I saw nothing beyond the farthest pin, lashed against the cedar posts that made it stand erect. My life at that moment measured no more than ten varas in scope.

I felt like a convict nearing the end of his sentence. I must not look ahead too far. I must take them one at a time. I must stay on the straight and narrow path until the end. Then and only then may I embrace my newfound liberty. Then and only then will I be free of chains.

". . . one-eighty, one-eighty, one-eighty; one-eighty-one, one-eighty-one, one-eighty-one . . ."

My only sound was the rattle of links—or was it the jingle of ancient coins? My eyes beheld only the wooden poles of the chaining pins—or were they tarnished silver? Five chains to go. Now four. Now three, now two. One chain. Precision! Don't look up! Don't lose the line. Move the pins, pull the chain, plant the staff. Line it up. There!

Don't look yet! Concentrate. Seven varas to go. How to measure them? Pace them off. Remember what Dub said. No need for pinpoint precision. The old Mexican and his party of surveyors would not have run a perfect line with Indians on them. You will come near enough by pacing off the last seven varas. Besides, the trove is huge. Too much treasure for the surveyors to have carried away with them.

I put my back against the chaining pin standing farthest to the northwest. I bent over and looked between my legs to align my course with the chain. I took a step of about one vara, then checked behind me again. Still on line. I took another step, lined myself up. I paced off the third vara. I tried the fourth, bumped my knee on something, felt thorns in my thigh. What was it? A rail covered with brambles. A rail to what? Never mind. Step over it. Five. Six. Seven.

My feet sank into soft soil. I stooped to grasp a handful of loam. What was that sound? A small stream trickled about twenty varas from me. I looked up the stream and saw it flanked by huge pecan trees draped with mustang grapevines. One marvelous specimen stood alone, cleared of vines, a ladder leaning against its trunk. Nearer to me I found smaller pecans, planted in rows. Some of their limbs wore bandaged splints.

Still nearer to me peach trees grew, also planted in orchard rows. Now I noticed trenches that branched out from the little spring-fed stream. They forked and carried water between the rows of trees.

I looked back toward the chain and compass. I had stepped over a rail fence covered with thorny dewberry vines. I could see beyond the chaining pins now, and on the southeastern horizon, at the other end of the line I had run, I saw the very peak of the hill of the zero stone. No wonder the surveyors had refused to move the zero stone for Eli. They chiseled it on that hill because they could sight its peak from the point of the buried treasure and plot a line to it!

And this tilled soil under my boots? I looked down the stream and saw a row of peas, killed brown by the recent frost. Then one of dead tomato vines tied to stakes and sagging as if still under the weight of the ripening fruits. Then a row of withered okra stalks. Then . . .

I staggered back from the point of the seventh vara, startled by the sight. It was Annie. Standing, staring, her hands on her hips, a bundle of dead plant stalks at her feet. She laughed. "Roy, what on earth are you doing? I've been watching you for the past ten minutes and for the life of me I can't figure it out!"

The facts were unspeakable. I couldn't admit that my greed for the treasure and not my concern for the well-being of the Standard family had been behind my quest for the zero stone all along. I resolved to utter the last lie she would ever hear spoken from my lips. I just didn't know what it was going to be yet. I stammered for a moment, but I did some pretty smooth lying under the influence of Annie Standard and I came up with a good one in no time.

"I was running a line. Dub got me to thinking. I figured I might like to take up the surveyor's trade. I just wanted to see how much I liked it before I had to take his equipment back to Austin."

"You might have asked for some help. You looked pretty silly moving those things by yourself."

I shrugged. "Didn't know anybody would be watching."

"Well, you were sure serious about it." She walked around the row of okra to approach me. "So, are you planning to make a surveyor of yourself?"

"No, I don't think so. I have an obligation to supply cedar posts for that barbed-wire salesman. Besides, surveyors have to wander too much. I'm looking to settle."

Annie wrung her hands in the apron she had tied around her slender waist and walked closer to me. "Where are you thinking of settling? Going back home to see your family?"

"Maybe to visit. But I won't live there. Too flat. I like these hills around here."

"Good," she said. "I was hoping you'd decide to stay here with us." She swayed gracefully toward me, smiling, her eyes fixed on mine. She walked in close to me and then stopped over the point I had stepped back from. She stood exactly 189 chains and 7 varas, 49 degrees northwest from the zero stone.

God bless the old Mexican for now and for eternity! That wise and aged vaquero had known my own fate better than I. I would never doubt him again. *El tesoro* stood where his map had said I would find it. The only mystery to me was whether he somehow knew I would find Annie there or whether the treasure marked on his map was of the pecuniary variety.

Treasure is a thing whose qualities lie open to interpretations. To Marion Harkey, treasure came in the form of cash money. To Dub Coe, it had taken the shape of everything from deer droppings to wildflower seeds. To Eli Flatt, treasure had been an elusive vision of streets, parks, and buildings. Paper-shell pecans were treasure to Annie Standard, and Annie was treasure to me.

I kissed her in the garden as a flock of wintering doves vaulted from the mother tree and swooped low over our heads. From that moment forward I have cast aside any thoughts of excavating buried treasure.

Make no mistake, the spell of the old Mexican's map will burn within me the rest of my life. I will never quench it. I will always wonder about that spot in Annie's garden. I go there often to stand over it. I have witched for the riches with forked sticks. I have probed for it with steel rods. But I will not dig. I will never make excavations for the buried gold, the bars of smelted silver, the jewels, the loot pilfered from the Mexican cathedrals. If it is truly there, that treasure will remain for someone else to unearth. I have mastered the lust. I have found something better to hold.

I would like for my sons and daughters to own the loot

if it is there, however. Annie, too, if she suspected treasure might lie under her garden, would want our children to own it. So I will, after a fashion, *order* the digging done someday. Then I will descend the shaft dug for me, slip the mortal bonds of rapacity, and let my soul find its lost peace in the cool river bottom soil under Annie's garden.

If a trove exists there, I will lie down in its place. For there is an odd clause in my will stipulating that when I die, my grave must be dug by my own children. They will bury me deep, on a line coursing 49 degrees northwest, exactly 1,897 varas from the zero stone.

Mike Blakely lives with his wife and son on a 1,500-acre ranch in the Hill Country of Central Texas. The author of *The Glory Trail*, he has written numerous articles on the history of the American frontier, and writes a monthly column on Texas folklore.

Available by mail from

TOR
FORGE

1812 • David Nevin
The War of 1812 would either make America a global power sweeping to the pacific or break it into small pieces bound to mighty England. Only the courage of James Madison, Andrew Jackson, and their wives could determine the nation's fate.

PRIDE OF LIONS • Morgan Llywelyn
Pride of Lions, the sequel to the immensely popular *Lion of Ireland,* is a stunningly realistic novel of the dreams and bloodshed, passion and treachery, of eleventh-century Ireland and its lusty people.

WALTZING IN RAGTIME • Eileen Charbonneau
The daughter of a lumber baron is struggling to make it as a journalist in turn-of-the-century San Francisco when she meets ranger Matthew Hart, whose passion for nature challenges her deepest held beliefs.

BUFFALO SOLDIERS • Tom Willard
Former slaves had proven they could fight valiantly for their freedom, but in the West they were to fight for the freedom and security of the white settlers who often despised them.

THIN MOON AND COLD MIST • Kathleen O'Neal Gear
Robin Heatherton, a spy for the Confederacy, flees with her son to the Colorado Territory, hoping to escape from Union Army Major Corley, obsessed with her ever since her espionage work led to the death of his brother.

SEMINOLE SONG • Vella Munn
"As the U.S. Army surrounds their reservation in the Florida Everglades, a Seminole warrior chief clings to the slave girl who once saved his life after fleeing from her master, a wife-murderer who is out for blood." —*Hot Picks*

THE OVERLAND TRAIL • Wendi Lee
Based on the authentic diaries of the women who crossed the country in the late 1840s. America, a widowed pioneer, and Dancing Feather, a young Paiute, set out to recover America's kidnapped infant daughter—and to forge a bridge between their two worlds.

Call toll-free 1-800-288-2131 to use your major credit card or clip and send this form below to order by mail

---

Send to: Publishers Book and Audio Mailing Service
PO Box 120159, Staten Island, NY 10312-0004

☐ 52471-3	1812 .... $6.99/$8.99	☐ 53657-6	Thin Moon and Cold Mist.......... $6.99/$8.99
☐ 53650-9	Pride of Lions .... $6.99/$8.99	☐ 53883-8	Seminole Song................ $5.99/$7.99
☐ 54468-4	Waltzing in Ragtime .... $6.99/$8.99	☐ 55528-7	The Overland Trail .... $5.99/$7.99
☐ 55105-2	Buffalo Soldiers .... $5.99/$7.99		

Please send me the following books checked above. I am enclosing $_____. (Please add $1.50 for the first book, and 50¢ for each additional book to cover postage and handling. Send check or money order only—no CODs).

Name _____

Address _____ City _____ State _____ Zip_____